The
Body
in the
Kitchen
Garden

PAULA SUTTON

The Body in the Kitchen Garden

RENE GADE

RENEGADE BOOKS

First published in Great Britain in 2025 by Renegade Books
An imprint of John Murray Press

1

A CIP catalogue record for this book
is available from the British Library.

Hardback ISBN 978-0-349-70379-4

Typeset in Berling by M Rules
Printed and bound in Great Britain by Clays Ltd, Elcograf S.p.A.

John Murray policy is to use papers that are natural, renewable and
recyclable products and made from wood grown in sustainable forests.
The logging and manufacturing processes are expected to conform to
the environmental regulations of the country of origin.

Carmelite House
50 Victoria Embankment
London EC4Y 0DZ

The authorised representative
in the EEA is
Hachette Ireland
8 Castlecourt Centre
Dublin 15, D15 XTP3, Ireland
(email: info@hbgi.ie)

www.dialoguebooks.co.uk

John Murray Press, part of Hodder & Stoughton Limited
An Hachette UK company

Dedicated To Duncan, Tobias, Phoebe,
Daisy and Lady Dashwood.

Also dedicated to Daphne Brewster – the character
who allows me to be the bravest version of myself.

Welcome to Pudding Corner...

Is there anything more heart-warming than being received into the welcome and open arms of the venerable English village? Ah, the bosom of country life – that perfect entryway into the vestibule of traditional Englishness. That conduit of all things green and pleasant. That gateway into a thatched-roof- and picket-fence-filled Narnia, where the quintessential patch of hallowed grass that makes up the village green reigns supreme and every stranger is a friend waiting to share pot of tea.

Welcome strangers one and all, for who can resist the allure of some harmlessly enthusiastic village community spirit? The helpful neighbours watching on kindly to ensure we never put a foot wrong ... straining their necks across the maze of narrow lanes to pleasantly observe that rules are followed, proffering the friendliest tips on what traditions must be upheld – and at what cost.

Hark, the charm of cottages that compete demurely for picture-perfect superiority. All for the greater good of course, and never for individual gain, for remember, there are no egos here in the countryside, just a gentle persuasion to do better. And who can deny the charm of the window box brimming with geraniums and petunias, the riot of colour – but not *too* colourful, the rusty iron gate – but not too rusty, the feigned autonomy, the faux individuality . . .

This place that a lucky few can call home. For all is safe and all is quiet when rural beauty is wrapped all around – just a cobbled street to trip you up here and a gaggle of ducks tottering by gently to pierce the silence there. This sleepy village is a place to belong to, a place to return home to, or perhaps even a place to disappear to. Time moves a little slower, everything has its place – and everyone must be kept in theirs . . .

Welcome my friends, to Pudding Corner. This bucolic stage of familiar delights where all take comfort in ignoring the little things to focus on the bigger picture – a picture that conveniently never seems to change . . . if they can help it.

Meeting the villagers . . .

Daphne Brewster: New-ish to Pudding Corner, having re-located from urban south London to rural Norfolk two and a half years ago. The village's Vintage Lady and amateur sleuth, she is a kind and inquisitive do-gooder who takes the side of the underdog.

James Brewster: Affable husband to Daphne, who is disapproving of her detective predilections.

Imani 'Immy' Antoinette Brewster: Daughter and eldest of the Brewster children.

Archie Brewster: Twin son to Daphne and James.

Fynn Brewster: Twin son to Daphne and James.

Byron: The Brewster family pet; a characterful miniature dachshund named after Lord Byron, the 1800s poet.

Aggie: Short for Agnes; Daphne's vintage beloved car, a 1969 Morris Traveller.

Marianne Forbes: A snobby and entitled ex-Sloane Ranger raging at the supposed injustice of her lack of financial clout and village social status.

Timothy Forbes: Long-suffering husband of Marianne, content with the simple life – unlike his other half.

Tarquin Forbes: Marianne and Timothy's son.

Augusta Papplewick: Self-appointed guardian of parish social and moral standards.

Minerva Leek: Quiet and unassuming friend of Daphne, outcast from the village.

Silvanus Leek (known to his friends as Silver): Young son of Minerva, best friend to Imani Brewster.

Nancy Warburton: Formidable village gossip and proprietor of the Pepperbridge Convenience Store.

Patsy Warburton: Younger sister of Nancy and fellow gossiper.

Reverend Gerald Duncan: Local vicar.

Mrs Musgrave: The headmaster's secretary.

Inspector Hargreaves: Local police inspector dreaming of exciting cases beyond bucolic village life.

PC Maxine Clarke: Former pupil of Pepperbridge Primary School, now a local PC.

Lord Hugh Darlington: Local gentry, recently returned from Australia after an extended period of estrangement from his now deceased family.

Lord and Lady Darlington: Hugh's parents, now deceased.

Edward Darlington: Hugh's older brother, now deceased.

Lady Sarah Kirdale: Edward's romantic interest.

Helena Carter: Former pupil of Pepperbridge Primary School. Known as the quietest and least troublesome of the five Carter girls, aka the H-Bombs. 'Significant other' to Hugh Darlington.

Mrs Freestone: Editor of the *Village Pump* parish newsletter.

Locations in the story . . .

Pudding Corner: A charming hamlet in West Norfolk. Home to Cranberry Farmhouse and the Brewster family.

Pepperbridge: A larger village next to Pudding Corner, and home to Pepperbridge Primary School.

Cringlewic Heath (commonly known as Cringlewic): A small domestic enclave situated in the middle of Cringlewic Woods and bordering Oxwold Overy estate.

Oxwold Overy estate: A large shooting estate owned by an unmentioned character.

Oxwold Overy: The largest local town.

Narborough: A local village located approximately five miles from Pepperbridge and Pudding Corner.

Cranberry Farmhouse: The country home of the Brewster family; a late-eighteenth-century farmhouse, complete with an ancient Aga, large attic and cellar rooms.

Darlington Hall: The Darlington family estate, known by locals as Old Hall.

A Fine Vintage: Vintage and antique furniture shop located in Pepperbridge belonging to Daphne Brewster.

Warburtons': Local Pepperbridge grocery and 'convenience' shop run by the Warburton family for three generations. Currently under the ownership of the Warburton sisters, Nancy and Patsy.

Chestnut Cottage: A typically modest brick and flint field workers' cottage in the centre of the village of Pepperbridge. Now extended and home to a longstanding member of the community.

Prologue

Early spring, March

Daphne Brewster absent-mindedly pulled on her worn leather driving gloves as she waited patiently for the youngest twin (by thirteen minutes) to slide into the back of the 1969 Morris Traveller van. Byron, her faithful little dog, was safely in the house and snoozing in front of the Aga, having been out for a much-welcomed run and a not-so-welcome digging break before the children had come down for breakfast. Now, with all three children in the car, and surprisingly ten minutes early, she was in no particular hurry this morning. She would rather take in the view and the crisp morning air than hustle the kids along and spoil the peacefulness of the moment. Moving to Norfolk had been all about finding some semblance of peace in an otherwise chaotic world and bar one blip she felt that at last she had found it. The Brewster family had settled comfortably into life at Pudding Corner after the rather unfortunate events – the blip – of the previous couple of years. It was as though the murder of Mr Papplewick, the headmaster of the local school, and Daphne's role uncovering who had been responsible for his untimely demise, had accelerated their acceptance into the fabric of village life. Daphne discovering, outwitting and subsequently incapacitating their former neighbour Doctor Ptolemy Oates, the unlikely perpetrator of the murder, led to a generous welcome that other newcomers had not experienced. It was a well-known fact that to become anything close to a 'local', one had to have lived in the county for at least ten years. It was only after a period of at least twenty-five years or so, with bonus points if you had a second generation living within the county perimeters, that you would reach the coveted status of actually 'being from Norfolk'. As luck would have it, Daphne's accidental sleuthing had inflated her currency to that of honorary local.

This was much to the annoyance of Marianne Forbes, who had been living in Pudding Corner for several years longer than the Brewster family yet was destined to remain a 'townie newcomer' despite her attempts to propel herself to the forefront of the village pecking order. It didn't help that these matters of social standing were decided on by a single omnipresent entity – in this case Augusta Papplewick: village doyenne and arbiter of parish rules. Augusta had only temporarily felt her crown of power shift during the confusion surrounding her husband's death. After a period of time away from the village – including a three-month stint on a luxury cruise ship touring the Caribbean and a 'Mozart and *The Sound of Music'* walking tour of Salzburg, her first proper departure from Pudding Corner since she had arrived as a less-than-trembling bride over forty years ago – she had returned refreshed, re-energised and surprisingly robust considering her newly widowed status.

Daphne sighed as she pulled out of the drive of Cranberry Farmhouse, listening to the old-fashioned click of Aggie's indicator and belatedly remembering to push in the choke. James will be listening and tutting, she thought, smiling wryly to herself as she pushed down hard on the accelerator to carefully glide around the curve that formed the 'corner' in 'Pudding Corner'. It was her favourite part of the drive and the children always giggled with glee as their bottoms slid to the left of the long bench seat despite their seatbelts being tightly secured.

The journey to the small village school in nearby Pepperbridge, the parish that was home to the hamlet Pudding Corner, took only a few minutes as they drove past the familiar expanse of countryside populated mostly by fields currently filled with pigs and sheep. The scenery, lit up by the spring sunshine, worked its magic on her senses even though she had passed it so many times before, and she caught her breath as she took in the crescent-shaped row of medieval cottages and marvelled at the view that evidently hadn't changed for several centuries. Before long they had parked on School Lane and the children trotted off in front of her, shouting out to friends and waving small hands covered in mittens to ward off the nip in the air. After two years at the school, they all knew the routine, but Daphne still walked behind them, knowing that if even one of her three-strong brood looked back as they lined up after the bell had been rung, and she wasn't there to meet their eyes or to match their smile reassuringly, there would be hell to pay at pick-up time.

Imani, a rather studious and confident ten-year-old (who had only this week decided – subject to change of course – that her nickname of 'Immy' was far too immature for her), had quickly found Silvanus and was showing him her solar system model made of large lumps of plasticine and ice lolly sticks. An equally studious although far more serious child, Silvanus was the son of Minerva Leek, Daphne's closest friend in Norfolk. Minerva was the person originally accused of Mr Papplewick's death, and who Daphne had been determined to prove innocent. In a shocking twist of events, it had turned out that Minerva was Mr Papplewick's secret daughter. So much for the serenity of the countryside ... Meanwhile, the twins, Archie and Fynn, now aged seven and entering a curious stage often involving insects and dirt, had run directly to the pond. They were on the lookout for frogspawn and wondering whether (rather prematurely, according to a matter-of-fact Silvanus, considering the time of year) there were any 'fat tadpoles' that they could bring home without Mummy noticing.

All in all, it was a very normal-seeming early spring morning – not too chilly, but certainly not mild enough to remove her gloves as Daphne waved goodbye to the children who walked in crocodile lines towards the classroom wings of the old Victorian school. She turned around quickly before Marianne, who she had just noticed stalking towards the school office, could see her. Even the sight of Augusta Papplewick waving goodbye to Silvanus was beginning to feel vaguely normal ... Or at least she no longer felt compelled to shield the little boy from Augusta's wrath. Daphne had witnessed several incarnations of Augusta. She started out as the disapproving matriarch of Pudding Corner, excluding Silvanus and his mother from the village, and she was now playing grandmother to her late husband's secret daughter's child. Not for the first time, Daphne thought that wonders would certainly never cease in this small village.

Having jumped back into her car and quickly sped off, narrowly avoiding Marianne and Augusta, Daphne parked less than half a mile away in front of her own shop which sat in a small row on what was grandly called the 'High Street'. Unlocking her seatbelt and twisting round to grab her bag and a tub of homemade Bakewell slices from the back seat, Daphne realised that she'd forgotten to bring milk so walked towards the Warburtons' store before opening up. Patsy and Nancy Warburton were purveyors of Pudding Corner's 'finest' (but often out-of-date) goods. Patsy was the younger sister of the formidable village oracle, Nancy, and was now one of Daphne's favourite people in the village. Getting to know Patsy, with her filthy sense of humour and a very kind heart, had been another benefit of solving Mr Papplewick's murder.

Daphne's shop, A Fine Vintage, was just a few doors down from the Warburtons', which gave them the excuse to share a cup of tea and a homemade biscuit most mornings. A Fine Vintage was one of her proudest achievements. A vintage furniture shop where she upcycled, restored and painted antique pieces, it was not only a long-held dream of hers but had gone from strength to strength and the business showed no signs of slowing down. Daphne was even being contacted by locals for interior decoration advice as well simply sourcing and selling furniture.

Today though, Patsy was nowhere to be seen. Through the glass window, Daphne saw Nancy's ankles, clad in wrinkled stockings, as the older woman stood sturdily on the wooden shop ladder stacking boxes of cereal on one of the highest shelves. Daphne wondered if Nancy knew how she looked from the other side of the window. Nancy's stockinged knees were a familiar sight through the distorted ripples of the Warburtons' glass, but for anyone passing through the village, it was a rather interesting spectacle. For non-Pepperbridge residents who entered the shop, their curious encounter continued when Nancy greeted them, revealing the deeply tobaccoed timbre of her surprisingly gruff voice. The most infamous East End gangster had nothing on Nancy Warburton's reverberating tenor.

'Good morning, Nancy,' Daphne chirped cheerfully as she entered the shop, the bell tinkling loudly and announcing her arrival as the door swung itself shut behind her.

'Morning, Daphne,' Nancy responded after a few seconds' pause.

She had a habit of doing that: tutting at the sound of the bell and leaving one wondering whether she was going to respond or not. It was always slightly unnerving. Luckily, Daphne was used to Nancy's little idiosyncrasies, and knew that most of them were intended to throw people off guard. For Nancy and Patsy, acting as though customers weren't in fact welcome was a sport. A bit of harmless fun. It kept the villagers on their toes. They didn't want anyone to get too comfortable – unless it was of their choosing – and if you were lucky enough to be welcomed into Nancy and Patsy's inner circle, then you had a loyal friend for life.

Pint of milk in hand, homemade Bakewell slices in the other, Daphne was just leaving the money on the counter when another customer entered the shop. It was Helena Carter, a hesitant woman of about thirty years of age, dressed in jeans, old riding boots and a tweed hacking jacket that looked about as old as she was. She wore her shoulder-length, mousy blonde hair back from her face with a velvet Alice band and had a rather timid countenance as her eyes darted around the store.

'Good morning,' she eventually aimed at Daphne shyly.

'Good morning – Helena, isn't it?' Daphne replied. She had seen her around the village before, mistaking her for one of the young mothers at the village school before Minerva had corrected her otherwise.

'Yes, that's right. I'm Helena Carter – from the Old Hall.'

'Hmrpphhh.' Nancy snorted and then muttered something indistinguishable under her breath.

Helena's cheeks flushed. 'I, I saw you through the window,' she said to Daphne. 'I was wondering whether I could ask you something – about your shop?'

'Of course, I'm just paying for this. Shall I see you outside my shop in just a second? It's not open yet but I won't be long.'

Helena gave a nod and took that as her sign to exit. 'Brilliant!' she said breathily while simultaneously backing out of the shop at speed. 'I'll see you there. Thank you.'

Nancy peered down from the ladder as the bell rung to

indicate the shop door closing. She 'harrumphed' again. This time Daphne couldn't help but laugh.

'Nancy! What's the matter? And please be careful coming down, your tights are down past your slippers.'

'Lady Helena of the manor, my arse!' Nancy said abruptly. 'She's one of the Carter girls – I remember her as a child and back then she was just plain *Helen* with shifty eyes. Started off as a cleaner, went off to university for two minutes and now look at her. Lady La Di Da at Old Hall. I'd like to know what position secured her *that* position!'

Daphne was slightly shocked; it was the most that Nancy had said to her in months. Not since the time she had poured her heart out about her long-standing feelings for Mr Papplewick, and her unsubstantiated fears for her sister Patsy, had Nancy revealed so much. She was normally a woman of few, and intimidating, words.

However, Daphne had heard this rhetoric before, unprompted from both Augusta and Marianne. Climbing above one's station was not-so-subtly frowned upon by certain stalwart members of the village. It seemed that Helena – who had started out as plain old Helen Carter and was now, due to her recent engagement, Helena Carter of Darlington Hall – had done just that when she'd returned to Pepperbridge with an 'a' at the end of her first name and a BA (Hons) at the end of her second.

An innate desire to keep people in their supposed place was one of the few things that Augusta, Nancy and Marianne had in common, albeit for different reasons. Marianne wanted to climb to the so-called top, Augusta wanted to *stay* on top and Nancy, being one of the longest standing members of the community and having seen many people come and go, taking their secrets with them and occasionally leaving a few behind, just liked to cause mischief.

The interesting thing about being a total newcomer was that you wouldn't necessarily be judged immediately – especially as a Black woman from south London who had ended up in the English countryside. As such, Daphne was slightly un-compartmentalisable. She had often seen people trying to figure her out, attempting to place her on the social scale. She was well-spoken and proud to say she was born in Croydon – although few could figure that one out, and Marianne certainly hadn't been able to. 'Croydon?' she had said with alarm when Daphne had given her a potted history of her life. 'You mean, *the* Croydon?'

'She seems rather nice,' Daphne said now to Nancy, being intentionally provocative.

'Who seems nice?' Patsy bellowed, walking in from the back of the shop.

'Helena Carter,' Daphne and Nancy said simultaneously – although Nancy inserted an extra-spicy expletive, emphasising her personal disapproval.

'Oh, not that again, Nance.' Patsy laughed. 'Leave the poor girl alone. We can't help who we fall in love with can we, and she never seems to take advantage of it or lord it over anyone. She's been quite dignified to be honest – or have you got evidence to prove otherwise in that secret notebook of yours?' she added pointedly. It was widely known that Nancy had a little black book filled with village gossip.

'Dignity does not consist in possessing honours, but in deserving them,' Nancy retorted, ' . . . and never you mind about my notebook!' she added snappily, peering sagely down at Patsy from the ladder and over the top of her half-moon glasses like a life-sized owl.

'Nancy! Are you quoting Aristotle?' Daphne couldn't help but laugh in surprise. Defying people's under-estimation of her was Nancy's superpower.

'What are you on about, Nance?' interjected Patsy. 'Doesn't everyone deserve a bit of luck and isn't it rather decent of him to want to marry a local girl rather than some socialite?'

'It's not her I'm bothered about . . .' Nancy muttered under her breath.

'What's that?' Patsy was only half listening now, checking if Daphne had anything of interest in her hands.

Choosing to ignore Patsy's question, Nancy went on, 'Aren't you going to serve Miss La Di Da then?' she asked, glancing at Daphne before turning back to her sister. 'Her Highness is requesting the pleasure of meeting Ms Brewster in her shop, if you don't mind!'

Daphne and Patsy both laughed; once she had the bit between her teeth, Nancy was relentless. 'I'll give you twenty minutes and then I'll come over,' Patsy said. 'What have you got today?' she added, eyeing the Tupperware tub in Daphne's hands greedily.

'Bakewell slices – homemade and fresh from the oven.'

'What's wrong with Mr Kipling?' Nancy muttered with faux irritation. She too had become partial to Daphne's baked offerings although she refused to admit it out loud.

'Nothing at all, Nancy, but these are my own special recipe – and they're still gooey and warm . . . I'll send one back with Patsy when I've opened them.'

Nancy grunted but didn't decline the offer.

Later that evening, back home at Cranberry Farmhouse with the children finally tucked up in bed and Byron, her faithful miniature dachshund, curled doughnut-like in her lap, Daphne was recounting the day's events to her husband as he sat nestled into an old George Smith sofa in the snug. The cosy, low-ceilinged room had been covered in the chintziest wallpaper that Daphne had ever seen when they had arrived at their new home. It had originally been first on her list of things to strip out, but she had fallen in love with its faded charm over time, and it had remained up. It gave the room a romantic air of cottage-core chic against the heavy rusticity of the wooden beams and was particularly beautiful in the flickering firelight. Daphne loved it.

Settling in for the evening, she reflected on the day's events. Helena had indeed been waiting at the shop, seeking Daphne's advice.

'She's the new fiancée of Hugh Darlington,' Daphne said.

'Who?' James mumbled absent-mindedly while scrolling through vintage car videos on YouTube.

'You know, Hugh Darlington – the one who returned to Darlington Hall after living in Australia for the past twenty years. He's the last member of the Darlington family and he inherited the house after his brother died several years ago. He's Lord Darlington, Earl of Pepperbridge.'

Daphne looked over to see whether James was listening and despite glimpsing a Jaguar E-Type on his phone screen, she decided to continue the one-sided conversation regardless. 'Apparently it took them ages to locate him in Australia because he was working on a 4,000-acre sheep ranch. Anyway, Helena Carter is his girlfriend – or fiancée now apparently – and while he's trying to get to grips with the estate, she has been tasked with sprucing up some of the rooms so that they can get going on Airbnb, and she says that she has no idea where to start. That's why she came to me, to ask if I can help her. Can you imagine? It's an incredible commission if it works out – Darlington Hall is huge!'

'That sounds great,' James replied automatically. The sound of sports cars racing around Le Mans played in the background; James's eyes tracked the progress of an Audi as it negotiated a particularly 'tasty' chicane.

She rolled her eyes; she knew when she was beaten. Her news may have been exciting, but cars were cars. For James, if it wasn't urgent, everything else came second.

Daphne didn't mind really; she was happy to daydream about the rooms she would be looking at towards the end of the week. She had often passed through the overgrown field bordering the grounds of Darlington Hall – known as Old Hall to the locals – on her dog walks. It looked beautiful, if a little rough around the edges. It was late Palladian in style, possibly built around 1780. She couldn't wait to get inside. And the gardens – oh, the gardens, they had the potential to be magnificent. She wondered what sort of budget Hugh Darlington had, if any. Just because one was in possession of a big house and a title, it didn't mean that one necessarily had money; she understood that. But it was still very exciting.

Just then her phone rang. She glanced at the clock on the mantlepiece and went through a quickfire mental checklist. It was 9.15 p.m., the children were in bed and her husband was by her side.

She walked towards the kitchen table and saw the name flashing up. *Patsy?*

'Hello, Patsy? Is everything OK?' At first, all Daphne could hear was the sound of laboured and jagged breathing at the other end of the line – had Patsy been running? However, there was soon a crescendo of moaning and ... was Patsy crying? Daphne felt her face drain of colour. 'Is it the shop ...?' she asked tentatively, praying that she'd remembered to file the insurance certificate somewhere sensible.

'It's Nancy,' Patsy wailed almost incomprehensibly on the other end. 'It's Nancy, oh my God, oh my God, it's Nancy. She ... she's dead!'

Chapter 1

May

The news that Nancy Warburton had fallen to her death from a stepladder while unboxing out-of-date country slices had hit the locals extremely hard. Even as the weeks had passed, it hadn't gotten any easier to comprehend that such a village stalwart was no longer around. It was still a shock, even for a village that had been unwittingly thrust into the spotlight due to the dramatic goings on of a murder (or 'The Pepperbridge Crime of Passion', as heaving-bosomed Mrs Freestone, editor of the *Village Pump* parish newsletter, described it to the smattering of 'trauma tourists' who occasionally turned up like circling vultures seeking out the most juicy and meatiest of details.

The truth was that prior to the events involving Doctor Ptolemy Oates and his hitherto lifelong best friend, Charles

Papplewick, Pepperbridge had enjoyed a distinctly prolonged lack of drama or tragedy (not forgetting the time that the village cricket team finally lost its unbroken winning streak to the Holt Ramblers in 1996). Pepperbridge and its close neighbour, Pudding Corner, could almost have been labelled unremarkable. Amid the beauty of its charming architecture, gently rolling fields and winding cobbled lanes, nothing out of the ordinary ever happened. That is, until Mr Papplewick's murder.

Nancy's accident had caused unrest to stir within the village. Mr Papplewick's murder may have come as a shock but, as time passed, it could be perceived as an unlikely and rather thrilling one-off. On the whole, in Pudding Corner and Pepperbridge, people tended to reach a ripe old age, expire quietly and without fuss, and then be buried in the local cemetery. This was typically followed by mourners congregating for tea and fruitcake in the village hall where embarrassing stories of the deceased were exchanged with cheerful relish. The second untimely death of a much-respected village bastion was an unsettling reminder that not everything happened in the expected natural order, and that it didn't take much to knock the village's reputation as a place of quiet beauty and a must-see heritage site on the Norfolk Brecks trail. After all, one unpredictable death could be regarded as misfortune; two would be seen as carelessness!

There was only one person who voiced their opinion that Nancy's demise had not been unpredictable at all. If there was one thing that the Reverend Gerald Duncan could be deemed good at (it was certainty not his ability to deliver a charismatic sermon), it was his uncanny ability to imply an all-knowing

'I told you so' to the end of any conversation covering any topic – ever. Reverend Duncan claimed that he had warned Nancy over the years that it was unsafe to climb the ladder and stretch out to reach the top shelves at her age. He even went as far as stating that he had suggested that she should invest in either a much younger assistant or one of those non-slip rubber stepladders with a safety handrail, to which Nancy had stared back at him with a deadpan face and an accompanying silence so loud that it screamed a thousand (undoubtedly less-than-savoury) words. Apparently, he had been forced to retreat, a bead of sweat forming at his dog collar as he swiftly paid for his Deep Action Toilet Duck without waiting for his change. This was unheard of for the vicar, who was known to run a tight ship with the church finances.

A sombre mood permeated through all who inhabited the village and surrounding areas – not least because Patsy had not felt up to opening the shop since her sister's death. The shop had been in the Warburton family for three generations, and although always rather erratic in its grasp of 'regular opening hours' – which appeared tauntingly on the window and were often obscured by a 'Be Right Back' sign – the store had never been closed for an extended period of time before. Not even when Patsy and Nancy's parents had died within a few months of each other back in the 1980s.

Today, however, marked the end of month two of the store's 'temporary' closure. The 'Be Right Back' sign hung sadly in the shopfront window as Daphne turned the key in the door and made her way in, closing it gently and locking it behind her.

'Patsy – it's me!' she shouted towards the back stairs behind the shop counter, peering into the gloomy darkness beyond. 'I've got you some bread and milk and a few of those chocolate brownies that you like . . .'

Daphne made her way towards the back of the counter, aiming to poke her head towards the living quarters to make sure that Patsy was up and out of bed. This had become a morning ritual of Daphne's before opening her own shop. She had started off politely knocking on the shop door and then ringing the doorbell with an increased sense of urgency after having not seen hide nor hair of Patsy for three days after Nancy's funeral. Up until then, Patsy had appeared to be functioning on autopilot, going through the necessary motions of planning her sister's memorial service and being carried along with the logistics of hosting distant family members who had shown up from Swansea. At first, Patsy had appeared emotionless, but not entirely incapable. Daphne had kept a watchful eye on her throughout, volunteering to help when and where she was allowed, and taking on a few of the more painful aspects of the funeral planning. (Would Nancy have preferred the pewter urn or the wicker . . . ? Who knew?) Patsy didn't have the heart to get involved with that particular choice, so pewter it had been. Strong, solid and sturdy – just like Nancy.

But once the funeral was over, the distant relatives long since departed, Patsy had indicated – quite understandably – that she would prefer a few days to herself to grieve in her own quiet way. Yet the days had turned into weeks and the weeks were now stretching into two months.

Daphne had tried not to interfere for almost two weeks – she hadn't wanted to appear insensitive and certainly didn't want to poke her nose in where it wasn't wanted. In the end though, concerned that the lights in the maisonette above the shop were never on, and the bins never out for collection, she needed to check that all was as well as could be expected.

Finally, having become fed up with Daphne's incessant daily banging and ringing – which showed no sign of abating – Patsy had reluctantly descended the stairs into the shop and opened the door to her. She had looked dreadful, a shadow of her former robust and (to the casual observer) slightly intimidating self. Deep bags under her eyes, a dejected slope to her shoulders, and what appeared to be one of Nancy's old housecoats stretched over her far broader shoulders. It had not been entirely unexpected, yet it was still a pitiful sight and Daphne had wanted to scoop Patsy up. She had proceeded to do just that, much to Patsy's initial surprise and then evident relief as she relaxed gratefully into the hug and started to sob.

It was one of the strange anomalies of village life . . . that you could live in close proximity to people who you had known you many years – if not your entire life – and yet still feel as lonely as a newcomer in a big city when it came to times of need. Daphne wondered how many villagers had come to see how Patsy was coping in the days and weeks following the funeral. Probably a handful, if that.

Since then, Daphne's daily visits to check on Patsy and bring her a few provisions had become a much-welcomed ritual for the two women. Patsy had eventually – and only half begrudgingly – handed over a door key so that she didn't have to descend the stairs every time Daphne popped by. Occasionally she would call down with a few mumbled grunts for Daphne to come upstairs where they would share a pot of English breakfast tea (dark and builders' strength for both women) and whatever delectable baked goods Daphne was proffering that day. The space in which Patsy now spent the entirety of her time was cosy but sparsely decorated – a maisonette where the sisters had lived together for most of their lives.

Sometimes, like today, Daphne's arrival would be met with silence. Daphne would be forced to call up with increasing volume before edging herself up the stairs with purposefully loud footsteps, not wanting to intrude on the older woman's privacy, but feeling the need to ensure the wellbeing of her friend, nevertheless.

'Patsy, I'm coming up!' Daphne forewarned now, making her way back to the stairs. 'Patsy? I'm here . . .' Daphne stopped short. Patsy was standing wide eyed and wild haired at the entrance to the sitting room. 'Patsy? Are you all right?'

'It doesn't make sense,' Patsy mumbled as if to herself. She had yet to make eye contact with Daphne, or even acknowledge her presence.

'What doesn't?' Daphne responded, knowing that she was likely to regret asking.

'Nancy falling . . .' Patsy glanced at Daphne. 'It doesn't make sense. Nancy was as steady as a rock. She's been climbing that ladder since she was a child. She wouldn't, couldn't have fallen . . . Someone must have been there. Someone must have been there to make her fall!' As she finished her ominous statement, Patsy looked directly at Daphne, staring hard into her eyes.

Daphne swallowed uncomfortably, shifting the weight on her feet from side to side. *Oh dear*, she thought to herself. *Here we go again . . .*

Chapter 2

In her short time as a local, Daphne had never seen Pepperbridge Village Hall like it was today. She had vowed early on that becoming part of village life meant throwing herself into every aspect of it – whether it was showing up to council meetings or volunteering to help with the Brownies. Life would have been far easier if she only showed up when she had to and disappeared into the sidelines at other times, but, as a Black woman in an almost exclusively white rural area who was already known for her part in solving a high-profile crime, the possibility of fading into the background had never been a real option. The hall was heaving with excitable parishioners wanting to share their tuppence worth at the monthly parish council meeting. Daphne had volunteered to put out some extra foldaway chairs after having been shocked to see dear old Pamela Whithorn, the octogenarian head cleaner at the church, valiantly struggling with them last time. The hall was already so full that anyone unwilling to stand would have to sit on one of the tiny chairs normally reserved for Pepperbridge Pumpkins playgroup.

With its curved vaulted ceiling, timbers painted white with black cross beams and large casement windows, Daphne always thought that the room resembled the inside of an upside-down longboat. The highly glossed wooden sprung floor had been reinforced for tea dances in the 1950s and the acoustics were loud and echoey, which meant that when one addressed a crowd at the top of the room it felt like the beginning of an acapella solo. Tonight, however, there was no concert. Daphne knew why there had been such a sudden influx of usually disinterested parties; it had nothing to do with the paper cups filled with Mr Beeston's recent rhubarb-and-beetroot wine experiment that currently sat untouched on a trestle table. There were seven topics on the evening's agenda, and Daphne guessed that 'item number one' had piqued most people's interest.

Suddenly there was the crashing of a gong and the hall immediately fell silent. All eyes had turned to the front where Augusta Papplewick stood wearing her signature pearl and diamond earrings, a casually tied silk pussy-bow blouse, sharply pleated navy blue slacks, and a pair of polished-to-perfection tan-penny loafers. In her left hand was a miniature gong that was still reverberating, and in her right hand, the tufted gong stick that had so recently sounded the commencement of the evening proceedings. Those attendees still standing shuffled quickly to their seats: naughty schoolchildren desperate not to attract Augusta's watchful gaze.

Augusta turned her attention to Mr Wittles, the parish council clerk, who was ever so eager to please Augusta – the chair. Mr Wittles jumped to attention and proceeded to announce the points of order.

Daphne was simultaneously aghast and mildly amused to watch Mr Wittles's eyes dart nervously towards Augusta at the conclusion of each of his sentences, before he handed the reins over to her with an alarming amount of reverence. He practically doffed his cap before slowly retreating backwards, head slightly bowed and eyes barely raised. It never ceased to amaze Daphne how Augusta had remained in control of the general populace of Pepperbridge and Pudding Corner, despite the behaviour surrounding her accusations of only a short time ago. Despite her bullying tactics and pinning the blame of her husband's murder on more than one innocent member of the village at various points during the investigation, Augusta had come up smelling of roses. Perhaps the fragile alliance she had recently forged with Minerva and Silvanus, having initially pointed her finger at the young woman, had simply bolstered the sense that she could do no wrong.

Daphne was abruptly shaken from her reverie by the sound of Augusta's firm voice.

'The parish council is very aware of recent concerns about youths exhibiting ANTI-SOCIAL BEHAVIOUR ...' Augusta held a slight pause, loaded with disapproval, before continuing, ' ... occurring around the village green next to Pott Row Lane.' She looked up pointedly from her reading glasses and scanned the room slowly for added emphasis, ensuring that her audience felt suitably chastised under her accusatory gaze.

Despite not one member of the audience being even remotely connected with the 'youths' in question, people shuffled uneasily in their seats and looked warily at each other.

'I cannot claim with one hundred per cent confidence that such despicable behaviour is undisputedly connected with the recent spate of thefts of farm machinery and domestic oil. However,' she continued, with a tone that implied otherwise, 'there has also been a bicycle theft from Mrs Bidwell's ram enclosure and apparently Reginald Urquhart's pet ferret has gone missing from its cage. I believe that it is *not* a coincidence that all of these events have occurred within three months of the youths starting to congregate on the green.'

There was a low murmur of agreement from the audience and a few 'hear, hears!' from fellow councillors, led by a passionate and surprisingly high-pitched 'YES!' from the direction of Mr Wittles, who was practically falling off his seat in his eagerness to show agreement.

'And they've been smoking pot – good-quality stuff it is, too. Clear as the day is long!' added purple-haired Julia Sugden. Julia was a seventy-eight-year-old former art teacher known for growing 'exotic herbs' in plain view of her front window, only shielded at certain times of the year by some of the most impressive hollyhocks Daphne had ever seen. Daphne couldn't quite work out whether Julia was complaining about the smell of cannabis or simply admiring its apparent potency.

Augusta looked directly at Julia, opened her mouth to respond, but then clearly thought better of it. With a sigh, she ignored her and carried on. 'It appears to me that said youths are a scourge—'

'I've also seen a tramp loitering around the cricket pitch!' came a clipped and clear-as-a-bell voice from the centre of the seated crowd. All eyes turned to Marianne Forbes.

'At least he looks like a tramp. Certainly, a thug,' Marianne stressed with conviction. 'Unkempt and dirty-looking and certainly not from either of the villages,' she concluded, more than happy to deflect the spotlight from Augusta, if only for a brief moment. Her application to join the parish council had, suspiciously in her opinion, been rejected without good reason on more than one occasion. If there was one thing that Marianne Forbes despised more than not having social clout, it was watching another woman abuse the exact same power that she herself coveted.

The truth was that Augusta Papplewick and Marianne Forbes were cut from the same scratchy cloth. Like two magnetic poles repelling each other, the mere presence of the other was enough to set off a battle of wills. Alas for Marianne, she had come close on a few occasions, but had yet to overthrow her older nemesis.

Daphne, who had witnessed many of the power struggles between the two, was in no doubt that out of the two formidably self-centred opponents, she would choose Augusta any day. Augusta may have had her faults – she was a snob, she was bossy, and she had an unbending sense of her own superiority – but she wasn't cruel. Marianne, on the other hand, was a different type of bully – the kind that puts people down to build themselves up.

'Your point being?' Augusta asked pointedly. Quick as a flash, the entire audience turned back around to face Augusta. 'What has this got to do with the youths on the village green?'

'Well, Augusta, perhaps he's the gang leader. Like Fagin and the Artful Dodger. Perhaps he's directing them to commit the crimes. Surely we should be trying to locate the centre of the criminal cell rather than just blaming the underlings,' Marianne finished smugly.

Looking around the transfixed crowd, Marianne triumphantly relished the fact that using such ambiguous terms as 'criminal cell' and 'underlings' – picked up from watching back-to-back episodes of *CSI: Miami* – had gone down rather well. All eyes had pivoted back to face her, the suddenly captivated audience warming up to the idea of a motley crew of Dickensian-style criminal teenagers and their trampish older leader wreaking havoc on the parish.

Daphne couldn't help herself. 'Sorry to interrupt, but we don't actually know that the youths on the village green committed any of the crimes, do we?' She had just become the centre of attention and she didn't like it one bit. But she also felt the need to prevent a witch hunt pursuing a group of harmless, bored teenagers who may have done nothing wrong other than drinking a few cans of lager, smoking some particularly potent weed, and making a silly amount of noise on the otherwise manicured green. 'I mean – has anyone actually *seen* them do any of these things? There's a big difference between syphoning off oil and stealing a ferret after all, and we can't start blaming them for everything and anything without evidence,' she continued fairly.

By now the parishioners didn't know which way to look. Heads had turned from Augusta to Marianne to Daphne before swivelling back to Augusta again.

'Well,' replied Augusta slowly, 'Inspector Hargreaves, who

unfortunately could not be with us this evening, has assured me that he will be looking into all of these matters – including, now, this mysterious Fagin-style tramp, Mrs Forbes.' She glared at Marianne with a pointed smirk. 'The inspector will be requesting the youths to move on as swiftly as possible.'

'National service!' barked Reginald Urquhart angrily from the back of the room. 'That's what they should be doing. The lot of them. National bloomin' service.'

'Thank you, Mr Urquhart,' Augusta sighed through gritted teeth. 'Now, shall we move on to the second point of order . . . any objections?' It was a question that wasn't a question – and everybody was well away of that fact. Nobody objected to moving on.

The rest of the meeting had dragged on as Augusta made an unnecessary meal out of each issue, eventually opening up the floor to a round of questions, the answers to which no one but Mr Urquhart and Reverend Duncan felt the need to know. The atmosphere had been reduced to that of a Latin class on a hot summer's day. Members of the audience were behaving like errant schoolchildren as they shuffled and fidgeted in their seats, staring wistfully through the windows or glancing longingly towards the exit – so close and yet so far. There wasn't a single attendee who felt brave enough to make their excuses and depart, and so when Mr Beeston's honking snores became too loud for even Augusta to ignore, the meeting came to a close with a sense of great relief. Not for the first time, and certainly not for the last, the residents of Pepperbridge parish were delighted for the effects of Mr Beeston's homemade wine concoctions . . . especially as tonight he had saved them all by succumbing to the potency of his own special brew.

Daphne joined the rest of the parishioners stretching out cramped limbs as they filed out of the village hall, blinking into the sunlight. She decided to take a stroll towards the gardens of Darlington Hall. It was a circuit that she had completed many times before in an attempt to reach her desired 10,000 steps per day, and it would take about forty minutes to get back to Aggie, who was still parked outside the shop. It had been quite a surprise to discover that, contrary to popular belief, more often than not a car was needed for even the simplest of errands in the country. But walking during her lunch breaks had been a wonderful way to get to know the parish. Exploring winding country lanes and discovering meandering farm tracks to nowhere had given Daphne an almost meditative pleasure – as well as upping her fitness levels – and she frequently tried to make time for a spontaneous jaunt when she could.

On her return from this evening's walk she would check in to make sure that Patsy had had something for supper, before driving the short distance home to James and the children, who she knew would not have batted an eyelid at her absence. James was currently obsessed with watching the most recent Goodwood Revival coverage and the children were enjoying playing outside in the garden as the late spring evenings grew longer and the lawn remained dry for longer periods.

The stroll to Darlington Hall consisted of a pleasantly flat walk of about a quarter of a mile down a country lane in the familiar direction of Cringlewic. She would then reach a stream straddled by a stone-arch culvert that preceded a fork in the road. In one direction, it led through dense woodland towards Minerva's enclave and in the other to acres of rolling farmland. At that point she would take the left fork and continue along the road for a further quarter of a mile before veering off left and heading diagonally through a public right of way that crossed the middle of a working farmland. This was the only bit of the walk that was uphill – rare for the flatlands of Norfolk – and as soon as she reached the top of the second field, she would access the tiny lane that signalled the border to the Darlington estate. If she had been driving, or if she chose to extend her walk by a further twenty minutes, she would have reached the estate's official entrance, past several rundown estate houses and a once-grand gated entrance. The gates were now permanently open and rusted, and the banks of grass on either side were overrun with weeds and overgrown hedging. The entire estate had obviously seen better days, hence Helena Carter's desperate plea for Daphne's assistance. Helena had explained that the long-term plan was to restore and refurbish the numerous derelict estate houses that bordered the land to create a boutique-style self-catering retreat, with the East Wing of Darlington Hall being sectioned off for paying guests, and the bulk of the formal rooms available for event hire. Helena had said that the West Wing would remain private quarters for 'myself, Lord Darlington and ...' But then her voice had trailed off inaudibly before she finished the sentence. Daphne had noticed Helena blushing, and she realised that the final word she had fumbled shyly over was 'family'. She wondered vaguely at how old fashioned and meek Helena came across – was that a result of rural living? Surely no one would be surprised that they might want to start a family of their own one day?

Now, Daphne swung one leg over the stile and crossed over into the field that would soon deliver a perfect view of Darlington Hall's distinctive fairy-tale turret – an architectural folly that served a purely aesthetic purpose. Once she reached the furthest corner of the field, she remembered that day, over two months ago now, when she had first met Helena. They had eagerly discussed the younger woman's plans for the home she now shared with the most recent and seemingly reluctant Lord Darlington, Earl of Pepperbridge. It wasn't just Daphne who had sensed his reluctance. He was rarely seen in the village and when he was spotted it was as a fleeting apparition, speeding past in his Land Rover.

Chapter 3

March, two months earlier ...

The antics of Nancy and Patsy Warburton never failed to make Daphne laugh. They were more than an unintentional comedy duo, they were a couple of loveable rogues who provided endless entertainment and – who would have thought it at first? – friendship.

Daphne had just left the shop, thankfully keeping hold of some of the homemade Bakewell slices. Despite Nancy's feigned disinterest, she practically hijacked six of them before Daphne could exit.

She was intrigued by the thought of Helena Carter waiting for her at the shop, and there she was, standing patiently and a tad timidly on the pavement outside.

'Sorry to keep you waiting!' she had called out cheerfully towards Helena.

'Oh goodness, that's no problem at all! I didn't mean to disturb you or make you rush.' Helena smiled gratefully.

It was clear that Helena would have felt happier to wait outside in all weathers rather than remain in the 'convenience shop' under the beadily watchful and openly judgemental gaze of Nancy Warburton.

Daphne opened up the shop and led Helena inside, indicating for her to take a seat as she walked straight through to the back and put the kettle on. 'These Bakewell slices are still warm from the oven – fancy a cup of tea with one?' she shouted back over her shoulder.

'Oh my goodness . . . Yes please, that would be amazing!' Helena gushed earnestly, as though Daphne had just offered to do her laundry free of charge for a week.

Surprised at such a heartfelt response, Daphne poked her head out from behind the curtain in the tiny kitchen while the kettle was boiling. Helena was sitting hesitantly on the edge of a high-backed, eighteenth-century dining chair, her face filled with belated regret that she hadn't chosen one of the comfier overstuffed armchairs that littered Daphne's pretty but chaotic little showroom. Daphne smiled and went back to making tea.

'So,' Daphne began when she eventually returned to the main showroom with a tray filled with a pot of tea, a cow-shaped milk jug, a little silver sugar bowl, two mismatched floral mugs and a plate piled with vanilla-scented frangipane slices, 'you live at Old Hall?' She sat down in one of the more comfortable armchairs opposite Helena and began to pour the tea.

'That's right ... er – yes, thank you,' Helena replied, nodding politely and acknowledging Daphne's gesture towards the milk and sugar. 'I live there with Hugh – he's my boyf—err, my ... umm ...'

Helena looked vaguely panicked, her eyes flickering about here and there. Anywhere but towards Daphne.

'Your partner ... Hugh Darlington?' Daphne offered up helpfully.

'Yes, that's right. Look, I'm sorry that I seem so nervous, it's just that ...' Helena was wringing her hands absent-mindedly now, still hesitating over her words. She looked up suddenly, a millisecond of bravery causing a tumble of words to spill from her mouth before she could regret them. 'You see, I grew up around here. I went to the local school, and the idea of me having the 'lord of the manor' as my boyfriend – let alone now my fiancée – feels as ridiculous to me as it obviously does to everyone else!' She glanced back down at her fidgeting hands, but continued, obviously wanting to articulate her thoughts while she could. 'I know what they say, you see. What they think ...'

Daphne listened quietly, methodically stirring her tea, not wanting to interrupt Helena.

Helena dashed Daphne a quick look, her shy green eyes momentarily glinting with exasperation, before looking down again. 'They think that I'm not good enough for him, that I'm a, a ... gold-digger!' She almost shouted the last words in frustration.

'I'm so sorry to hear you feel that, but I'm sure that they don't think that ...' Daphne replied unconvincingly.

There. She had said it. Daphne had guessed that that was

where this was heading. Nancy Warburton had inferred as much. There was no situation more limiting than being surrounded by the people you grew up with and who could only see you as the one thing you no longer were, Daphne sighed inwardly. Here, it seemed that if your grandfather had been a pig farmer or had worked at the local sugar beet factory – both good and honest careers – then you could achieve every degree and qualification possible; you could build an empire, become the next Bill Gates and accumulate a multi-million-pound fortune; but in the parish of Pepperbridge, you would *always* be known as the child of the pig farmer or the sugar beet worker. Woe betide you put on airs and graces, thinking that money could change your place in the village hierarchy.

Now that she had started, it seemed that Helena couldn't stop. She had come from humble beginnings, she explained to Daphne. She was one of five daughters, having grown up in a modest but bustlingly happy home with her mother and grandmother. They had been known collectively as 'Those Carter Girls'. Both mother and daughter had been as pleased as punch that Helen – as she had then been called, despite having always had an 'a' at the end of her name – had been the first member of the family to attend university. Helena's sisters had not been so complimentary about what they had seen as a waste of time and money, but nevertheless, Helena – the most reserved of the boisterous Carter girls – had pursued her dreams to study art history. Admittedly, it hadn't been proven to be the great escape from provincial life she had hoped for; after her three years of relative freedom were over, she had returned to the village without hopes of a relevant job or the financial ability to pursue life elsewhere. She had fleetingly thought about travelling, backpacking to Florence and Paris and taking cash-in-hand jobs to see the Old Masters, but had instead remained at home with her mother who had been diagnosed with breast cancer shortly after Helena's grandmother had passed away. Three of her four sisters had remained in the village, some with children. Helena was the only one who hadn't partnered up early with a childhood sweetheart. Instead, she had taken odd jobs nannying and cleaning for the influx of city types who were increasingly moving into the area. One day, she had seen a small advert in the village post office asking for a 'household manager and assistant' at Darlington Hall. It had been scrawled in almost illegible handwriting, buried under a pinboard of dog grooming and childminding adverts. One thing for sure was that she was the perfect 'Jack of all trades and master of none', and an advert for such a muddled job description was befitting of her abilities. At least while she thought of what she could do next.

Turning up for her interview and entering Old Hall having seen it only from afar for most of her life had been a surreal moment, but not as surreal as the moment Lord Hugh Darlington himself had opened the oversized front door and stood before her in old jeans and a moth-eaten jumper, with a tanned and youthful face that belied his forty years, and a smile as shy and awkward as her own. The rest – as they say – was history.

Daphne had sat in silence, fascinated as Helena explained how they had fallen in love with each other almost instantly. Hugh had not long returned to his family home after a twenty-year period in Australia. He had returned friendless and without any close family – at least none known to him.

Both of Hugh's parents had been only children, so there were no close uncles, aunts or cousins to speak of. His brother – a relative stranger to him being older by thirteen years – had never married and had died prematurely in a car crash, and so it had been left to Hugh to take up the helm of the family estate. A role that, estranged from his parents, he evidently hadn't anticipated inheriting, let alone taking on.

'So, you see, we were both like two fish out of water when we met, and I think that's what drew us to each other,' Helena explained. 'He's not like a typical Hooray Henry from around here. In fact, he sounds more Australian than English. No airs or graces. He worked on a sheep farm for two decades. Not running it – just working on it! Apparently, none of them knew he was titled. He was just run-of-the-mill Hugh . . . and that's what he is to me. Just Hugh.'

She looked up at the end of her huge outpouring. Daphne could see Helena's shoulders begin to relax once she realised that Daphne was only listening with kindness.

'Well then. It sounds as though you two are made for each other.' She had smiled reassuringly, sensing that despite her own burgeoning interest in this most unlikely love story, now would probably be a good time to change the subject. 'So, tell me your plans for the Old Hall.'

'Yes, yes – Old Hall . . .' Helena closed her eyes and let out an almost imperceptible sigh before she continued. 'Well, for starters, it's huge! So many rooms – too many rooms in my opinion. It was bad enough trying to clean the place, but at least I was only cleaning the rooms that were in use . . . the kitchen, the lounge – er, I mean the "drawing room".'

Helena had corrected herself quickly, Daphne noted.

'There's such an awful lot to do and sort out, and Hugh has so much on his plate already, trying to make the estate work for itself with the tenant farmers and such. So, he – we – decided that getting the East Wing bedrooms up to scratch would be my job, except I haven't a clue where to start. Most of the rooms are filled with junk and old furniture, except maybe it's not all junk, some of it may be precious. It's his family's stuff after all. It's just so much responsibility – what if I mess up and throw out the wrong things? What if he doesn't like what I do? It's just a bit, well—'

'Overwhelming?' Daphne suggested.

'Yes, that's exactly it. It's overwhelming and I don't want to cock it up – oh, sorry!' Helena stopped abruptly and glanced up red-cheeked. She looked as though she was about to cry. In fact Daphne had feared she might cry from the moment she took her first sip of tea.

'Look ... firstly, you're not going to "cock" anything up.' Daphne said with a grin – her use of the word certainly brought a grateful smile to Helena's face. 'Do you have a budget to work with?'

'Yes, but not a huge one,' Helena replied, her voice filled with apology.

'That's OK, it sounds as though there may be a few ways to raise some funds to help with the revamp – especially if the rooms are filled with furniture that can be sorted and maybe a few bits sold?'

'That's exactly what I was hoping,' Helena blurted out. 'When I saw that you buy as well as sell vintage furniture, I just *knew* that you might be able to help us! Then when I spotted your sign stating that you do interior design, I was *so* relieved. I love art – but interior design is not my strong point I'm afraid. I only had a bedroom to myself for the first time a couple of years ago,' she exclaimed, her mind clearly returning to her childhood home filled with sisters. 'And I don't even live in that room now that I'm with . . .' She stopped short, about to disclose something that may have been obvious to all and sundry, but still felt like a rather intimate topic in front of a relative stranger.

However, it was obvious that Helena had almost immediately felt comfortable in Daphne's company. She had opened up quickly about the new life that she had unexpectedly found herself living; the relief of being able to share even just the tip of the iceberg of her new-found situation had been palpable. Perhaps it was Daphne's lack of familiarity with Helena's family's reputation and the village snobbery that had followed her into adulthood. Daphne provided a clean slate for people who felt the weight of judgement hanging heavy on their shoulders.

'So, here's my suggestion. Why don't we arrange for me to come up to Darlington Hall one morning and we can go through the rooms and your plans together. It all sounds rather exciting to me, and I would love to help.'

Helena practically jumped out of her chair – not hard considering how upright and stiff it had been – and launched herself towards a startled Daphne, hugging her (and almost knocking over the mug) with unbridled gratitude.

'Yes, yes!' she exclaimed, her earlier shyness momentarily forgotten in her enthusiasm. 'When can you come?'

Later that day Daphne received the shocking news of Nancy's fateful fall, and helping Patsy – as well as looking after the children and managing the shop – occupied all of Daphne's time in the weeks following the accident.

It was at least three or four weeks before Daphne found herself at the large oak door to Darlington Hall, taking a moment to admire the cast-iron bell pull that extended down from the arched stone entrance. A flushed and eager Helena opened the door herself before Daphne's hand had even had a chance to tug on it, leaving Daphne momentarily disappointed at not hearing what sound it made. It was an imposing entrance and Helena looked almost childlike framed within its huge proportions. She enthusiastically ushered Daphne inside.

Daphne was pleased to have done a little research about the building before arriving – the history of architecture and period buildings was a particular passion of hers. At its epicentre, Darlington Hall incorporated a manor house built in the later sixteenth century, though most of the rest of the house dated to the seventeenth century when it had been significantly remodelled and enlarged; wings had been added in the eighteenth and nineteenth centuries. The building was of rubble carstone with brick dressings and slate-and-black glazed pantiles, and a central entrance gable. It was handsome if slightly imposing. From the central 'Great Hall' (which must have hosted a grand banquet or two in its time, Daphne imagined), a myriad of doors and corridors led into darkened areas filled with shadows. On the first floor, to the left, was a minstrel's gallery, and if she turned round to face back towards the front of the house, two enormous stained-glass windows flanked the entrance, giving the room an ecclesiastical air. Under the staircase sat a concert-sized grand piano.

'Amazing, isn't it?' Helena said quietly – evidently still in awe of the grand building that she now called home.

'It really is, isn't it?' Daphne agreed. 'What a wonderful place to live.'

Helena seemed pleased with the compliment. She offered Daphne a cup of tea and a slice of cake, which Daphne politely declined, too excited to discover the rest of the house.

It took them the best part of an hour to explore the whole house and, even then, Daphne was aware that there were still rooms and corridors that they hadn't ventured down or into. This included the attic, which Helena explained was 'vast, filled with servants' rooms, and stocked with furniture', and also an area that Helena vaguely nodded towards before moving on swiftly and indicating that it led to Hugh's office. He was busy with work, she said, and couldn't be disturbed.

Their partial tour of Darlington Hall had worked up their appetites for cake and conversation, and Daphne and Helena eventually stopped for a much-needed break in the Great Hall.

'Well, I can understand how overwhelmed you must have felt, but to be honest, there's a logical way that we can begin the whole sorting process before we start decorating the rooms,' Daphne explained. 'The house is in the shape of an 'H', so we can section off areas bit by bit, starting with the topmost tip of the East Wing and making our way downstairs, room by room, along the side. Does that sound good to you?'

Helena nodded eagerly, looking relieved that someone was taking charge of the task. She was a hard worker, but she was happy to admit that she was more of a 'second-in-command' sort of person – this suited Daphne fine.

'It will be fun!' Daphne said. 'I'll make a plan of times and dates that I can come and help, and I'll give you a list of what you can be doing in the meantime. Once we identify pieces that you're happy to part with, we'll get those over to the shop and hopefully we can raise some extra funds that way too. Then there will be the best bit – creating mood boards for each room. Don't forget to start collecting inspiration pictures and images of rooms that you like so that I can get an idea of your style.'

Helena seemed delighted by the plan, and by the time Daphne was ready to leave, she was grinning from ear to ear and practically pirouetting with relief. 'Thank you so much, Daphne. I'll start clearing the green room first and then I'll await your instructions on which room I should work on next. I'm sure I'll love whatever decorating schemes you come up with. I haven't a clue – everything in my house came from car-boot sales and Ikea!'

'Don't knock a car-boot sale – they're my favourite places to shop.' Daphne chuckled.

'Hels!' A booming voice with an Australian twang startled both women out of their amiable chat. It echoed from the depths of one of the hallways behind the cantilevered staircase. 'Hels – where are you? Has she left yet?'

Daphne almost jumped out of her skin. Her shock escalated when two Border collies careered eagerly towards her at breakneck speed, only to be expertly halted by the disembodied sound of their owner's voice, who was evidently following behind them. Although she knew that Hugh Darlington was around somewhere, he had been conspicuously absent, and the house had seemed so quiet and still that she had quickly forgotten that he was at home. Not even the distant sound of a radio or a phone call had been audible during their tour, and certainly no whining or scrabbling of dogs.

Hugh Darlington walked into the Great Hall looking flustered and slightly embarrassed as he realised that Helena wasn't alone. 'Oh!' was all he said as he stopped, stock-still, in the doorway adjacent to the grand piano.

'Hello. I'm Daphne. Daphne Brewster.' In the absence of any sign of an introduction from Helena, Daphne walked towards Hugh, offering her hand. He remained still and unmoving in the doorway. A mixture of surprise and discomfort had fleetingly crossed his face before he evidently remembered his manners and took a reluctant step towards Daphne, half-heartedly proffering his own hand. 'Hugh. Hugh Darlington,' he said, stating the obvious.

'Pleased to meet you ... Hugh? Or should I call you Lord Darlington?' Daphne asked, only half joking, unsure of what to make of this not-so-friendly and rather unassuming man who was apparently Helena's Prince Charming. He was tall and ruggedly handsome, peering down at them with an enigmatic air.

'No!' he almost barked at Daphne, causing her to take a startled step backwards. 'Sorry – I mean, no, there's no need for that. Titles I mean. Haven't used one in years and I've no intention of doing so. We don't stand on ceremony here.' He finished speaking in a softer tone, almost mumbling towards the end, perhaps embarrassed by the strength of his own reaction.

There was a slight pause when Daphne hoped that Helena might smooth the way and interject, but she remained quiet, standing behind them and leaving Daphne at the front.

'Righto. Well, you have a very beautiful home, Hugh. It's the first time that I've visited it. We've only lived in Pudding Corner for a couple of years, and I've still got so many places to explore in the area,' Daphne said amiably, hoping to diffuse the awkwardness of the moment by keeping the chat light and friendly.

It seemed to do the job. Hugh appeared to relax when he realised that she hadn't been offended by the abruptness of his initial reaction. He walked further into the room and towards Helena, who was looking on quietly as though unsure of what to say.

'Helena mentioned that you were coming to discuss the refurb. I'm sorry that I wasn't here to greet you when you arrived, but I had a business call to attend to.' His voice sounded slow and controlled; his accent was a hybrid of an Australian drawl mixed with the clipped tones of the British upper class.

Is there also something else in there too? Daphne wondered. Whatever it was, she couldn't quite make it out, but with his weathered skin, sandy hair and stocky, muscular build, he definitely sounded and looked like someone who had spent the past twenty years wrangling sheep in the Australian out-back rather than a lord of the manor who had spent a lifetime on the polo field.

'Don't worry. I was in good hands,' Daphne replied, smiling and nodding towards Helena. Awkwardness still pervaded the atmosphere as she tried to make polite small talk with Hugh. 'Do you play?' she asked him, gesturing towards the piano.

'Regrettably, no,' he replied, quickly closing that avenue of conversation.

'Anyway, I must be off, but it was a pleasure to meet you. No doubt I'll be seeing you again as we start sorting out some of the rooms.'

Driving off, she saw Helena and Hugh standing in the doorway in the reflection of her rearview mirror. Helena waved Daphne off, Hugh's arm gripping her waist tightly. Their heads were close together – almost resting on each other. As Daphne drove the rattling Morris Traveller slowly down the long drive and out of sight, she reflected that at least they seemed comfortable in each other's company now she had left. The last thing that Daphne noticed as their figures faded from sight were the two Border collies sitting obediently on either side of the couple like a pair of sentinels.

Chapter 4

May – Back in the pasturelands of Darlington Hall

Still lost in thought, Daphne made her way over the stile and was about to reach to pinnacle of the steeply sloping field before it gently receded back down towards Darlington Hall. She stopped to catch her breath. This marked the end of her evening walk and, if she had calculated correctly, she ought to have walked about 3,000 steps – give or take a few. This would push her total towards a hefty 6,000 by the time she got back to Pepperbridge High Street, popped in to see Patsy, checked on her own shop, and finally returned home to her waiting husband and children.

At this rate I'll have buns of steel by the end of summer, Daphne chuckled contentedly to herself, trying her hardest to ignore the twinging threat of cramp that was creeping into the sole of her right foot.

Reaching the pinnacle, she was rewarded by what she now regarded as the best view in Pepperbridge. The back façade of Darlington Hall looked majestic, and from this vantage point, Daphne had a stunningly clear bird's-eye view of the entire walled kitchen garden on the left-hand side of it. It was by far Daphne's favourite view of the estate. The historic, half-crumbling kitchen garden was a thing of beauty with its double borders, once-ornate flower and vegetable beds, overgrown herb beds, and long-abandoned octagonal dovecotes. There were still a few old fig trees trained against the south-facing wall, rows upon rows of heritage apple trees, a few rotted wooden obelisks, and the remains of a derelict old orangery. But, most excitingly of all, two large Victorian glasshouses stood alongside the east wall. Despite a decade of neglect, their original internal workings remained, including complex heating and ventilation systems. The main timber structures were rotten in a few places but not entirely beyond repair, and thankfully, much of the brickwork was structurally sound. The same could not be said about the sloped glass ceiling. While the side panes were in miraculously good condition, the roof had several gaping holes, as evidenced by shards of glass that now resided on the floor.

Alas, even if the walls did not present an immediate danger to all who entered, then the perilously sharp fragments of glass that clung precariously to the ceiling frame certainly did. In Daphne's humble opinion, the two beautiful structures should have been high up on the list of planned renovations. Repairing them could enable the estate to retain as much historical integrity as possible. But it wasn't her money. She also knew that even with the best will in the world, although the walled garden had the potential to attract many visitors when it was restored, it wasn't going bring a healthy income to an ailing estate as quickly as well-fed heads on beds would.

There was time for one last lingering look at the walled garden, imagining its bountiful and productive past life, then Daphne caught her breath enough to make the journey back to the heart of Pepperbridge. The evening was mild, but as the light started to dim, she knew that the late spring chill would enter the air quickly and so she ought to get a move on.

Wait . . . what was that?

Daphne had only just turned away when out of the corner of her eye she sensed a sudden movement in the distance. Glancing towards the gardens, she saw what looked like a man exiting one of the glasshouses. She squinted to see if she could identify the blurry figure. *It must be Hugh*, she thought. There wasn't currently a permanent gardener at Old Hall – she'd already asked Helena if anyone was helping to keep the garden under control and she'd said that she wished there was but they were mostly managing the estate themselves for the time being. Despite local gossip to the contrary, Helena had explained that the only help they had was from the tenant farmers who tended the adjoining fields and a couple of ladies who had been recently enlisted to help clean the intended B & B bedrooms and bathrooms, plus the visitors' sitting room, bar area and a couple of other rooms in the East Wing that were intended for public use. Helena and Daphne dealt with the furniture removal and planning themselves.

Perhaps Hugh was having an early evening walk too, Daphne thought. She scanned the garden for the Border collies who were never far from their owner, but they were nowhere to be seen. She noticed that the figure had paused and seemed to be staring in her direction.

'Oh!' she exclaimed, startled to see who she thought was Hugh seemingly meeting her gaze, even if it was from a discreet distance. She raised her hand in an attempt at a polite wave. *Can he see me properly from that far away?* she wondered. Although, as she was one of the only Black women in the area, it would be patently obvious it was her. Looking closely, she could only be sure it was Hugh from the waxy finish of the Barbour jacket he usually wore, his unruly shock of sandy hair and his stocky frame. Not for the first time, she cursed the limitations of her short-sighted vision.

The Hugh-like figure looking up at her failed to raise his hand and so she eventually dropped hers limply to her side. She suddenly felt like a voyeur, a peeping Tom, intruding on someone's personal space and peaceful time alone. On the few occasions that Daphne had met him since their first stilted conversation in the Great Hall, Hugh had been pleasant enough but he was clearly a distracted, serious man preoccupied with worries. Judging by the enormity of his inherited estate, he probably had significant financial stress on his mind. Embarrassed, she raised her hand once more towards the still-watching figure in a farewell wave, turned quickly on her heel and retreated hastily back down the field towards the village.

It was a few minutes before 8 p.m. when Daphne passed the familiar 'Welcome to Pepperbridge' sign. It was flanked by pretty, petunia- and lobelia-filled hanging baskets, their bright, fragrant blooms giving visitors the impression of arriving in a rural idyll.

Augusta's commanding influence was visible in every corner of Pepperbridge's public spaces. Particularly the manicured front gardens and inoffensive front-door colours of even the most private of properties. Neat, tidy and pretty – with a tastefully restricted colour palette in line with Augusta's specific sensibilities – were the hallmarks of the village. Woe betide any offender who lived on Pepperbridge's main stretch and didn't meet Augusta and the committee's carefully constructed vision. It took a firm hand to win the silver medal for Norfolk in Bloom's 'Village of the Year' five times in a row.

The sun would be setting in about twenty minutes and Daphne wanted to be home before it got dark, but popping in to check on Patsy would only take a few minutes. Once she reached the topmost end of Pepperbridge's long and winding high street, Daphne decided to half jog the final few hundred metres to give her a little more time with Patsy. She noticed the 'youths' hanging out on the village green as she jogged past. They were loud, like teenagers letting off hormonal steam often are. Their portable stereo boomed out rap tunes as they filmed themselves attempting synchronised dance routines for TikTok and yelling playfully at each other. Daphne didn't see anything suspicious or out of the ordinary, beyond a few cans of Red Bull, that evidenced the 'anti-social behaviour' documented at the parish meeting. *Boisterous yes – menacing – no*, Daphne surmised to herself. She put the fearmongering in the council meeting down to the hysteria of a few local fuddy-duddies whose vision of village life was perhaps a little too stuck in an idealised, mothballed past. Presumably the same villagers who had once 'volunteered' an easily coerced Reverend Duncan to ask Madge Ripperton to halt her popular yoga classes in the village hall on the basis that her use of incense indicated sect-like behaviour or was even a sign of a devil-worshipping cult.

Patsy had been surprisingly pleased to see Daphne and even raised a half chuckle in response to Daphne's retelling of the council meeting – particularly the description of Mr Beeston snoring away in his rhubarb-wine-induced inebriated state.

'That must have infuriated Augusta no end!' Patsy rasped with a gentle laugh.

Daphne wondered whether Patsy was finally beginning to miss the outside world and might soon be ready to face life once more, without Nancy by her side. With any luck she had also moved past any thoughts that Nancy's tragic accident had not been an accident at all. Daphne was all for investigating a conspiracy theory – who didn't like a bit of true crime – but this one was too close to home and didn't make any sense at all. Plus, it was certainly not a healthy one for Patsy to obsess about.

'I'll pop in again tomorrow. Scones or teacakes?' Daphne called out as she opened the door to leave, the tinkling door-bell filling her with nostalgia for a time when Warburtons' was still a functioning shop.

'Teacakes,' shouted Patsy from the top of the stairs, and with that Daphne made her way home, relieved that there had been no further mention of foul play.

Chapter 5

June

Over a week had passed since Daphne had ventured up to Darlington Hall after the parish council meeting. In that time, she had had quite a bit of success selling some of the less historic, more run-of-the-mill brown pieces of vintage furniture on behalf of the Darlington estate through her shop and through online auction sites such as Vinterior and eBay. There were other pieces of furniture with lovely details or great bones that she was still in the process of restoring or upcycling with new upholstery or paintwork, and some more significant antiques with a clearer history that Hugh had agreed to sell. Daphne had organised for those to be valued professionally and taken to auction on his behalf.

All in all, the big Darlington clear-up was well on its way

to proving itself to be a financial winner. They were on the cusp of the most inspiring part now – the revamp and re-design of the allocated bed-and-breakfast rooms. This was an opportunity for Daphne to try her hand at interior design on a larger scale; the thought left her positively breathless with excitement.

It wasn't the only positive change that Daphne had witnessed since her evening walk to the fields overlooking Darlington Hall. Non-committal about reopening Warburtons' at first, Patsy had slowly returned to the shop. The opening days and hours were even more random than during the shop's heyday, and there was no promise of regularity or longevity, but it almost felt like things were getting back to normal. *Almost.* The absence of Nancy's imposing yet sturdy, reassuring pres-ence had left a gaping hole in village life as well as in the often rollercoaster ambience of the 'convenience store' itself.

Entering Warburtons' and asking for a specific product had once been a task to take on at one's own peril. Such risky behaviour had allowed Nancy to exercise her enjoyment of verbal blood sports. More fortunate victims would simply receive a fierce look and an ominous silence, while the less fortunate quickly regretted their well-meaning queries about where to find the milk or bread. Now, however, if a customer was fortunate enough to stroll by when the shop was open, an innocent question would be greeted by a gruff but at least semi-informative answer from Patsy.

Daphne smiled to herself as she opened the door to A Fine Vintage, pleased that Patsy was slowly but surely emerging from her maisonette and returning to village life. She hadn't had time to pop in to say hello this morning yet, but she had been delighted to notice that Warburtons' was already open for business when she had parked her car. At a glance, she'd seen Patsy stood at the counter, already conversing with a customer. Daphne had instantly identified this customer as Augusta from the back of her perfectly cut bob, tastefully neutral camel cardigan and matching 'slacks'. Just as well that Daphne had a client coming in and she hadn't interrupted that particular conversation. She wasn't in the mood for one of Augusta's habitual 'inquisitions' regarding the goings-on at Darlington Hall.

Daphne surveyed the jam-packed showroom of her vintage and antique furniture emporium with a quiet sense of satisfied pride. She now advertised herself as a vintage trader, restorer and upcycler, taking on individual commissions and small interior design projects. She also worked on behalf of clients to find professional restorers and auction houses who were better placed to handle valuable and historic pieces. What had started as a huge leap of faith after she had sold a few painted chairs, plus the sort of vintage knick-knacks that she liked to display around her home, had become a fully-fledged business. Much to Daphne's surprise, it was already proving to be rather profitable.

She walked through to the little kitchen at the back of the shop to put the kettle on and wipe down some linseed-oil-covered brushes when she heard the shop bell ring and the door open. 'I'll be right with you, Mr McClean,' Daphne shouted, assuming that he had turned up for his appointment a few minutes early.

The seventeenth-century-style ladder-back dining chairs from Darlington Hall that Mr McClean was coming to check out were already set out in the rear half of the shop. They were looking rather marvellous, with polished oak turned legs, deep red leather seats and large brass upholstery studding. They had scrubbed up beautifully, if she did say so herself. If they were what she thought they were – she had guessed that they were made in Derbyshire by craftsman Rupert Griffiths – then she suspected that she would get a good price for them, which would go a long way to helping Hugh and Helena with the renovations after Daphne had taken her seller's percentage.

'Would you like a tea or a coffee?' Daphne called from the kitchen to the shop.

'Neither, thank you.'

Augusta's unmistakably haughty tones shook Daphne momentarily out of her good mood. Rolling her eyes inwardly, she leaned backwards to look through the doorway that led from the tiny kitchen and into the back section of the shop. The older woman was peering at a few price tags and disdainfully lifting up an item here and there, only to place it back down with ill-concealed displeasure.

'Augusta? What a nice surprise. I wasn't expecting to see you here this morning!' Daphne said with a brightness that belied her mild irritation at Augusta's presence. She knew exactly what the woman was there for.

Augusta's interest in Hugh Darlington and Darlington Hall went way beyond the usual Pepperbridge nosiness that Daphne had become used to. As the largest estate in the area, it was perhaps understandable that people were fascinated by Old Hall's new caretaker. The mystery surrounding Hugh Darlington, who, despite being born in the house forty years ago, had not been part of the local community since he was nineteen, only added to locals' curiosity. To villagers both old and new, Hugh was an alluring and intriguing figure, and attempting to catch a glimpse of him was a regional sport.

It amused Daphne how, despite being firmly entrenched in the twenty-first century, many villagers were fascinated with land-owning gentry. The social divisions of class appeared to be as alive and thriving in many small country villages as they had been during the days of Jane Austen. Hugh Darlington had assumed the role of Pepperbridge's very own Mr Darcy. In recent weeks, there had been multiple occasions when Daphne had been sought out by a budding Mrs Bennet in the hope of a much-coveted invitation to Darlington Hall. Most of these characters would ignore Helena's relationship with Lord Darlington – dismissing her presence as an upper-class gentleman merely temporarily sowing his wild oats at best or, at worst, Helena as an unworthy gold-digger.

Augusta's interests, however, were neither of these. Rather, she had already positioned herself as Lady Catherine de Bourgh, the indignant and meddlesome grand dame furiously opposed to the mixing of a classless girl with a member of the aristocracy. With no actual reasoning behind her annoyance beyond profound irritation at social mobility, Augusta had taken it upon herself to pepper her conversation with critiques regarding the 'timid and undeserving' Helena's every move. Augusta had been constantly interrogating Helena's motives for infiltrating herself (via cleaning no less!) into the world of the last Darlington standing.

'He was rich yet easy pickings for a girl with unchecked

ambition and loose morals,' Daphne had overheard Augusta stage whispering for all to hear at a Pepperbridge Primary School PTA meeting a few weeks ago. 'I knew his mother and she would have been aghast!' she had continued.

Every time Daphne begrudgingly hoped that Augusta had changed her snobbish ways, she would do or say something to prove the exact opposite. Augusta may now have a blossoming (if less-than-perfectly grandmotherly) relationship with Silvanus, her late husband's biological grandson, but she remained decidedly judgemental about everything and everyone else.

'How can I help you?' Daphne asked Augusta with strained politeness. She was in no doubt that the woman had a clear purpose. Most likely she was choosing her words before administering her sting. Augusta was nothing if not punctilious in every detail of her life: she made no accidental remarks or spontaneous visits.

'Oh, I just happened to be walking past . . .'

Mmmm – highly unlikely, Daphne thought.

'I was wondering whether you knew if Lord Darlington might be willing to host any events in his gardens this year – the summer fete perhaps? What with the worrisome youths taking over the—'

'They're hardly "taking over", Augusta!' Daphne couldn't help but laugh at the overblown fear of the teenagers who had started hanging around the village green.

Augusta raised an eyebrow and continued despite Daphne's mild scoffing, ' . . . taking over the village green, as well as a homeless vagabond hanging around, I thought that it might be prudent to make alternative arrangements for the fête, for example. It was historically held at Darlington Hall after all, it was only after the present lord left for Australia that they stopped hosting it, so this could be a lovely opportunity to reintroduce that tradition. I, of course, will be more than happy to meet with his lordship to discuss things in detail, but I wondered – since you seem to be the only person to see him regularly' – Augusta sniffed disapprovingly – 'if you might mention the idea and tell him I'd like to come to discuss it.'

Was that all? Daphne wondered. It was a relatively modest ask, although she knew how hard it must have been for Augusta to admit that she had yet to buddy up with the elusive Lord Darlington despite having been on friendly terms with his mother.

'Well of course I'll ask for you, Augusta. I can't imagine why Lord Darlington wouldn't be happy with that arrangement, although the walled kitchen garden may be out of bounds due to the glasshouses' state of disrepair. Anyway, I'll ask him – or at least I'll ask Helena to mention it and arrange a proper meeting.' Daphne referred to Helena with barely concealed delight, knowing that this would irritate Augusta even more than asking for a favour in the first place.

Augusta sniffed again before turning on her heel and directing a curt 'thank you' at Daphne.

Good, that was short and sweet, thought Daphne, her eye on the time. It was twenty past nine and Mr McClean was due to view the chairs between 9.30 and 10 a.m.

'The Blackamoor waiters!' Daphne heard Augusta suddenly exclaim.

She jumped in shock, having been sure that Augusta had already left the shop.

'Ah yes ... The Blackamoor dumb waiters,' Daphne repeated, sighing under her breath.

'From Darlington Hall? Why on earth are these being sold? Lady Darlington *loved* her Blackamoors! They're Art Deco, aren't they?'

'Indeed they are, Augusta. And yes, from Darlington Hall.'

'I remember having tea with Lady Darlington in the morning room and admiring them. Such beauties! Why is Lord Darlington getting rid of them? What an extraordinary decision. Don't tell me – it's that young Helen Carter, isn't it. She hasn't got a clue about the integrity of Darlington Hall – these are a historical feature!'

'That might be so, Augusta, but some would say that regardless of its historical significance, a dumb waiter in the caricature of a Black servant is offensive and has no place in a contemporary interior. It was Hugh Darlington's decision to sell them, not Helena's – and I wholeheartedly agree. There is more than one way to honour the past without succumbing to unnecessarily offensive design tropes – no matter how old!'

Suitably chastened, Augusta opened her mouth to object and then thought better of it.

'Well, his mother would be devasted to see everything being sold,' she eventually grumbled.

'Not everything, Augusta. Only the pieces that don't need to be kept and that are taking up space. Helena and Hugh need to start making money somehow or Darlington Hall will end up being sold to strangers anyway or – heaven forbid – pulled apart by a developer. They've been very sympathetic to the idea of continuity in the interiors, but they do need to be updated. The wallpaper and curtains were practically hanging off the walls in places – it had been neglected for over a decade.'

'Possibly longer than that,' Augusta agreed reluctantly. 'Lady Darlington lost interest in everything once the former Lord Darlington pushed her beloved Hugh away.'

'Pushed him away?' Augusta had piqued Daphne's interest. Since meeting Hugh, she had often wondered why he had spent so many years far away from his family seat in England. It was one thing disagreeing with your parents as a teenager, but what magnitude of event could have kept him away for so long, even from returning immediately after the deaths of his parents?

All family dynamics were different of course, but Daphne couldn't conceive of not seeing her own family for over two decades – despite her parents having recently retired back to the Caribbean, making their meetings less regular than ever before. There must have been more to this family estrangement than a mere quarrel. After all, despite the now-crumbling Old Hall, Lord and Lady Darlington couldn't have been short of a penny or two. It was hard to imagine that they didn't have enough money to fly their son over to see them from time to time, or to make a trip to Australia themselves. *Surely Lady Darlington must have wanted a reconciliation with her son?* Daphne's mind was whirring just thinking about it.

Sensing a shift in the balance of power after registering that Daphne wasn't aware of Hugh Darlington's backstory, it was Augusta's turn to take the moral high ground and smile.

'Well, I'm not one to gossip, of course. I'm sure that Helena will fill you in on everything.' Augusta paused, watching

Daphne smugly, fully aware that the younger woman was dying to hear more.

'Perhaps ... But tell me, why did—?' There was a sudden tinkle from the bell on the shop door.

'Daphne Brewster?' called a friendly voice from the front of the shop.

Damn. Just as this was getting interesting, thought Daphne. 'Mr McClean – welcome! Tea or coffee?'

Chapter 6

Augusta felt more than a little bit smug as she left Daphne to deal with her customer and began the short stroll back to her house beside the church. The weather had hit a mild spell and the clouds floated fluffily against a pleasantly blue sky, obscuring the sun only occasionally. It created a picture-perfect backdrop to the houses in the village – reminiscent of an illustrated tourism poster from the 1930's – with her own house sitting idyllically among the rest. The Old Vicarage was as pretty and quaint as her former house had been elegant and regal. She hadn't been sad to see Wellingborough House with its Georgian splendour go. She had lived in it since the start of her marriage to Charles when the house still belonged to her in-laws – Mr and Mrs Papplewick senior. For that reason, it had never really felt like home, and she had never felt able to put much of her own stamp on it, despite her mother-in-law moving out into a nearby cottage when John's father had died. The Old Vicarage had provided a clean slate, a much-needed new beginning. Although the circumstances surrounding the change were far from the best, she had welcomed being able to start this new chapter of her life in fresh surroundings. The house may have been pretty and quaint, but, having belonged previously to the diocese until the church decided to sell it off, the interior had been functional and basic, so Augusta had finally had the opportunity to make it her own.

She walked along the High Street, wondering – contrary to Daphne's aversion – whether the Blackamoor dumb waiters might add a frivolously grand touch to her modest drawing room with its low-beamed ceiling and inglenook fireplace.

Augusta had just reached the start of the village green and was about to cross the road towards Ploughman's Walk and then on to Vicarage Lane when she noticed two things. The first was the annoying reality that the youths hanging about on the green at all hours of the day and night, weekday and weekend, looked as young and harmless as Daphne had indicated. *What a nuisance*, she thought. Their mythical menace had resolved the mystery of the recent spate of oil and poultry thefts rather nicely. Augusta's second observation was that the unkempt-looking stranger mentioned in the parish meeting seemed to be loitering under the shade of Gertrude Epsom's overgrown laurel hedge. *Note to self: the distance of that over-hang is totally unacceptable. I must mention it in the minutes of the next council meeting*, she reflected with irritation. Of course, she could just politely knock on Gertrude's front door and remind her to tame her unruly hedge discreetly and without the public embarrassment of a judgemental village audience, but Augusta vaguely remembered that Gertrude had failed to back her on opposing a planning application – the one for the erection of a single-storey extension to the house of the new Americans in the village. Augusta had yet to forgive her.

Anyway: the stranger. A bearded man wearing incredibly scruffy clothes – *were those army trousers?* – with feet wedged into those ugly casual sandals that she absolutely could not bear. From here, his feet looked so dirty they could almost be tanned. It was all most odd. Usually, Augusta could identify almost everyone in the village; even if she didn't know them by name, she certainly had a good eye for who they were or at least why they were in Pepperbridge. Tourists and people visiting relatives were easy to spot. The former usually walked far too slowly along the pavement, heads darting from side to side as they admired historic buildings; they constantly wielded their dreadful camera phones and wore hideous hooded cagoules and sensible walking shoes whatever the weather. The latter group were often holding a cake aloft or carrying gifts of wine and flowers. It was highly unusual for Augusta to spot anyone who did not fit the profile of a villager, tourist or visitor. Bar a few ghoulish tourists who had hung around shortly after Doctor Ptolemy Oates had been convicted of murdering his old friend in a potting shed, strangers tended to be the type who possessed a copy of *Britain's Most Beautiful Villages* or grown-up children visiting their elderly parents on a Sunday.

This type of stranger – the 'homeless' type – was a rarity in these parts. The main reason being that Pepperbridge was in the middle of nowhere. Surrounded by agricultural fields, it was one of a series of small villages separated by secluded lanes and roads. It took at least forty minutes of driving to reach anywhere remotely 'bustling' or accessible by foot or train. In the humble opinion of Augusta Papplewick – chairwoman of the West Norfolk charity committee K.I.N.D., which stood for Kindness, Inclusivity, Nurturing and Dedication – this type of stranger could *not* be tolerated. Standards must be upheld to retain the much-coveted Norfolk in Bloom prize, after all.

Crossing the road determinedly and without giving it a second thought, Augusta began to approach the man with her arm held aloft in his direction. 'Excuse me!' she barked, startling him with her commanding tone and steady footsteps.

He turned around in fear, grabbed the sleeping roll and rucksack that he had dumped at his feet and hightailed it in the opposite direction.

'I say, young man! Wait just a minute! I want a word with you!' Augusta shouted after him but to no avail. Within seconds he had disappeared into the distance and round a corner towards the north end of the village.

'Well!' Augusta stood in frustration, her hands on her hips, outside Gertrude Epsom's front gate, with an overgrown laurel branch tickling her right cheek.

Back at the Old Vicarage and annoyed at her foiled citizen's arrest, Augusta decided to call Inspector Hargreaves at the police station and report the stranger. Something must be done to hold back an influx of ne'er do wells entering the village and cluttering up the doorways.

'But what did he actually *do*, Mrs Papplewick?' Inspector

Hargreaves asked once more with incredible restraint and patience. 'I need to establish whether there is a crime that needs investigating or whether he was seen to be acting in a suspicious manner?'

'Well, he was menacing and yes, extremely suspicious-looking,' Augusta surmised confidently.

'In what way was he menacing? Did he approach you? Did he say anything to you or threaten you?' he said, hoping to find legitimate motivation for Mrs Papplewick's phone call.

'No, Inspector Hargreaves – I approached him. Or at least I tried to approach him. He ran off before I could reach him. Just as I explained the first time,' she added slowly, as if speaking to a child who could not grasp something profoundly obvious.

'The point, Mrs Papplewick, is that he doesn't seem to have committed an actual crime. You have just described a man you've seen in the village, walking around minding his own business—'

'Looking scruffy – he was wearing camouflage trousers!' Augusta exclaimed with indignation.

'Looking scruffy,' continued Inspector Hargreaves, pausing with growing exasperation, 'and otherwise causing no reason to be concerned. He wasn't lying on the floor or seeming ill? Did he appear inebriated in any way? I'm sure you can understand where I'm coming from, Mrs Papplewick. There hasn't been a crime committed.'

'Inspector Hargreaves – may I remind you that there has been a spate of poultry thefts and oil-tank drains in the area of late?'

Inspector Hargreaves sighed. 'Yes, yes, Mrs Papplewick.

I understand.' He evidently knew better than to continue contradicting Augusta Papplewick. 'I'll have a look for him this evening when I'm doing my rounds and I'll find out how long he intends to be in the area and whether he is of any fixed abode.'

'Very good, Inspector. I feel much safer already.'

'The poor lad has more to fear from you than you do from him,' Inspector Hargreaves murmured under his breath.

'What was that?' said Augusta, sharply.

'Nothing, Mrs Papplewick. Happy to help.'

Across the village, Daphne was clapping her hands with glee and celebrating her significant sale to Mr McClean, the gentleman who had popped by to view the formal dining chairs. Along with the chairs, he had also purchased a dining table, a grandfather clock, a Royal Doulton and Bruce Oldfield dinner service and several framed etchings. *What a result!* Not all of it was from the Darlington estate either, so she would get full price for many of the items and still have good news for Helena. Days like this reminded Daphne why moving from the city had been such a good idea. She had wanted to try something new, to be her own boss. It had come at considerable risk – she had exhausted most of her savings in renting the shop and buying the initial stock – but now business was levelling out and becoming lucrative. Most importantly, she was enjoying her work–life balance for the first time in years.

Reaching for her handbag, Daphne decided to drive up to Darlington Hall and give the good news to Helena in person. As Mr McClean had paid in cash, she would also be able to hand over Hugh and Helena's portion of the sales immediately, rather than carrying it around with her. Although she wasn't concerned by the youths on the green, especially having seen how harmless they seemed, she was still cautious enough to know that someone was responsible for the minor thefts around the village. She didn't want to tempt fate by carrying a few thousand pounds in her handbag for too long.

Daphne would take her lunch with her and hand over the money to Helena. Perhaps she could have a quick picnic on the grass beside the kitchen garden if Helena didn't mind, and then make her way into Oxwold Overy to deposit the rest of the money into her business account. She could fit all this in comfortably before school pick-up time. It was a sensible plan, and on a fine spring day like today when the cloud-free sky was bright blue and the sun was shining, it sounded like a perfect one.

Helena was equally excited when Daphne arrived on her doorstep, holding a large envelope of cash.

'That's absolutely brilliant, Daphne – Hugh will be so pleased!'

'I've written out a separate receipt with Mr McClean's name and details for your accounting records, so everything should be in order.' Daphne grinned happily.

'Amazing, thank you. Will you come in for a mug of tea?'

'Well, I'd love to, but I was rather cheekily hoping that I could have my lunch sitting in the shade of the chestnut tree overlooking your kitchen garden. It's such a beautiful day and it's so peaceful there.'

'It really is. I'll join you!' Helena said immediately – clearly keen to get outside and enjoy the sunshine after hours of cleaning and clearing out dark, dusty rooms. 'Just a sec – you go on ahead and I'll make myself a quick sandwich and bring out a flask of tea.'

'Super, I'll see you in a while.' With that, Daphne headed off in the direction of the kitchen garden, eager to have a quiet stroll and take a closer look at the glasshouses.

The minute Daphne opened the creaky wooden gate to the walled garden she felt as though she had entered a bucolic fantasy land. A secret garden filled with overgrown vegetable plants and sprouting herbs, plants gone to seed and towering into majestic shapes that bore no resemblance to their better-known forms; they were almost exotic in their untethered wildness.

From a distance, the kitchen garden appeared relatively neat and well structured, but up close it possessed an unruly beauty. The wide gravel paths between the beds and borders were still walkable, but the plants on both sides reached towards each other, forming wispy archways overhead. It was both romantic and daunting. *Where would one start?* Daphne wondered, lost in imagining returning her surroundings to being a working kitchen garden once more.

She walked slowly towards the glasshouses, taking it all in. She felt incredibly at peace walking among this verdant oasis of calm that had been abandoned for so many years before taking on a life of its own.

Daphne knew that she shouldn't enter the glasshouses – they needed a structural survey before anyone could take that risk – but she wanted to get a closer look so that she could imagine how they might look if they were restored.

She particularly loved the huge, ornately shaped Victorian cast-iron radiators that had once heated these glass sanctuaries, providing the lushly elegant retreat for generations of horticulturists past.

As she approached, she felt the thrill of their grand scale. The glasshouses were huge, awe-inspiring structures built against a long supporting red-brick wall. Not like her own relatively tiny greenhouse at home. These would once have transcended the confines of time and climate, producing humid, jungle-like heat. *If you close your eyes*, Daphne thought – indulging in a spot of fantasy – *you could perhaps imagine being in the exotic climes of the Caribbean rather than a field in rural Norfolk.*

Opening her eyes, it took her a second to see the pile of clothes in a corner of the glasshouse, along with a basic camping stove and a pair of shoes peeping out from what appeared to be a rolled-up sleeping bag. Walking close enough to the entrance to have a proper look inside, but not close enough to risk standing beneath the fragmented glass roof, she could also smell the remnants of cigarette smoke. Someone had either been sleeping in the glasshouse or they had stashed some belongings there. Daphne backed away quickly, suddenly realising that it was likely to be the homeless stranger that had been seen wandering around the village in recent weeks.

Poor chap, she thought. *Not the safest place to rest your head for the night.*

There was no sign of the man himself – if indeed these things even belonged to him – so Daphne decided to simply mention the possibility to Helena, perhaps even offering him assistance if he needed it. Having volunteered for Shelter when she lived in London, Daphne could empathise deeply with someone who had found themselves sufficiently down on their luck enough to have to sleep outside. *Perhaps they could help him to find a half-way house or some part-time work?* Maybe he could even help with clearing the kitchen garden for a while? She knew that she was getting ahead of herself, but she had a habit of rooting for the underdog. It was how she ended up proving Minerva's innocence when Mr Papplewick was murdered.

Daphne walked back to the edge of the kitchen garden just in time to see Helena approaching the chestnut tree with a tray filled with a flask, two mugs, a plate of sandwiches and two blueberry muffins.

'I just had another walk around. It's so beautiful in the kitchen garden – I'm obsessed with it!' she explained, slightly out of breath and trying to think of a way of bringing up the homeless stranger without alarming Helena.

'I know – it's lovely, isn't it? Hugh says that we don't have enough money to deal with it right now, but one day we'll definitely restore it to its former glory.'

Daphne was delighted. It would have broken her heart to hear that Hugh wasn't bothered about its restoration, although she completely understood that it would be expensive and, for now, the money was best spent elsewhere.

'Actually, I could be wrong but I think that you may have an unexpected guest living in one of the glasshouses. I saw a camping stove and some clothes, and it smelled as though someone had been sleeping rough in there relatively recently.'

'Really?' Helena asked, wide-eyed.

'Yes, I think it might be the homeless man who's been hanging around the village. A few people have mentioned him. I'm sure he's harmless,' Daphne added reassuringly, seeing Helena's eyes widen even more, 'but it might be worth getting Hugh to check out the glasshouse. If nothing else, it's not exactly the safest place to sleeping with the glass roof looking so precarious. Those shards are like a million swords of Damocles hanging over you.'

Helena was looking increasingly anxious, her eyebrows knitted together. 'Goodness – that's a bit of a worry. I think I'd better tell Hugh. I'd hate to think of someone sleeping rough in there – you, you don't think he's dangerous, do you?'

'Please don't worry, Helena,' Daphne said. 'I'm sure he was just looking for somewhere sheltered and quiet to sleep.'

At least she hoped that was the case.

Ten minutes later, Lord Darlington came steaming down from Old Hall towards Daphne with Helena trying to keep up behind him. He looked furious; his face was contorted in silent rage, his eyes darkening. 'Show me where!' he barked without greeting or even looking at Daphne, although his question was clearly directed at her.

'Um . . . in the left-hand corner of the furthest glasshouse. I only saw some clothes and a camping stove – I didn't actually see anyone . . .' Daphne almost regretted saying anything at all.

'Wait here!' Hugh raised his palm only inches from Daphne's face, stopping the two women from following him in no uncertain terms.

Daphne felt the hairs on the back of her neck begin to

bristle. She wasn't used to having orders barked at her, regardless of whether he had a title in front of his name or not, but she was a guest on Hugh Darlington's property so she would do as he had requested – and keep her mouth shut – this time.

Daphne waited beside Helena under the chestnut tree where they had a clear view of Hugh storming along the path towards the glasshouse. His stride was forceful and fast. When he arrived, they saw him enter it without hesitating.

'Oh damn,' Daphne said under her breath. She suddenly felt responsible for Hugh striding in there and knew that she wouldn't be able to forgive herself if anything happened to him. Perhaps she ought to have encouraged Helena to mention it to the police rather than Hugh. Not because she was fearful of the stranger, but because she was slightly fearful of Hugh's mood, and of what he might do to the stranger if he did indeed come across him.

The stranger was nowhere to be found. The women watched Hugh searching futilely around the walled kitchen garden before charging back to them.

On his return, Helena tentatively offered a suggestion, clearly hoping to calm Hugh down. 'Perhaps we should inform the police?'

'No!' Hugh practically shouted at her, recovering his composure when he sensed Helena practically jumping out of her skin – all under Daphne's watchful eye. 'No,' he repeated, this time more calmly. 'There's no need to involve the police. It's just a homeless man. I don't want to get him in trouble, I just want to make sure that he's OK, that's all.'

In Daphne's opinion, the way he'd thundered towards the glasshouses only moments before looked more like he was about to whack the living daylights out of someone than 'make sure they were OK'.

'Right,' Daphne announced, desperate to extract herself from this fraught conversation. 'Well, I'd better be going. I've got to get to the bank before I pick the children up from school.' She made a theatrical point of looking at her watch, feeling an urgent need to leave despite her uneaten sandwich.

Daphne's obvious desire to escape seemed to release Hugh from his angry trance and restore him to his senses; his face softened and he turned towards Daphne with a self-conscious smile. 'I meant to say thank you for organising that sale. It's helped us immensely and I'm very grateful.'

'Well, let's hope it's the first sale of many – I'm sure it will be,' Daphne replied, forcing an upbeat tone.

She had already decided to call the local police station to tell them where the homeless man was sleeping. She didn't want to get anyone into trouble either, but thinking about Hugh's irrational reaction, anything she could do to prevent the situation from escalating was surely in everyone's best interests.

Who exactly was this man she was hoping to protect? Daphne wondered as she walked back to Aggie, relieved to be leaving the tense atmosphere at Darlington Hall. If her escapades investigating Pepperbridge's last mystery were anything to go by, it wouldn't be long before she found out.

Chapter 7

As it happened, Inspector Hargreaves had several reasons to make the short trip into Pepperbridge to search for Mrs Papplewick's 'suspicious stranger' that afternoon. He wasn't simply following Augusta's orders, he had been quick to clarify to his colleagues.

That woman infuriated him no end. She was judgemental, snobbish and bullying, but he had to admit, with the heat of an uncharacteristic blush partially concealed under the whiskers of his bushy moustache and beard, that she was also extremely impressive. She reminded him of his school dorm matron as a matter of fact . . .

'Inspector!' PC Maxine Clarke put an abrupt halt to his boarding-school daydream, trying to get his attention, and not, it appeared, for the first time.

'Sorry – yes, Clarke?' Inspector Hargreaves cleared his

throat and unnecessarily adjusted his tie before looking guilt-ily over at PC Clarke. She had a telephone receiver dangling from her right hand and someone evidently on hold.

'There's been another theft in Pepperbridge. This time it's a dozen eggs and fifteen pounds from Dilly Wittock's honesty box.'

Inspector Hargreaves sighed. It was the third call they had received in as many hours about a petty theft in typ-ically crime-free Pepperbridge. It was hardly a riotous crime rampage, and certainly not as dramatic as the Doctor Oates situation last year, but it was an oddity nonetheless to be receiving so many calls. Yesterday they had had at least two calls citing thefts from people's front gardens or doorsteps, and there had been half a dozen or so others during the previous week. Individually, such thefts were insignificant, but a pattern was emerging that was worth investigating. Something was definitely up, and top of the 'likely suspects' list were the youths congregating around the village and the tramp-like stranger who had been seen skulking around the lanes and alleyways.

The final straw was a call from Daphne Brewster: the woman who had been inadvertently – and infuriatingly – caught up in the Ptolemy Oates case. Annoyingly, she also ended up being the one to entrap Doctor Oates – leading to his conviction and robbing Inspector Hargreaves of a career-defining moment of glory. How he'd longed to identify the murderer of Mr Papplewick. In his dreams he would have chased down the conniving doctor, dramatically throwing himself across the floor *CSI*-style to grab his escaping feet, pinning him down and apprehending him on the spot. He had often fantasised about the glowing praise and thunderous applause he could have attracted from an awed crowd watching the impressive scene unfold. This was how working in the police appeared on the television. *Alas, not in real life.* In real life, a meddling woman from south London took down the suspect singlehandedly, leaving just the bare scraps of glory as he handcuffed the already-unconscious Doctor Oates. Now that same woman was meddling some more, phoning to tell him that she knew where his current 'suspect' had been sleeping rough.

'Would you rather I went down on my own?' PC Clarke once more interrupted his idle reverie, still holding the receiver and waiting patiently for something to tell Dilly Tamworth.

'No, no – tell her I'm on my way.'

As she waited for her children to bundle out of their classrooms, Daphne stood in the playground with Minerva Leek standing shyly at her side. It amused Daphne how hilarious and cynically witty Minerva could be once she warmed to you, yet in public she assumed the guise of a nervous child.

Years of being made to feel like an outsider in her home village had left Minerva fearing criticism and confrontation. Even now, she still preferred to fade into the background, swathed in her unassuming black ankle-length skirts and hand-knitted sweaters, as far removed from the Boden-wearing yummy mummies or Dubarry-stomping horsewomen that dominated the school gates as one could possibly get. Her overbearing instinct was to hide her anxious-looking narrow face and intelligent eyes behind a long, dark fringe and observe quietly in the hope that she would be left alone – despite being a grown woman who was more than capable of defending herself and her son when necessary. She was a strange mix of stoic intelligence and self-conscious anxiety. The former enabling her to stand her ground in the unlikely event that she was publicly challenged and the latter causing her to retreat when she was given half the chance, even when people were trying to be pleasant. Of course, now that she had been openly acknowledged as the late Mr Papplewick's daughter – with the cherry on top being her unexpected tenuous friendship with his widow, Augusta – few challenges or sneers were directed at her these days. Even Marianne Forbes was forced to be on her best behaviour when it came to Minerva and her son Silvanus, despite her instincts being to the contrary. In Marianne's estimation, Minerva was what she would have called 'prime sport' at school – a 'weirdo' who should have been an easy target – and it was most frustrating that she was now out of bounds for light-hearted one-upmanship.

'The poor man!' Minerva was saying to Daphne after hearing the story about Hugh, the potential rough sleeper and the glasshouse. 'If you ever see him, please let him know that he's more than welcome up at Cringlewic. He probably just needs a helping hand to get him back on his feet. We've got a few empty cabins up in the commune and he's fine to bunk in one if he wants. The others won't mind a bit – it's what we do.'

'That's an excellent idea, Minerva, and such a generous offer. If I see him, I'll let him know. I'll also tell Inspector Hargreaves that that offer is on the table. It'll be reassuring for him to know that they're not just moving him on to the same situation in another village – or worse. Everyone deserves a roof over their head, preferably not one that's made from broken glass.'

In the distance, Minerva and Daphne spotted the unmistakeable figure of Marianne Forbes charging through the school gates and judgementally surveying the playground. They both let out a quiet groan as they registered her steaming towards them with torpedo-like determination.

'Hello, ladies!' Marianne barked loudly, looking around brightly to see who else had noticed her arrival. She always wanted to give the impression that she was having the most fun and the wittiest conversation, and there was no point in doing that without an audience to appreciate it. Despite being permanently disappointed that she was forced to send her children to Pepperbridge Primary School rather than the deliciously covetable and smart prep school in town, she was determined to make the best of a bad situation. Taking the view that it was mind over matter, she aimed to treat every school playground appearance with as much sparkling pomp and ceremony as a lunch (that she could not afford in any case) with the girls at Claridge's. She was, after all, the biggest fish in a very small pond, and the other parents deserved to be reminded of what they should aspire to daily. 'What's on today's agenda then?'

'We were just talking about the poor man who's been seen around the village. If you see him again, please could you let him know that there's a bed in Cringlewic for him?' Daphne had been reluctant to tell Marianne, but then she realised that the more people who knew there was somewhere welcoming for the man to stay, the better.

'Urghhh – yes – how ghastly!' Marianne exclaimed, barely

listening and instantly getting the wrong end of the stick. 'I mean, what on *earth* is he doing around here? Aren't there laws to stop tramps from being near schools and preying on decent villagers? I mean, lord knows what he would do if he caught one of us women on our own. He's probably not eaten or washed for weeks – let alone had . . . you know . . . !' Marianne paused for a second, the sudden thrill of that horrifyingly filthy but strangely enticing image clouding her thoughts for a second.

'Marianne, I imagine that the last thing on his mind is ravaging you on the school run. He probably does want a hot meal and a hot bath though,' Daphne interjected in exasperation, while Minerva suppressed a laugh. She could count on Marianne to overlook anyone else's welfare, especially in favour of a more titillatingly imagined outcome.

To Daphne and Minerva's relief, the school bell rang, signalling the end of the day and bringing their conversation with Marianne to a premature (and convenient) close. Excited children poured into the playground in a cacophony of noise and chatter.

Daphne nodded goodbye to Minerva, with the giggling twins Fynn and Archie on either side of her, clinging to each of her arms and attempting to swing while the more sensible Imani hastily swapped a book of Greek mythology for Silvanus's portable chess set, before they departed in their separate directions.

'I've just got to pop back into the shop to grab the dog bed – it's in desperate need of a wash,' Daphne told the children who were safely strapped into the back seat of the Morris Traveller. Byron, the miniature dachshund who often accompanied her, was today more than happily ensconced on an oversized floral cushion back at Cranberry Farmhouse with James in his home office. On days when Daphne needed to visit a client's house, she usually left her ever-faithful little companion at home, although she missed having him by her side during the day.

Daphne had just pulled out of School Lane when she spotted the man. He had stopped to stroke a cat that was miaowing for attention. Hearing the car, he instantly crossed the road and began hustling quickly along the opposite side. He had a large kitbag slung over his shoulder, and he was wearing a misshapen jumper that hung over a dirty pair of combat trousers and battered Birkenstocks.

She pulled over quickly and told the children to remain where they were.

Sensing Daphne's car slowing, the man had begun to speed up into a half jog, half run in the direction of Bernard Close.

'Excuse me!' Daphne got out of her car and trotted after him with her hand raised. 'Please don't worry, I don't want to bother you! I just want to tell you about somewhere you can sleep!' she called out.

He slowed down and hesitated before pausing to turn around to look at her.

'Honestly, I mean you no harm. It's just that – well, I think I saw your things in the Darlington Hall kitchen garden, and I wanted to let you know that there's a place at the Cringlewic commune in the woods where you can stay if you want a proper roof over your head. They'd be happy to help you. The glasshouse is dangerous and well, obviously, it's private property. I wouldn't want you to get into any trouble or anything . . .' Her voice trailed off. Daphne was aware that she was beginning to sound like a proper busybody who was hellbent on not minding her own business.

The stranger was standing at a distance from her, his hand shielding his eyes from the glare of the low afternoon sun. There was something vaguely familiar about him, and then it came to her: this was the man who had watched her standing at the top of the field from the kitchen garden the evening after the parish council meeting. Not Hugh Darlington. That's why he hadn't waved back. She'd caught him trespassing on the Darlington property without realising, and then she had gone and waved at him. Looking at the stranger now, she saw that it had been an easy mistake to make. He had a similar height and stocky build to Hugh and close up she could see that they had similar colouring too. But looking at this man's threadbare clothes and scruffy hair, it was obvious now that it was him that she had waved at, and she smiled at her error.

The stranger paused for a few moments more and smiled back. 'Cheers. I'll remember that,' he called back to her. With that, he turned and fell back into his half jog, accompanied by the cat, who had by now caught up with him and was still meowing by his side.

'He seemed normal enough to me,' Daphne was telling James back at home in Pudding Corner later that evening. She watched her husband dice her home-grown leeks and add them to a delicious-smelling casserole before accepting the glass of red wine she held out to him in an extended hand.

'Still, probably not necessarily the wisest decision to approach him with the children in the back of the car—'

'But he was nowhere near the children,' Daphne replied, 'and, as I said, he seemed incredibly normal . . . He was stroking a cat!'

'Whatever that proves!' James interjected, sipping his wine and looking at his wife in amusement. Her fearlessness never ceased to entertain, amaze, and worry him in equal measure.

'I mean that he wasn't threatening or weird, and he didn't seem out of his head on drink or drugs. Just rather calm and almost affable.' She paused to take a sip from her smooth and intensely fruity glass of Chilean red (was that a silky note of plum she had just tasted?) before coming up behind James and adding a pinch more salt and pepper to the casserole dish. He grimaced affably in faux disapproval. 'I hope he takes my advice and heads over to Cringlewic. I hate to think of him sleeping in that glasshouse – or worse, Hugh Darlington finding him trespassing on his property!'

'Well, listen, Mother Teresa, you can't help everyone and at least you've done your best to try to help this man. Can you try to stay out of trouble this time? Now, where are those pistachios?'

Just down the road and across the fields in Pepperbridge, Inspector Hargreaves had concluded a mini-investigation of his own. With PC Clarke in the driving seat, he had just got back in the police car after chatting with Dilly Tamworth about her stolen eggs. Apparently it hadn't been the first time that her eggs or the money from the honesty box had been stolen, and normally she wasn't too bothered, but this week she'd added a few country boxes filled with potatoes and tomatoes, as well as a couple of bunches of daffodils from her garden, so there had been a bit more money left out front than usual, including some notes.

'It's an unfortunate business,' Inspector Hargreaves had agreed after listening to Dilly complain about the concerning state of young people, general moral slackness and a failing society for over fifty minutes.

'Things aren't what they used to be,' Dilly had lamented. 'Back in the day you could leave a hundred pounds out on your front lawn and no one would touch it. In fact, you'd most likely wake up to find more money since people would assume you were collecting for charity! I've known me neighbours for over fifty years and I'd trust them with me life. They even helped me look for Mr Tiddles, me cat, when he went missing. It's a shame that things are changing so quickly. New people arriving all the time and youths hanging around every street corner. Where are the old ways? Where's the trust? Where's the community? It's all gone to pot I tell you – and now me eggs!' Dilly had wailed in despair.

'Indeed. Well, I can assure you that we will be doing our very best to find the perpetrator – or perpetrators – involved,' Inspector Hargreaves had reassured her, patting his brow with a handkerchief as he attempted, for the fifth time, to leave before she restarted her tirade. It was perfectly understandable of course. She was quite rightly upset that someone would have the bare-faced cheek to walk up to her front garden and steal money from an old woman without thinking twice. However, his time was better spent trying to find the thieves rather than sitting and hearing a million different ways in which society had fallen apart over multiple cups of tea and slices of cake – even if he agreed with her and her Battenberg slice was top-notch.

'Where to next, sir?' PC Clarke asked patiently. She had been sitting alone in the car for the past fifty minutes while Inspector Hargreaves had 'popped' in to ask Dilly Tamworth a few questions. No tea and Battenberg slices for her; she tried her best not to feel bitter about it.

'Darlington Hall, methinks,' the inspector replied, shifting about in his seat. 'Damn, Dilly's Battenberg slices are good!' he exclaimed before letting out a long and, alas, not-marzipan-scented belch.

Truth be told, the welcome that Inspector Hargreaves and PC Clarke received at Darlington Hall was rather less warm than they had anticipated. Helena Carter had been surprised to see them on the imposing doorstep but she had been affable enough – in no small part because she and Maxine knew each other from their time at the village school. But it all went steadily downhill when Helena attempted to get the latest incumbent Lord Darlington to come and greet the two police officers.

Helena had left them standing in the entrance hall while she had disappeared down a long, echoey corridor and through an ornately carved, heavy-framed oak door, leaving it slightly ajar. At first all they could hear were dogs barking in a worryingly aggressive manner, but after a few admonishing commands from their owner, they quietened down, allowing the echoing hallway to act as a giant ear trumpet, funnelling all sounds back to the entrance hall. Inspector Hargreaves and PC Clarke had heard the hissings of what appeared to be an ill-contained argument between Helena and Lord Darlington, with the young woman trying her best to coax the man out of his study.

Eventually, having finally persuaded him, Helena re-appeared. An openly resistant Lord Darlington followed with his two Border collies trotting beside him.

'Lord Darlington, I presume?' Inspector Hargreaves held his hand out towards the other man, slightly nervous of the two large hounds standing silently, but with their teeth occasionally flashing in warning, on either side of Hugh.

'Hmm,' Lord Darlington leaned in, reluctantly shaking the proffered hand and nodding his head in agreement before taking a step backwards and waiting silently to hear what Inspector Hargreaves would say next. The two dogs looked attentively at their quiet master, just waiting for him to say the word.

'You probably don't remember me?' the inspector continued nervously, eyeing the poised collies.

Lord Darlington's eyes widened with interest as he peered intently at the police officer, trying to place his face.

'There's no reason why you should. I was a young bobby on the beat when I last met you. Fresh-faced and bushy-tailed, straight from the academy. You couldn't have been more than seven or eight – it was just before you went off to boarding school, I believe.'

Lord Darlington's face clouded over, and his inquisitive expression changed rapidly to one of deep irritation. Inspector Hargreaves felt it best to move the topic swiftly on. He recalled that boarding school hadn't been a particularly happy time for the seemingly privileged youngster. In fact, it had proven to be the start of things going wrong for the young lad. *Hadn't he been found hitchhiking and trying to run away from home on more than one occasion?*

'Err – yes, well – the reason I'm here, Lord Darlington, is that there have been a number of thefts around the village in recent weeks. I've been informed that you may have a had a stranger loitering around your greenhouse and we'd like to have a few words in connection to them.'

Lord Darlington's face remained impassive for an uncomfortably long time. Three pairs of eyes staring expectantly at him for several seconds, awaiting his response, failed to prompt him to speak.

Finally Helena – eager to break the silence – interjected, 'Yes, that's right, we found some belongings hidden in one of the Victorian glasshouses. We're not sure who they belong to of course, but it looks like someone was squatting in there. Isn't that right, Hugh?' Helena looked over at her fiancé, her eyes pleading for him to be at least a little bit accommodating.

Hugh Darlington expelled a long sigh, finally finding his tongue and coming to his senses. 'Yes, of course, darling,' he confirmed in a clipped and dismissive tone. He turned to Inspector Hargreaves and spoke carefully. 'We assumed he was a harmless vagrant, but should we be worried, Inspector?'

'No, not as far as we're aware, although I wouldn't approach him if you do see him – just in case, as you never know who has been taking what these days.' The inspector gave Lord Darlington a knowing look and silently mouthed 'DRUGS' rather dramatically, as though the women present couldn't see and, if they could, might faint at the word being said aloud.

PC Clarke rolled her eyes at Helena, and Helena responded with a stifled smile of acknowledgement.

'Would we be able to take a look at said greenhouse please, sir?'

'Of course,' Hugh replied. 'I'll take you there myself. Piper! Damascus! Heel!'

On the stroll down, PC Clarke and Helena strolled amiably behind the men, taking the opportunity to catch up on gossip about former classmates and village life. Hugh Darlington strode out purposefully in front, with Inspector Hargreaves trying desperately to keep up with the much fitter, younger man.

'Truth be told, Inspector; I do believe that we've had a few thefts from around Old Hall recently. I hadn't thought much of it as it's only been small things so far, but now you've explained your reason for being here, I've started to put two and two together, and it's all beginning to make sense.'

'Ah, interesting!' Inspector Hargreaves managed to catch up with Lord Darlington, almost puffed out of breath by his efforts. He was simultaneously excited by this new information and halfway to being too exhausted to react.

'Yes, you may have heard that we're in the midst of clearing out a few things from the hall in order to get things up and running for holiday accommodation, so when the odd thing goes missing it has been easy to assume that things have simply been misplaced by accident.' Hugh turned to make sure that the two women were a good distance behind before he quickly flicked his eyes back to a ruddy-faced Inspector Hargreaves. 'You see, between you and I, Inspector Hargreaves, the estate that I have inherited is in a bloody awful state of affairs. Financially, it's on the brink of ruin and structurally it's falling apart. So understandably, I must do everything I can to save it and keep it going. That hasn't been easy or straightforward.'

Inspector Hargreaves puffed and nodded beside him, happy to allow Hugh to continue speaking as they reached the south gate to the walled kitchen garden.

'Unfortunately, my brother – and my father before him – mismanaged the estate finances and I'm only now beginning to see to what extent. It's a complete mess and the paperwork is endless.'

He pushed the old gate open, leaving it ajar so that the women could follow through behind them.

'I see,' Inspector Hargreaves managed to mumble. Thankfully they were on flat ground now and Hugh's pace had mercifully slowed to a brisk stroll.

'It means that I'm often tied up speaking with solicitors and accountants. I've had to fire my brother's old business manager since he seems to have been helping himself to the pot in my absence.'

'Yes, I imagine that he had ample time in the years it took them to locate you . . .' Inspector Hargreaves blurted without thinking.

Hugh looked over at him sharply and Inspector Hargreaves felt compelled to compensate for potentially overstepping the mark. 'I, err . . . I didn't mean to imply that it was in any way your own fault, of course. Who could have predicted that your brother would pass away in such tragic circumstances?'

The 'tragic' circumstances surrounding the early demise of the eighth Lord Darlington – playboy, all-round *bon vivant* and

Hugh's elder brother – had involved him falling from the deck of a privately chartered casino yacht in Port Canaveral wearing nothing but a pair of gold lamé carnival knickers, a coconut-shell bralette and a pair of bespoke John Lobb foil boat shoes. The coroner had said that if he hadn't drowned then the alcohol levels in his bloodstream would have killed him anyway. He'd left the Darlington estate in a dire state of debt.

'No, Inspector. I hadn't imagined for one second you would think that,' Hugh said pointedly.

They had reached the entrance to the glasshouse and the four of them stood peering in.

'His things are over there – see?' Hugh nodded his head in the direction of the pile of clothes that lay in the far-left corner. They spilled out from behind a radiator: a small camping stove and a few half-opened tins were scattered around. 'He's clearly been living in here,' he added solemnly.

Inspector Hargreaves proceeded to raise his foot to enter but was caught by Hugh, who prevented him with a sharp arm across his stomach, almost winding the inspector in the process.

'Look up,' he indicated with his other hand, eventually releasing the inspector from his hold and pointing at the glasshouse roof.

'Goodness me!' the inspector exclaimed, looking up to see the mosaic of intricately cracked panes and broken shards of glass glistening and twinkling menacingly from a great height in the late afternoon sunshine.

'Daphne said it was like a million swords of Damocles – and she was right!' exclaimed Helena, looking up in awe and horror.

'Well, I think the first thing we ought to do is to put some police tape across these structures to prevent anyone – our stranger included – from entering and getting hurt.'

'I totally agree, Inspector,' Hugh Darlington said, nodding sagely in agreement. 'And are there any other measures that you think we should take? For our own security? Until we know what sort of chap this homeless man is, at least.'

'Just be vigilant, Lord Darlington, and give me a call if you see anything or anyone suspicious or worrying. At the moment, we can't be sure that the homeless stranger is the same person responsible for the petty crimes that have been going on, but if there is any evidence to make that connection we can haul him in for questioning. To help us in the meantime, if you wouldn't mind putting together a list of the things that have gone missing from Darlington Hall, perhaps we can see whether we can find anything during our enquiries. You'd be surprised how many stolen goods are stored close to the locations of burglaries for thieves to retrieve later.'

'Right you are, Inspector. Good advice. Thank you.'

Helena looked questioningly at Hugh. He suddenly seemed to be being incredibly affable towards the inspector. It was rare for him to be so friendly around strangers; normally he was on his guard, stressed and suspicious of everyone. From the stories he had told her, it was clear that life had dealt Hugh some tough blows, leaving him with trust issues that affected the way he interacted with everyone – except her, of course.

After Inspector Hargreaves and PC Clarke had said their goodbyes, Helena turned to Hugh and asked the question that she could not shake from her mind. 'You've noticed things missing? Inside the house?'

Hugh had been about to return to his office, but hearing her concerned voice, he turned towards her, put his arm reassuringly around her shoulder and told her not to worry.

'I'm sure it's nothing, bits of paperwork and a few trinkets – a paperweight and some silver frames. Possibly things that I've mislaid. It was just something I mentioned in passing to the inspector.'

'No one has been in the house – have they?' she asked again, her stomach churning.

'No, darling. No one's been here that we don't know about. It's all fine.'

But staring into the distance over Helena's head, Hugh's worried eyes belied the calm of his voice.

Chapter 8

It was the burglary at Chestnut Cottage that finally convinced the Pepperbridge community to start taking the petty thefts seriously. What seemed to have started as opportunistic pilfering – a few eggs here and a garden tool there – appeared to be turning into a far more sinister crime spree.

The Chestnut Cottage burglary had come straight after another burglary on School Lane where only a few items were snatched from a doorstep. This one had been a professional break-in while the occupants had been visiting relatives in Cornwall. The back door had been kicked open, the back windows had been smashed, and electrical goods worth several hundreds of pounds had been stolen. Thankfully nothing of personal value had been lost, except perhaps the sense of peace and ease within the village. The entire parish of Pepperbridge and Pudding Corner had long prided itself on being the type of locality where you could comfortably leave your doors unlocked or ask a friendly neighbour to pop into your house to feed your cat while you were out working.

This trusting neighbourly atmosphere was one of the things that had drawn Daphne to the county of Norfolk in her family's search for a slower and more rustic life. Not that she would ever willingly leave her doors unlocked. Once a city girl, always a city girl, and that was a level of trust that she didn't think she could ever relax into. She remembered standing in the kitchen in her bra and knickers one weekend morning, hair wet from the shower, kettle whistling noisily on the stove, and Byron happily chewing on something questionable at her feet. It was early and James and the children had still been in bed the last time she checked. She had been about to take her husband a hot mug of tea when there was a tapping on her kitchen window and there, on the other side, was the postman cheerfully staring in and waving a parcel.

Bearing in mind that the kitchen was located at the back of the house, so he would have had to walk all the way round and open the gate to tap on that particular window, Daphne's soul almost left her body. It was a level of neighbourly familiarity that she had never experienced – or expected.

Raising a tea towel to her front she'd walked to the back door in shock, thanked the postman for delivering the package, briefly chatted about the weather, and said goodbye as though it was the most normal thing in the world to have a conversation standing in your underwear covering yourself with a tea towel that barely reached your tummy button. Daphne had wondered what surreal *Truman Show*-esque place she had found herself in. The memory still made her face flush, and from that day forward she always remembered to wear a dressing gown.

The possibility that there was a thief in the midst of this friendliness and familiarity was a shock to everyone who had heard the news. Serious burglaries were unheard of in Pepperbridge and Pudding Corner. Bras, knickers and underpants disappearing from clothes lines for a bet – yes; doors broken down and windows smashed – no. Not in these pleasant pastoral surroundings.

Worse still, and particularly distressing for the residents of a village obsessed with outward appearances, was the graffiti that had appeared on the churchyard walls. In large curling letters were scrawled the words, 'PIGS', 'SCUM' and 'ARSE'. It was rather juvenile and crude, but unsettling and scandalous nonetheless.

An emergency parish council meeting had been called and most attendees were villagers with at least one anecdotal story about something going missing over the past few weeks. An overwhelming sense of dread was beginning to creep over the parish as, one after the other, the villagers expressed their fears.

Inspector Hargreaves attempted to stem the rising tide of panic by explaining that the police were already working on several leads. 'The local constabulary are very aware of your concerns. Please rest assured that we are doing everything in our power to hunt the criminals down,' he shouted above the noise of people swapping burglary horror stories that they had read in the national news.

'Please, please, ladies and gentlemen. Can we have calm,

please?' The inspector raised his voice, glancing at Augusta Papplewick who looked smugly amused at his lack of crowd control.

They both knew that it would have taken her less than half a second to gain control of the rowdy room had she chosen to do so, but instead she sat with pursed lips, letting him suffer.

He tried thumping his hand on the table but accidentally hit one of the vicar's silver trays, which had been used to transport teas and coffees from the tiny kitchen. It smashed to the floor with a resounding crash. Suddenly everyone was silent and staring at Inspector Hargreaves. At a loss for what to say, in desperation he adapted his favourite lines from a film. 'We, at the West Norfolk Police, have a particular set of skills. Skills that we have acquired over very long careers. Skills that make us a nightmare for criminals like this ...' He had everyone's full attention now so he couldn't stop talking. 'If they stop now then hopefully that will be the end of it, but if they don't, we will look for them ... we will find them ... and by Jove, we will CHARGE them!' He ended by slamming his fist once more on the table, and the room erupted into rapturous applause.

After the meeting, Patsy and Daphne slowly wandered back to Patsy's shop. It was mild enough to take their time, with only a slight nip to the breeze that gently rustled the trees. Daphne was delighted that her friend had finally ventured beyond her shop doorway, even if the parish meeting wasn't the most exciting social engagement.

'Wasn't that Liam Neeson's famous speech from that film?' Patsy asked Daphne.

'*That's* where it's from! *Taken*. I've been wracking my

brains thinking about it – I knew I recognised it from some-where!' The women laughed companionably. 'Well,' Daphne continued, 'he certainly got everyone's attention with those words and thankfully not everyone is as obsessed with action films as you are, Patsy, so they're probably none the wiser!'

'It's quite worrying though, isn't it? I've never known of proper robberies in the area, and I've lived here my whole life. It does make me wonder whether that's what happened to Nancy.' Patsy's eyebrows furrowed.

'What, a robbery gone wrong? But nothing was stolen, was it?' Daphne asked, although they had discussed this at the time, and she already knew that the answer was no.

'I know, but it still doesn't make any sense to me,' Patsy replied wistfully. 'Nancy wouldn't just have fallen from a ladder that she climbed every day of her life!'

Daphne thought back to the loose, wrinkled tights that Nancy was wearing on the morning that she died, but she kept quiet. At the time, she had warned Nancy to pull them up and be careful, as a joke. Heartbreakingly, the thought of Nancy tripping over them did not seem as unlikely to her as it did to Patsy.

'I'm so sorry, Patsy . . . We all miss Nancy so much.'

Patsy smiled weakly, eyes darting away. 'Anyway, here we are. I'd better head straight home.' They had reached the doorway of Warburtons'.

'Are you OK to lock up or would you like me to wait?' Daphne said.

'Don't be daft,' Patsy replied gruffly as she turned the key in the shop door, ' . . . but thank you for asking.'

*

Daphne had arranged to meet Helena at Darlington Hall the following morning. After clearing three bedrooms and two bathrooms, they were now at the design stage, looking at the beautifully proportioned and now empty rooms that were ready for decorating. Daphne had already prepared mood boards for each of these rooms and this morning they were going to order paint and wallpaper samples.

Having come directly from school drop off, Daphne had arrived twenty minutes earlier than their scheduled meeting time. Conscious that although Helena wouldn't mind, one could never second guess what mood the unpredictable Lord Darlington might be in, she decided that rather than surprise them she would take an early stroll down to her favourite place, the walled kitchen garden, have a quick mooch around, and then walk back up to the hall in time for the meeting at 9.30 a.m. While her snooping days were meant to be behind her – especially if Inspector Hargreaves had anything to do it – she couldn't resist.

Walking through the kitchen garden was like a morning meditation; even the prospect of bumping into the stranger was not enough to put her off. Sadly, seeing homelessness up close was not something new for anyone who had lived in a city and so it didn't deter her – despite James's reservations about her wanderings. Besides, if she saw the stranger again she could ask if he needed help or at least raise the alarm if he appeared menacing.

All Daphne could hear was the wind rustling through the plants to the melodic accompaniment of birdsong. She imagined how wonderful it would be to host a yoga session within these peaceful walls. In fact, that could be the perfect money-making scheme for Hugh and Helena: a wellness retreat where people stayed in the bedrooms, ate food grown in the kitchen garden, and practised yoga surrounded by plants. *How utterly blissful*, she thought, making a mental note to suggest the idea to Helena.

She had reached the first glasshouse, and she couldn't help trying to suss out whether the mysterious stranger was still using it as his base. There was a difference this time: the glasshouse was bordered by blue-and-white police tape gently flapping in the breeze.

Oh dear, Daphne thought as she walked the length of the building towards the entrance. Now she could smell the remnants of a fire through the cracks in the glass. There was a rancid edge to the lingering scent of woodsmoke. It looked as though the man had not only continued sleeping and cooking in there, but through the rippled panes of glass she could vaguely see that he had moved an even bigger pile of things to his precarious residence. The stranger appeared to have no intention of taking up Minerva's offer to stay at Cringlewic commune. Hugh would undoubtedly be furious.

Despite her earlier bravado, Daphne wondered what she would actually do if she discovered that he was still asleep in there. *What if he was the thief, and what if he was dangerous after all?* But she had a strong hunch that he wasn't. He had seemed understandably reticent the day she had approached him, but he had also come across as non-aggressive and, in truth, rather polite. From the little she had seen of his face, his eyes had seemed sad yet kind, and she'd had the sense that he hadn't wanted to be any bother at all.

She peered in cautiously. The distinctly unpleasant stench

filling the building and the burning smell was getting stronger by the minute. The pile of clothes she had seen through the glass was even larger than she had thought and in the middle of the floor. There was an open holdall bag filled with what appeared to be brass candlesticks, picture frames and various other shiny objects jumbled chaotically within and what remained of a recently smouldering campfire with a few embers silently twinkling. Except the more she looked, the more she realised that she wasn't looking at a pile of clothes at all. She was looking at the body of a man dressed in multiple layers of clothes who was slumped over the fire, collapsed.

Goosebumps erupting on her skin, Daphne ran inside without hesitation, not thinking of her own safety for a second. She grabbed the body by the shoulders and leaned his head back to see if he was conscious. Half of his face was charred and burned, and his eyes were open. Gagging at the smell of burned flesh, which had become overwhelmingly noxious, and stifling a scream, Daphne realised that the man wasn't just unconscious, he was in fact very much dead. Worse still, he had a large shard of thick glass sticking directly out of his back and through his chest, as she belatedly realised her hands were now damp from the sodden patches of blood that had seeped through his darkened clothes. Horrified, she could no longer contain her scream. Dropping the body and frantically wiping her hands on her trousers she leaped up and looked at the glass roof.

Panic and confusion engulfed her. *Surely he hadn't been killed by a falling shard of glass? Dear God.*

In shock and at a loss for a brief second, Daphne pulled herself together and realised that there were two things she needed to do. She needed to call the police, of course, but first she must move away from this half-shattered glass ceiling before another deadly shard fell.

Her phone had no signal in that part of the garden – in fact, the signal in and around the estate was notoriously bad at the best of times – so she ran desperately back up towards Darlington Hall, her heart thudding, dialling furiously. She needed to raise the alarm to Hugh and Helena so while she continued trying to call 999, she ran towards the front door and started banging. She had only just hung up after finally getting through and frantically informing the emergency services when Helena flung open the door wailing, her tear-stained face in a state of panic.

'My goodness, Helena! What's happened?' Daphne asked in confusion. *Had Helena already seen the body?*

'It's H-H-Hugh.' She gulped hysterically. 'He's been attacked – we've been burgled ... Oh Daphne, he's really hurt!'

Chapter 9

The screeching sound of sirens cut through the early morning air as the police and two ambulances arrived almost simultaneously, scattering gravel up the drive.

Daphne had followed the panicked Helena into Darlington Hall and down a corridor towards Hugh's study. It was a beautiful room – Daphne couldn't help noticing despite the circumstances – but it had been truly ransacked; papers, books and furniture had been toppled over and lay strewn around. Somebody had thoroughly searched the room – drawers had been pulled out and tables upended – but what had they been looking for? On the floor behind the large mahogany breakfront desk, just out of sight from the doorway, Hugh Darlington was slumped unconscious with a gash to the back of his head. His hands were covered in blood, as if he had been attempting to defend himself, and an ornate, blood-stained candelabra lay on the floor next to the carved claw-and-ball foot of the desk.

Hands shaking and in disbelief, Daphne checked for a pulse. A faint throb in Lord Darlington's wrist reassured Daphne that she wasn't on the cusp of discovering two corpses in one morning. She instructed Helena to stay with him and ensure that his airways were kept clear while she waited for the police and ambulance to arrive to show them where to go. She didn't want to mention the body to Helena in her panicked state; that could come later. The poor girl hadn't stopped to question why Daphne had seemed equally as flustered when she had flung open the door earlier and Daphne was worried that it would be too much for her to bear under the circumstances.

Daphne had witnessed some things in her time, particularly over the past two years living in Pudding Corner, but this morning topped the list of her most surreal experiences. In fact, this had to be the weirdest day she had had since moving to Norfolk – and considering that she had once found herself fighting for her life with a previously innocuous neighbour, that was saying a lot.

Could the body in the glasshouse and the burglary at Darlington Hall be a coincidence? Daphne doubted it. Judging from the bag of loot by the side of the body in the kitchen garden, it seemed at a first glance that the mysterious stranger may have attempted a robbery, encountered Hugh in the study, attacked him and run off. But why would he have run off to the exact place where everyone knew he had been hiding, and then sit down and start a campfire? It didn't make any logical sense. Surely if you had just burgled and attacked someone, you wouldn't escape to their garden to cook a meal? Wouldn't you want to get as far away as possible as fast as you could?

Perhaps he had been trying to get away, Daphne reflected. *Maybe he had only returned to the glasshouse to collect a few things and burn some evidence?* It would only have taken a second or two for a shard of glass to fall from the fractured roof and pierce him through the back.

Daphne began to feel sick. The horrific image of that poor man impaled by a huge shard of glass didn't bear thinking about. But no matter how hard she tried, she couldn't shift the terrible sight from her mind.

Inspector Hargreaves had come to the same conclusion as Daphne after questioning her and Helena. A burglary gone wrong, he surmised, followed by the deceased stranger's ill-fated attempt to gather his things from the glasshouse, burn the evidence of his crime, and run away. The bag that Daphne had seen upon discovering the body was filled with the stolen silverware, some ornately framed pictures of the Darlington family, a few wallets – including Lord Darlington's – and other random household goods that had been reported stolen from the village, with more missing items found stashed away around the glasshouse. There was no indication that anyone else was involved, and with most reported items now accounted for, it certainly pointed towards him acting alone.

If Inspector Hargreaves had read the situation correctly and if his officers played their cards right, they would in all likelihood be able to trace all of the missing items to the glasshouse or the other places in the walled garden, where the man may have stashed them to come back for at a later time. It might even turn out to be a nice and neat open-and-shut case with no loose ends. Just how he liked them. He'd rather leave the complicated crimes to the Met and be home in time for dinner. And while meddling Daphne Brewster somehow managed to be at the scene of the crime *again*, at least she wasn't stealing any of his glory this time.

Daphne looked on as the officers searched the house and grounds. She felt a twinge of sadness that the priority seemed to be finding the stolen possessions, when one man was dead and another seriously injured. It seemed all wrong.

It appeared that Hugh Darlington was going to be fine – thankfully. After the ambulance crew had arrived and administered medical aid to him, he had regained consciousness, although he had little recollection about what had taken place. He was still extremely woozy and needed to be taken to hospital to be put under observation for potential concussion. Whatever had happened had only taken place in the last couple of hours and although Hugh had no recollection of the burglary now, it was possible that time would restore his memory.

Daphne asked Helena if she would like her to stay for a while and she gratefully agreed. The news of the body in the kitchen garden had obviously been the last straw for the poor girl's already frayed nerves. Hugh's study had been cordoned off for further investigation and two police officers remained there taking photos and notes. With Helena having already answered as many questions as she could, she was allowed to clean herself up and get ready to follow Hugh to the hospital so that she could bring him home after he had had his once-over. It was only when Helena was released from questioning that Daphne realised that she was still in a nightie and dressing gown, looking bewildered and childlike, her eyes wide and permanently on the verge of tears.

'You go and have a shower and get dressed and I'll make us some sweet tea to calm our nerves,' she told the younger woman, who was obviously in no fit state to drive to the hospital on her own just yet. Aware that she still had some blood on her own shirt, Daphne didn't want to distress Helena any further, and thought better of asking her for a clean top, instead buttoning up her cardigan discreetly to cover the offending stains.

In the kitchen, she filled a battered old copper kettle with water from an oversized brass tap over the huge Belfast sink. She placed it on the stove top, found the mugs and tea bags and then leaned back against the scrubbed-oak kitchen counter, replaying the awful events of that morning. If she hadn't arrived early and headed straight for the walled garden, they still wouldn't have known that there was a body there. She was aware that since finding out about the trespasser, Hugh had taken to patrolling the garden at different times of the day, but with Hugh lying unconscious in the study, would anyone have gone down to the kitchen garden? *The body could have lain undiscovered for days.* The thought sent a shiver down Daphne's spine. And what a bizarre twist of fate that the homeless stranger would suffer such a freakish fatal accident presumably minutes after leaving Hugh for dead.

It was a tragic end to the story, but at least it alleviated concerns about who might be the next victim of a burglary in the village. He hadn't seemed like a violent person in the few short minutes she had spoken with him, but what did she know? Perhaps her instincts weren't so accurate after all. Doctor Oates hadn't seemed violent either.

The kettle began its high-pitched whistle, making her wince, and Daphne realised that she was suffering from the beginnings of a bad headache. She was overthinking things again, her mind obsessing over every detail she had seen and her temples straining from the stress of frowning as she tried to make sense of everything. It was a bad habit of hers that often resulted in a severe headache when her thoughts started tying her up in knots. But she had just seen a dead body, after all. And although it was the second dead body she had witnessed in Pudding Corner, it wasn't something that one could get used to.

Daphne promised to check in on Helena that evening owing to Hugh being kept in hospital overnight for further investigation. He didn't appear to be suffering from concussion, but he had some memory loss surrounding the break-in and attack, and the doctors needed to double check that he was fit enough to be released.

As the two women sat quietly in Darlington Hall's elegant drawing room, sipping yet another cup of much needed, restorative tea, a tearful Helena recounted her conversation with Hugh in the hospital. The gentle early evening light cast faint shadows across the room as she sat upright in an old Howard chair and spoke with an expression filled with quiet anxiety.

'One minute I was putting some cash in an envelope and

the next thing I was waking up inside an ambulance,' Hugh
had told Helena weakly from his hospital bed. 'I have no idea
what happened in between.'

'Hugh has been incredibly stressed about money,' Helena
explained. 'He'd been fretting over things into the early hours
of the morning, spending hours in his study and coming to
bed later and later every night. Last night, I went to bed alone,
leaving him in the study – as usual . . .' Helena looked up at
Daphne, slightly embarrassed. This was certainly not the
fairy-tale relationship nor the *femme fatale*-style entrapment
that many in the village imagined. 'But when the dogs barking
downstairs woke me up at about three, he still hadn't come
to bed. I went downstairs to try to urge him to have at least
a few hours rest. When I got downstairs, he was just coming
in through the front door from outside with the dogs, and—'

'But you'd heard them barking downstairs?'

'Yes?' Helena said with a frown.

'And he was coming in through the front door with them?'

'Yes . . . well, actually, no, the dogs were already inside,
I think? They must have come in ahead of him. Anyway, I
told Hugh that he really ought to be coming up to bed, and
he said that he'd be up in a minute but he wanted to make
a hot drink first. He brought me one too in fact, and we sat
and chatted with our cups of tea for a while. I thought that he
was coming to bed at that point, but he must have gone back
downstairs when I fell asleep. The next thing I knew I was
waking up in bed alone. I realised that his side hadn't been
slept in so I went downstairs immediately – furious that he
hadn't had any sleep or at least expecting to see him asleep
at his desk – he's done that before. But when I walked into

Hugh's study it was chaos. And then I saw him – on, on the floor – covered in blood!' Helena had started crying again, and Daphne closed her arms around her in a reassuring hug.

'Please don't worry. It's all going to be fine,' Daphne said reassuringly. 'Hugh is fine, you're fine and the dogs are fine; that's all that matters. There was nothing else you could have done. I'm sure that he's relieved that you weren't down there with him when the man broke in!'

'Yes, you're right, Daphne,' Helena agreed. 'He's going to be OK and that's really all that matters.'

Chapter 10

Daphne couldn't remember the last time that she had seen Marianne Forbes looking as smug as she did right now at the latest Pepperbridge parish emergency council meeting, which were becoming a regular occurrence. If an expression could exemplify the phrase 'I told you so', then the one plastered across Marianne's face was screaming the words in flashing neon capitals. However, silently conveying her triumph wasn't quite enough for Marianne. Once she had felt the musky, bloodied scent of glory within her grasp, she would always choose to hang on to the moment for as long as she possibly could. To further underline her foresight and superiority in the eyes of the parish, she made sure that there was no room for doubt by repeating the words 'I told you so' to anyone who misguidedly chose to listen, as well as to those who tried their best not to.

'Forgive me but does this actually bear any relevance to the question at hand, Mrs Forbes?' asked Augusta with barely concealed sarcasm. 'After all, the floor was opened up in order to put to rest any further concerns about the thefts ...' It was meant as a rhetorical question with the aim of bursting Marianne's irritatingly buoyant balloon; however, Marianne being Marianne, she was prepared to publicly fight Augusta for the upper hand.

'Yes, Mrs Papplewick, but I thought that it might be recorded as a much-valued – and it seems much-needed – learning experience for the committee with regards to taking the concerns of parishioners seriously in the future. It is clearly vital to act on the intuition of those with prior experience of witnessing different facets of society at first hand,' Marianne continued gleefully. 'I hate to say "I told you so",' she paused to let the significance of her words settle in, 'but I did mention the presence of the tramp quite early on. If only the committee had acted on my words immediately and done something about him then ... well, who knows what heartache could have been avoided?' She ended her speech triumphantly, cocking her head to the side and coyly making eye contact with the audience: an undisguised attempt to win as many hearts and minds as possible with her most sincere Princess Diana impersonation.

Augusta said nothing and allowed a silence to hang in the air for slightly longer than was comfortable. She waited until people started shuffling in their seats and clearing their throats awkwardly, no one daring to say a word as the two women faced off against each other. Finally, once she was satisfied that even Marianne had started to feel awkward, she looked down at her agenda with absolutely no acknowledgement of Marianne's final comment and moved straight on to the next topic.

At the end of the meeting, Daphne and Patsy once again walked back towards their respective shops together, this time accompanied by James. Unlike the recent episodes of crisp, bright sunshine, today the inclement weather of drizzle and a gloomy grey sky matched their mood. Not normally present at these meetings, James had wanted to hear confirmation that this whole unpleasant business had been put to bed.

'Well, thankfully that should be the end of that little period of disruption,' James said with relief, feeling satisfied with Inspector Hargreaves's assessment that as they had managed to retrieve most of the items stolen during the burglaries within the glasshouse, they were now no longer looking for anyone else in association with the thefts. The case could be closed – or at least it would be once they had cross-checked criminal records across the country and identified the body.

'Mmm, I'm not so sure ...' Patsy murmured under her breath.

'What do you mean?' asked Daphne in surprise as James failed to suppress a groan.

'Well, the stranger turned up shortly after Nancy fell from the ladder—'

'Yes?' Daphne asked, intrigued as to why this was relevant.

'Well, that means that it wasn't him who spooked Nancy when she fell from the ladder, and I doubt he would have hung around if he had just caused someone's death. It would count as murder.'

'But Nancy's fall was an accident, wasn't it?' said James, confused.

'Yes, Patsy – there was no indication that Nancy fell due to a burglary. I know that you're trying to make sense of things, and I totally get that, but—'

'I've said it before and I'm saying it again: Nancy would not have simply fallen from the ladder for no reason,' Patsy shouted angrily. 'Something happened that night, I am one hundred per cent sure of it. Nancy would never have fallen like some doddery old geriatric – I know that. She was as steady as a rock and as strong as an ox!'

Daphne exchanged a quick side glance with James. She didn't want to distress her friend any further by undermining her theory, so they walked the rest of the route in silence until they finally arrived outside Warburtons'.

'Look, I'm sorry, Daphne,' Patsy said as they parted ways, 'I didn't mean to lose my temper, but I just know that Nancy couldn't have fallen out of carelessness that night. Someone was in the shop with her, and I won't rest until I find out who.'

Daphne reached out and gave Patsy a hug. Having comforted James through the loss of his father a few years back, she knew the toll that grieving could have on a person. It was understandable that Patsy didn't want to imagine that her sister had fallen by accident. It was too senseless and frustrating to think that something as simple as a slip could end someone's life. And Patsy was correct about one thing: Nancy had never been doddery or careless.

Nancy had lived in Pepperbridge for her entire life. She had known every house and every family in the village by name – and considering how much the village had grown in the past fifty years, that was no easy feat. She had watched most residents grow up and had seen dozens more come and go. She'd seen people born and she'd seen others buried – what Nancy hadn't witnessed was probably not of much consequence, as Patsy had claimed in her eulogy. The village would never be the same without her.

'Night night, Patsy,' Daphne called out to her retreating friend.

'Night night, Daphne; night James.'

And with that they pulled away from the kerb in the direction of Pudding Corner. James was driving this time, with Daphne lost in her own thoughts as she watched Patsy pull down the shop window blinds through the reflection of the side mirror.

The following morning, Daphne returned to Darlington Hall with James in tow to help with some of the heavy lifting of furniture. Hugh Darlington was back at home after spending a couple of days under observation in hospital. The mess in his study had been tidied away by Helena in his absence, but rather than immediately returning to managing the estate, he remained with his feet up in the snug at Helena's insistence. She had firmly demanded that he continue to convalesce for a few more days. Hugh had vigorously complained and attempted to do the opposite, of course – he had so much work to do – but even the doctors had insisted that he needed to take it easy for at least a week after his head injury, so he had reluctantly agreed.

Daphne and Helena had decided on the final decorating schemes for the three bed-and-breakfast rooms, and the paint would be arriving soon. The fabrics, an Ian Mankin sage green check and a chintzy Jane Churchill floral in complementary blue and green, had been chosen and a lady from the village had been tasked with making up the curtains and other soft furnishings. The upholsterer in nearby Narborough village, just a five-mile drive away, was ready and waiting to receive three ornately shaped Victorian nursing chairs, one for each room, with bespoke fabrics selected to match each scheme. Within the next few weeks, three bedroom suites would be up and running. If emotions hadn't been dulled by dramatic recent events, it would have been an exciting time. They were about to see the fruits of their labours finally come to life, and cavernous Darlington Hall would soon be paying for itself.

James was carrying the final chair into the back of the hired van, preparing to deliver the chairs to the upholsterer before returning to work back at his home office.

It was all going to plan when one side of the chair slipped out of his grasp, landing on his foot. 'Oooof – fudge!' he called out in pain, trying not to turn the air a fruitier shade of blue.

Hobbling back to the main hall in search of the kitchen and some ice to numb the pain, James passed a door that was slightly ajar and a voice called out.

'Helena – is that you? Daphne?'

'Err, sorry – no it's me, James. I'm Daphne's husband,' James responded, poking his head around the corner of the door.

Hugh Darlington sat with his legs across the sofa and a tartan blanket covering most of his body. He was surrounded by newspapers and a radio quietly broadcast the cricket in the background.

'Oh, James! Hello, it's good to finally meet you. Sorry about this, I feel awful not helping but . . .' Hugh said apologetically, his hands motioning to the large plaster stretched across his temple.

'Goodness, it's no problem at all – happy to help. You've been through the wars, you deserve to put your feet up. Daphne and Helena are happy enough bossing me around,' James said cheerfully.

'Yes, yes, good stuff,' Hugh replied, self-consciously struggling to keep up the small talk in his reclined state. 'Well, I suppose everyone in the village was happy to hear that the suspect won't be bothering them any more?'

'Oh absolutely!' agreed James, absent-mindedly easing the pressure from his left foot which was still feeling rather painful. 'I mean, it's a sorry state of affairs – no one deserves to go that way – but yes, at least everyone can feel safe again. Although . . .' James said, recalling Patsy's doubts the evening before.

'Although?' Hugh repeated, his head slightly tilted to the side as he looked at James with interest.

'Oh, it's nothing really. Just something that Patsy Warburton said last night.'

'Patsy Warburton – the woman who owns the shop?' Hugh enquired politely. 'Who lost her sister in an accident recently?'

'Yes, that's right,' James affirmed. 'Except the poor thing is still grieving heavily. She doesn't think it was an accident, she thinks that it may have been a burglary gone wrong – like yours.'

'Oh lord – so she thinks that this same chap may have been

behind that too?' Hugh asked, looking horrified. 'How awful! Has she mentioned that to the police?'

'No, that's the funny thing. She doesn't think it was the same man at all for some reason. She thinks that it was someone else entirely. Bizarre, I know,' James said, seeing incredulity flash across Hugh's face.

'Someone else entirely . . .' he repeated. 'Not more thieves going about the area, surely?' Hugh looked aghast.

'Sorry, I didn't mean to alarm you!' James instantly regretted taking the conversation in this direction. Of all the things to say to a person who had just been attacked during a break-in, the theory that there may be more burglars on the loose was probably not the best. 'I'm sure it's just Patsy over-thinking things. There's nothing indicating that there was a break-in at Warburtons' so it's doubtful that it was anything but a nasty accident. The poor woman just slipped and fell – I imagine it would have been caught on their security cameras anyway.'

'They have security cameras?' Hugh asked.

James shrugged his shoulders. 'To be honest, I'm not a hundred per cent sure.'

Hugh, who had started lifting his torso up from the sofa during the conversation, suddenly looked as though he'd been toppled by a wave of tiredness. He dropped his head back onto the pillow, closing his eyes in exhaustion. 'Good for them. Sadly, there's no budget for extra security like that here.'

James, seeing that Hugh looked utterly spent, made his excuses and left, his pursuit of ice for his painful toe now forgotten. Walking back to the van, he berated himself for putting the fear of God into a man recovering from another ordeal. He'd get a reputation for meddling if he wasn't careful.

Daphne and James had arrived at Darlington Hall together that morning in the hired van, leaving Aggie at the shop. While James had taken the chairs to the upholsterer and returned the van to the local garage in Pudding Corner, she had decided to walk back to the village though the fields. Helena had kindly offered to drop her off but Daphne had insisted on walking. The crisp blue sky was lit up by the bright sunshine, and the fresh air was perfect to clear the cobwebs of her mind. Plus, with all the recent drama, she had fallen behind on her goal of 10,000 steps per day.

She hadn't walked past the walled garden since discovering the man's charred body, and Daphne wondered whether she could ever dare enter that once bucolic place again. Horrific images of his body constantly replayed in her mind.

That's it. I'm going to force myself to get over this, she thought, making an about turn towards the garden's south-facing gate. If she didn't return immediately, she feared that she would never visit this special place on her own again.

Opening the gate, she was confronted by the same overgrown and wild beauty as before. The wind had picked up and was blowing gently, and although the sun had been out just moments ago, it was now hidden behind a stream of puffy white clouds, the obscured sunlight casting a bluish-grey filter over everything. Perhaps it was her imagination, but the walled garden didn't feel as joyful as it had before. *Maybe these walls can sense loss*, Daphne thought sadly.

She wasn't intending to stay in the garden for long, just long enough to ease off the metaphorical Band-Aid that could stop her visiting it in the future. Daphne couldn't explain why but she felt compelled to continue along towards the glasshouses, walking slowly and measuredly until she arrived at the entrance to the furthest one. The last time she had been in this exact same spot, she had witnessed such an appalling scene that it took all her restraint not to turn and run away. But she was determined to get a handle on her emotions. Taking a deep breath, she kept her feet firmly planted on the ground and stayed where she was – directly in front of the entrance. Police tape still sealed the doorway, not that Daphne would have ventured in anyway. It was a stark reminder of the events that had unfolded there only a few days ago.

There was nothing much to see really; another area was cordoned off in the middle of the glasshouse and there was some tape on the floor. Inspector Hargreaves and his team had spent the past few days going through the building with a fine-tooth comb and checking for any additional stashes of stolen goods, as well as any other evidence that could help them with their enquiries.

Daphne's mind was cast back momentarily to the man's face when she had stopped him in the village. He had seemed so normal, and his smile had been so grateful. He hadn't seemed particularly desperate or harried, only a little skittish and tentative. *What had driven him to attack Hugh?* Perhaps he hadn't expected to see anyone downstairs at that time in the morning. That must have been it, because she was sure that the man she had seen gently stroking a cat and trying to avoid any confrontation with her would not have readily hurt someone. Her gut instinct told her so, even though the evidence seemed to go against it. Questions cascaded through Daphne's mind: *Who had he been? What had happened to him? What drove him to steal? And how did he end up in a quiet little village like Pepperbridge?*

It was time to leave the walled garden for now, although she was relieved that she had been able to return, even if there was now an air of melancholy about it. Turning back and retracing her steps, Daphne saw that several gardening-related items had been placed on top of the cold frames that bordered the side of the glasshouses. They must have been things that the police had found inside that weren't relevant to the cases of theft. There were a few old rolls of twine, some terracotta saucers, a pile of baskets and a few rusted old hand tools. More interesting was a bundle of old yellow, faded newspapers tied together with string. Luckily it hadn't rained during the past few days or they would have been ruined. Daphne took a closer look; they were old local newspapers that she presumed gardeners had once used to line seed trays, or perhaps they had been intended to be added to the heating stove. They dated back decades – the top paper on the pile was dated 5 August 1972.

How fascinating, she thought, flicking through to look at some of the headlines. But she quickly noticed that the news-papers all had something in common: they were all dated 5 August 1972.

How odd! Intrigued, Daphne pulled a copy out and started taking a more thorough look through. She was soon rewarded with another fascinating discovery when she came across a centre-page spread featuring a photograph of the Darlington family all sat stiffly in the main drawing room of Darlington Hall. They were posing for an official family christening photograph, with a distinctly uncomfortable air about it. Lord Darlington looked grumpy and as though he would rather be anywhere but posing for a photograph. One could imagine him looking repeatedly at his watch wondering how much time this inconvenient gathering was going to take. Lady Darlington looked neatly prim and proper in a shift dress with matching princess coat, hat and white gloves, holding a chubby-cheeked Hugh dressed in a long and presumably ancestral christening robe. A young Edward looked straight at the camera with a cheeky smirk, and a man and a woman unknown to Daphne stood behind the seated Darlington family with strained smiles. The byline read: *Lord and Lady Darlington at Darlington Hall with the Honourable Edward Darlington and godparents at the Christening of Master Hugh Aubrey Charles Darlington.*

It was Hugh's christening photo. *How incredible!* They must have bought as many copies as possible to keep for posterity. How sad that they had ended up as a pile of would-be mulch beside a dead body.

It suddenly occurred to Daphne that she hadn't seen any photographs of the complete Darlington family in any of the rooms. There was a black-and-white wedding portrait of Hugh's parents, the seventh Lord and Lady Darlington, on the untouched grand piano that sat in the corner of the entrance hall, and ancestral family portraits hung in the dining room and along the gallery on the first floor, but she hadn't noticed any others. She wondered whether they were tucked away in the private areas of the house or whether Hugh had hidden them away after his family estrangement.

Maybe Hugh would like to see these, she thought. Hopefully this little discovery might give Hugh something semi-positive to smile about at last, although one could never be sure. Scooping up a couple of copies, she decided to take them with her and bring them back to Darlington Hall the next day. For now, she needed to get back to the shop and her own family.

Chapter 11

'I've never seen any photographs of Hugh as a child before! Oh, Daphne isn't this so sweet?' Helena exclaimed the next morning when Daphne presented her with the newspaper spread.

'I thought you might like it. I noticed there weren't any family photos on display here, so I wasn't quite sure whether you had seen this one before,' Daphne said as they both peered closely at the grainy image in the yellowing newspaper.

'No, there aren't any family photographs anywhere. Apparently Hugh's brother removed them all and sold the silver frames for cash at some point. Hugh has no idea what he did with the actual photographs, which is such a shame. Mind you, there are so many untouched attic rooms stuffed to the rafters with furniture and old steam trunks and things, so who knows what might be packed away up there.'

Helena's list of items stowed away in the attic piqued Daphne's interest.

'Old steam trunks and more furniture, you say?' Her eyes had lit up. 'Perhaps we could use the trunks as bedside tables in the rooms? It would be lovely to try and reuse as many things as possible that are originally from Old Hall. Maybe we should go up there one day and have a scout around for useful things? You never know, we may even come across the family photos.'

'Good idea,' Helena agreed. 'I've never fancied rooting away up there on my own to be honest – it's far too dark and spooky, and Hugh is always too busy with work to explore with me. I've always wanted to take a look though. There must be some amazing treasures hidden away among the tat. I've poked my head up there a few times when I've been brave enough to but sorting the attic rooms out felt overwhelming. There's so much stuff to go through – files, paperwork, furniture, clothes, and boxes and boxes filled with a lifetime's worth of stuff.'

Daphne nodded in agreement. 'I suppose as exciting as it seems to us, the prospect of trawling through it all must be dull for poor Hugh. Imagine having to sift through generations worth of family paraphernalia with no other family members around. I know that he has you to help him, thank goodness, but it must feel quite isolating to suddenly be responsible for all of it – especially when he didn't expect it,' she said thoughtfully.

'Exactly, but maybe that's why I should go up there and make a start on it. Take a bit of the burden off, don't you think?'

'Yes definitely, one day maybe, but for now you've got enough on your plate!' Daphne gestured towards the two crates of paint that had been delivered that morning. Both women sighed and laughed companionably.

'Anyway, thanks for these,' Helena nodded down to the newspapers in her hand. 'I'll show them to Hugh when he wakes up. He's snoozing in the snug at the moment; he's been locking himself away for hours on end. Sometimes he won't even let me in. I don't think he's recovered from being hit over the head yet. It was quite a blow – the doctors were amazed that his skull wasn't fractured . . . The shock of it all has really knocked him for six too.' She looked down with a frown. 'Sometimes I've caught him just staring into space and shaking his head. Looking so dazed and sad.'

Helena was looking quite dazed and sad herself, Daphne thought. The poor woman had found herself becoming the unexpected crutch to a man facing overwhelming personal challenges. She was glad that they had each other – even if Hugh's emotional reticence and unpredictable mood swings had startled Daphne at times. But as long as Helena was happy, that was all that mattered.

Later that day, as the clock crept towards school pick-up time, Helena and Daphne took a well-deserved break from wall-paper stripping. The rooms they were tackling first had high ceilings and layers of ancient paint clogging up the promise of impressive decorative mouldings beneath. After much deliberation, Hugh had reluctantly agreed to commit to professional decorators doing the bulk of the painting work, but with the aim of speeding things up and keeping professional labour costs down, it had been agreed that Helena and a far more conservatively priced Daphne would sand, strip and prep as much as was feasibly possible themselves. It was dirty work, and it wasn't proving to be quick or easy, but they were getting through it slowly and amiably, fuelled by Daphne's retro jazz playlist, numerous cups of tea and slices of home-made carrot cake.

They were sat wearily on the floor of the third and final bedroom, with only an hour to go before Daphne needed to head back to the village.

'The architraves and coving in these rooms are just so beautiful, aren't they?' Daphne said, looking up at the ceiling. 'It's one of the things that I love most about old buildings – all the distinctive architectural details. Like icing on a giant wedding cake,' she continued admiringly, brushing crumbs from a recently eaten country slice off the front of her overalls and onto a side plate.

'Oh yes, it's one of my favourite things about the place. They make every room look so effortlessly romantic!' Helena agreed. 'One day, I'd love to restore the mouldings in the drawing room. It's such a shame that they've been ripped out. That vast room looks so plain and bare without them – so much of the character is gone.'

'You know, I wouldn't be surprised if it's all still there,' Daphne said before sipping her tea. 'The first time I saw that room, I thought the ceiling was unusually low for a building like this. It felt strangely oppressive with the ceiling almost touching the top of the window frames.' Daphne looked over at Helena to ensure that she wasn't causing any offence with her observations, but Helena was nodding enthusiastically.

'I wonder whether they had a false ceiling put in at some point. Lots of grand houses – and not so grand ones, to be honest – put them in to cut down on heating costs. Countless period properties in England have the most intricate period details boxed in or covered up,' she explained.

'I know!' Daphne said, struck by an idea. 'Do you have one of those newspapers from this morning? That photograph was taken inside Old Hall, wasn't it? Perhaps we can see which room it was taken in and what the ceiling looked like?' It might have been easier to ask Hugh directly, but he was resting, plus Daphne liked nothing better than to dabble in a little architectural sleuthing.

'Brilliant idea!' Helena agreed, jumping up from the floor with new-found energy. 'Just a minute, let me get a copy. I think I left them in the main hall.'

Helena was soon back by Daphne's side with a newspaper. They scanned the large, faded picture of the Darlington family. Sure enough, the photograph had been taken in what appeared to be Darlington Hall's drawing room. In the background was evidence, albeit faint, that the ceiling was much higher than the architrave around the windows and did indeed have beautiful carved mouldings of its own.

'You see!' Daphne announced triumphantly. 'I knew it. How exciting. Obviously, uncovering these mouldings will probably need to be part of the long-term renovation, but it would be lovely to restore the room to its former glory – budget allowing, of course.' Beautiful as it was, she was conscious that maintenance and repair costs for a house of this size were prohibitively high.

'That would be amazing,' Helena agreed as she stared

intently at the newspaper. 'It's a shame that the picture is so grainy though. I'd love to have a clearer look at the ceiling – and at Hugh's chubby baby face!' She laughed.

'I wonder whether the original photo will be in the local library archive?' Daphne mused.

'The what?' asked Helena.

'The library archive. It's a local newspaper and sometimes libraries keep preserved copies and images from over the years, don't they? Surely they must have a better-quality copy than one that's been kept in a glasshouse for four decades. Especially as this is a significant estate belonging to a notable local family. Might be worth taking a look to see if there are photos featuring the other rooms too?'

'That's a great idea – you've got a knack for investigating things! Why don't I look into that myself though? Hugh's family history is a rather touchy subject, so I'd better handle it delicately.'

'Honestly, it's my inner history nerd,' Daphne joked, but it was true. Her fascination with history and architecture was one of her many quirks. It was the thing that had drawn her to Cranberry Farmhouse, her quaint, dollhouse-like Georgian home in Pudding Corner, and the same interest that had kickstarted her ill-fated 'friendship' with her history-loving former neighbour, Doctor Oates. 'It's no bother at all, just let me know if you want me to and I'll pop into the library next time I'm in town. I have to return some books for the children soon anyway, so it wouldn't be a problem. In fact – I'll enjoy the excuse to do a little bit of historical research.' She chuckled.

'OK ... great. I'll let you know – thank you.'

'In the meantime, we'd better get back to work if I'm going to be able to pop into the shop before school pick-up time.'

Back at the school gates, the atmosphere was humming with talk and the mood was panicked.

Daphne walked in to find Marianne in a state of hysterical excitement; she was evidently stirring up alarm by buzzing from person to person, collecting and spreading gossip disguised as news, feigning as much gravitas as she could muster in the process. Groups of parents were huddled everywhere, and Daphne was relieved to see a solitary Minerva standing looking calm and unaffected, waiting patiently in the corner of the school playground for the bell to be rung.

'What on earth has happened?' Daphne asked, feeling mildly anxious.

'There's been another burglary,' Minerva said stoically, apparently being one of the few adults present who knew that panicking was not going to help anything.

'No – surely not!' Daphne uttered dejectedly. 'I thought this was all over and done with.'

'It seems not. This time it was a house on Benedict's Mews. In full daylight apparently. Old Mr Rogers had left his back door open to bring his shopping in from his car when he was suddenly knocked over from behind, just a few feet up his garden path. The shopping was taken, along with his wallet. He didn't see a thing.'

'Poor Mr Rogers . . . Is he all right?' Daphne asked.

'He's OK, apparently – just had a nasty shock and a bruise to show for it.'

'Thank goodness for that. Do the police think it's connected with the other thefts?'

'I have no idea. No one seems to be talking any sense. Just wails of despair and doom as to what the world is coming to. Marianne is the main harbinger of the "End of village life as we know it" prophecy, of course,' Minerva explained, tongue only ever-so-slightly in cheek.

As awful as this new turn of events was, Daphne felt relieved to have a friend like Minerva to share their mutually cynical yet often humorous take on life in a small village. Their friendship had developed quickly within Daphne's first few months of arriving in Norfolk. With both being outsiders of sorts, they had recognised a kindred spirit in each other, and Daphne was eternally grateful for their friendship.

'End of village life, eh? I blame those Londoners,' Daphne retorted with a raised eyebrow and a slight smile, owing to the fact that Marianne herself had only moved up from Fulham, south-west London, the year before Daphne relocated to Norfolk with her own family. A fact that often seemed to escape Marianne's memory banks when she made reference to any pesky 'newcomers'.

Receiving instructions from the local constabulary telling residents to lock their doors and exercise vigilance was an unexpected twist in the past week's events. An unnerving and fearful atmosphere had crept over the parish. It was heightened by the knowledge that the thefts could no longer be fully attributed to the deceased man in the kitchen garden. It was still widely assumed that he had been partly responsible for the previous burglaries, but the new hypothesis presumed that he had only been a cog in a wider gang of thieves who had chosen to target sleepy Pepperbridge.

'Welcome to the sleepy countryside, eh!' James had said with a heavy sense of irony when Daphne had arrived home to them him the news, with three rambunctious, just released-from-school children in tow.

'First wash your hands and take off your school clothes!' she called out to the kids as they overtook her in the entrance hall and raced straight through to the kitchen in the direction of the biscuit jar in search of Jammie Dodgers.

'Not quite the serene and safe idyll we imagined when we left south London, is it?' James continued embracing his wife in a reassuring bearhug.

'No, not quite, I suppose,' Daphne agreed sadly. The children were safely out of earshot, and were now getting changed out of their school uniforms upstairs as Byron yapped happily on the upstairs landing, thrilled at their return. 'But let's hope that this is just an unfortunate blip in an otherwise perfect landscape. A second blip, I mean . . .' She looked at James and they couldn't help but grin at each other. Despite the recent events, Daphne didn't doubt for one second that their home in Pudding Corner in the parish of Pepperbridge was the only place she wanted to be. She had grown to love their home and the surrounding area fiercely, and she was determined not to let anything – not even a spate of worryingly out-of-character burglaries – dull that feeling.

Chapter 12

Hearing PC Clarke's voice on the other end of the phone the following morning was a surprise. Daphne had just returned home after dropping the children at school when her phone had started ringing.

'Good morning, Mrs Brewster. Would you mind popping down to the station at your earliest convenience please?' the constable said apologetically. 'The inspector would like to ask you a few more questions about the events in Darlington Hall garden, if you don't mind. It's nothing serious, he just wants to clear up a few loose ends. Thank you so much.'

'Of course. I'll be there in just under the hour, if that's OK?' Daphne replied, her mind whirring. She put the phone down and wondered idly to herself whether it was something to go with the recent robbery. Did they have a new lead?

Deciding that she may as well try to kill several birds with one stone, Daphne gathered the children's library books and grabbed a handful of reusable shopping bags so that she could do some errands after popping into the police station in Oxwold Overy. *If I'm going to be in town, I may as well be productive,* she thought as she emerged from Cranberry Farmhouse into a warm day, not a cloud in the sky.

'Thank you for coming in, Mrs Brewster,' Inspector Hargreaves said pleasantly when Daphne entered his office at a little after 10 a.m.

'No problem at all, Inspector. How may I be of help?'

'Well, it's a decidedly unpleasant matter I'm afraid, Mrs Brewster, not one for the faint of heart.' He stalled uncomfortably for a moment, clearly struggling to find suitable words.

'Don't worry, I'm not very squeamish,' Daphne reassured him, intrigued by his silence.

Inspector Hargreaves cleared his throat, adjusted his tie without cause to – as he often did in moments of uncertainty – and went on. Thanks to her prior experience at the police station, much to Inspector Hargreaves's chagrin, Daphne recognised this tie-adjusting as a familiar prelude to the inspector saying something difficult.

'When you came across the body of the man in the Darlington greenhouse—'

'Glasshouse,' she corrected. 'Sorry to interrupt, but it's called a glasshouse,' Daphne explained, sensing that she was risking throwing him off track but being unable to resist. 'It's a common mistake – they're often used interchangeably, but there is a historical difference between the two, you see.

Glasshouses were traditionally made entirely of glass panes while greenhouses are made of wood or metal frames with glass panels. It's why glasshouses are so rare and special – they were far more expensive to build from an engineering point of view . . .' Daphne trailed off, registering the bewilderment in Inspector Hargreaves's eyes. 'Sorry – do carry on, Inspector. We were speaking about me not being squeamish.'

'Yes, well glasshouse, greenhouse, whatever. When you came across the man's body, did you notice anything else after you saw that he had fallen into the fire?' he asked impatiently.

Chastened, Daphne thought back to that awful morning in the walled garden. 'Hmm, well, I was so shocked to find a body and seeing the glass sticking out of the poor man's back that I'm not sure whether I noticed anything else unusual—'

'You didn't notice his hands?' Inspector Hargreaves asked.

'His hands? Umm – no, I don't think so. I was concentrating on his face – which had been burned – and his back and chest, of course. When I realised there was blood on him I sort of jumped back and didn't see anything after that . . .' Having claimed not to be queasy, Daphne was beginning to feel decidedly nauseous at the memory.

Noticing her face go pale, the inspector pressed a button on his phone and called through to the front desk. 'Could we please get a glass of water in here for Mrs Brewster,' he barked through the intercom, before turning back to Daphne, 'or would you rather a cup of hot sweet tea?'

'No, water will be fine – thank you, Inspector,' Daphne said appreciatively. 'Why are asking about his hands? Do you know who he is . . . or was?' she corrected herself as she gratefully accepted a glass of water from PC Clarke, who had entered the office within seconds of her superior officer's request.

'Well, you see, Mrs Brewster, that's the thing. We can't identify him. It's his fingertips that are complicating the process.'

'His fingertips?'

'Yes, his fingertips. They were burned off, you see. It looks as though they'd been placed in the fire.'

'You mean that they had fallen into the fire surely – when he fell forward?'

'Perhaps,' the inspector replied, sounding more than a little unconvinced.

Daphne was shocked into silence. Was the inspector insinuating that the stranger's hands had been purposely placed in the fire? *If so, by whom?* Surely he didn't think she was involved?

'We're thinking that it might be some sort of gang violence. Torture or revenge perhaps. I've heard of this sort of thing before, but I was just wondering whether you had noticed anything else since you were the first person to come across him. Any unusual gang signs or warnings that you might recognise? I imagine that when you were living in south London you may have come across things like this . . .' The inspector shuffled uncomfortably in his chair, his eyes avoiding Daphne's for a few embarrassed seconds.

Reeling from the inspector's misguided assumption that as a Londoner she was familiar with gang warfare – this wasn't an episode of *Luther*, after all – Daphne paused before breaking the awkward silence. 'So, you think that he may have been murdered?' What had already been a traumatic experience was becoming more disturbing by the minute.

'That's what we're trying to work out, Mrs Brewster. The glass certainly fell from the ceiling. There were correspond-ing shards in the same area. Of that we have no doubt,' he clarified.

'Anyway, if there's anything else you can remember from that morning ... or any intel on gang habits,' Inspector Hargreaves tentatively added, 'I would appreciate if you could let me know as soon as possible.' He ended the conversation abruptly and stood up, looking profoundly relieved that their discussion was over.

Slightly shaken, Daphne mirrored his actions and stood up, but not before taking a final sip of water.

'Are you all right to find your own way out?' he asked, indicating the door while fumbling with his tie.

'Yes, of course. Thank you, Inspector, and yes, if I remem-ber anything else, I'll certainly let you know.'

Daphne's mind was racing. *Why would the man's fingertips have been burned off? Could such a horrific thing really have been intentional?*

She had parked Aggie in the supermarket car park because it was within walking distance of the police station and the library. After picking up a few essentials from the supermar-ket, including pasta and cheese to make macaroni cheese (at Imani's request) that evening and dog treats for Byron, she finally made it to the library. Completing her last errand of the morning, Daphne returned the children's books, and then decided to enquire about finding old newspapers and local

records. Helena hadn't officially given her the go-ahead ...
but, well, she was already here and she herself was intrigued –
so why not!

The librarian behind the counter on the second floor
seemed delighted by Daphne's query, clearly relieved to take
a short break from the mundanity of stamping children's
books. She had a soft Scottish accent, a pie crust collar and
her amber hair was coiled up into a tight bun. Judging from
the size of the neatly wrapped bun, Daphne guessed there
was a lot of it as she followed along behind the woman who
had insisted on showing her the way personally.

'You'll need to search for the newspaper's title here in the
catalogue to see whether it's available in print, online or on
microfilm,' she explained enthusiastically. 'If it doesn't appear
in the index, you can try searching the secondary indexes for
regional newspapers to narrow the search. Sometimes the
index is included on the microfilm reel instead of in print, but
if it's local to us, we should have it. When you find the paper,
just click 'view dates', enter the relevant time frame and Bob's
your uncle. Let me know if you need me to help you search.'

After thanking the librarian, Daphne settled down ready to
focus on finding the original photograph of Hugh's christening, but she was soon distracted by the archive of aristocratic
history in the local newspapers of forty years ago. They had
liked nothing better than to write about the landed gentry
and their various social events. Dozens of articles featured
dinner dances, horse trials and concerts, as well as weddings,
christenings and even a few fancy funerals. There were birth
announcements, death announcements, and articles announcing cricket and golf club presentations and award ceremonies,

each occasion marked with a proud and posturing formal family portrait. The Darlington family and Darlington Hall appeared frequently until the mid 1990s, and then their presence in local society seemed to abruptly wane. Subsequent decades brought announcements of the deaths of the seventh Lord and Lady Darlington in the mid 2000s, followed not long after by an announcement of the premature loss of Lord Edward Darlington, Hugh's playboy brother.

Remembering the purpose at hand, Daphne started trying to focus on finding photos of Darlington Hall. Clear pictures of the interior could provide clues about the original layout and structure of the many rooms. But despite her interest in the architectural detail, it was proving hard to concentrate on interiors alone. The photos featuring the Darlington family were infinitely more fascinating. She found pictures of Hugh as a toddler in his parents' stiff and formally posed arms, and of Hugh and his brother Edward sitting on a pony and a horse respectively while their mother held the reins of Hugh's pony with a serious expression and a bored Edward sat astride his horse looking as though he'd rather be anywhere else than with his family. In another image, the family stood outside Darlington Hall with Edward leaned up against a vintage Porsche and a much younger Hugh clinging to his mother's skirt. In a picture in an edition from the mid 1980s, an older Edward, looking as though he were in his early twenties and dressed in black tie, accompanied 'Lady Sarah Kirdale' to a party in an extremely grand-looking marquee in the grounds of Darlington Hall; the walled garden was visible in the background. A later picture of Hugh, looking about twelve and sat at the grand piano in the entrance hall, was captioned:

Master Hugh Darlington shows off his Grade 8 piano skills at an impromptu concert at the birthday of his mother, Lady Elisa Darlington.

Daphne's eyes lingered on a photograph of the family standing solemnly together at the funeral of an elderly relative. There were also extended family members in the picture this time, but the middle of the group featured Hugh's parents, Lord and Lady Darlington – both looking decidedly miserable, and a slightly more grown-up Hugh standing sullenly next to his taller and far more cheerful-looking brother. They were all on the lawn on what appeared to be a sunny day – the weather at odds with their sombre funeral clothing. It was obviously a very bright day because several people were squinting into the sun, and Hugh was half shielding his eyes with his hand, looking straight at the photographer with sad, soulful eyes. *Not much has changed in that respect*, thought Daphne.

She looked again. There was something familiar about this particular photograph; perhaps she had seen it before in the house? No – she was certain that she hadn't seen any family photos in the house. Perhaps it just reminded her of grown-up Hugh? Yet that wasn't it either. Strangely, it didn't remind her of grown-up Hugh at all – the expression was very different – but it was definitely reminiscent of something – or was that someone – she had seen before. Anyway, she had found what she had been searching for. A whole host of images showed Darlington Hall's interior architectural details including architraves, ceiling roses and intricate coving. She could even identify many of the pieces of furniture that they had found stacked up to the rafters in various rooms. Her library visit had been productive, but best of all, it had taken Daphne's mind off her unsettling conversation with Inspector Hargreaves. For just a short while, her thoughts had been free of the burned body in the kitchen garden, though she knew it wouldn't last.

Dropping off the groceries at home in Pudding Corner, Daphne could feel the onset of a headache. Something was niggling her at the back of her mind; she was overwhelmed by unanswered questions and her exhausting to-do list. She had been spending so much time with Helena at Darlington Hall that she had been neglecting her commitments at A Fine Vintage, and she felt guilty that her routine of regularly popping in on Patsy had slipped too. Warburtons' had been open almost daily for a while now, so at least she knew that Patsy was interacting with people, but she was conscious that her friend was still struggling with grief – not to mention coming up with all sorts of theories about her sister's death. She decided to make a concerted effort to see her today – perhaps she would pop by with some of the apple Danish pastries that Patsy loved.

Taking a couple of headache pills to quell the mounting headache, Daphne took a short stroll around her garden with Byron scampering happily by her side, checking on her raised beds planted with tulips and early growing fennel and lettuces. She sat down on the steps of her little potting shed and absentmindedly stroked a delighted Byron's tummy while she tried not to think about anything else other than what she intended to grow in the vegetable patch that summer. *Maybe pumpkins this year?* she thought, before remembering how well her courgettes had grown last season. *Wouldn't it have been natural to fall into the fire hands-first after being hit in the back?* 'Stop it!' she shouted out loud. 'No intrusive thoughts!'

She really needed to think about planting out the sweet-peas now – and the dahlia tubers ... *Why was that photo somehow familiar?*

'That's enough!' she said to herself, desperately trying to clear her mind and seek distraction. 'I'm off to the shop.'

Daphne had just parked outside A Fine Vintage when she saw Patsy striding angrily along the road away from Warburtons'. 'Is everything all right, Patsy?' she called out as she locked the door of her Morris Traveller.

'No, it bloody well isn't,' Patsy barked without dropping a stride. 'I caught one of those scallywags trying to pocket a packet of Murray Mints yesterday and now there are at least three packets of Tic Tacs unaccounted for. He must have pilfered something after all.'

'Oh Patsy, you can't just go after them yourself – shouldn't you let the police know? They may be dangerous!'

In truth, Daphne wasn't as worried about what the boys on the green might do to Patsy as what Patsy might do to the boys on the green. The last thing her dear friend needed right now was to get in trouble. Patsy looked utterly furious, and she was certainly no shrinking violet who was afraid of confrontation. In fact, Daphne couldn't think of anyone that she would place a bet on to win a fist fight against Patsy – and certainly not when she was in this mood.

'What the hell will the police do? Slap their wrists and tell them to go to bed without supper?' Patsy spat out sarcastically. 'Besides, I'm certain that someone came into the shop the night that Nancy died and I'm ninety-nine per cent sure that it must have been one of them. I'll get to the bottom of this if it's the last thing I do!'

Ah, now Patsy's explosive tirade made sense. The gradual build-up of her festering suspicions was coming out full throttle. Patsy had been wanting to confront someone about Nancy's death for months, and now she had the perfect excuse and opportunity.

They had nearly reached the village green – Patsy steaming ahead with Daphne in pursuit, pleading with her friend to stop – when Daphne almost ran straight into Marianne.

'What on earth? What the hell is going on?' Marianne exclaimed.

'So sorry, Marianne – I need to stop Patsy!'

Sensing drama, Marianne gleefully did an about turn and followed the two women to wherever their intended destination might be. Patsy was striding along furiously and Daphne stood little chance of restraining her. Marianne crossed her fingers in the hope that Patsy's target might be Augusta Papplewick. 'Now wouldn't that be a fun sight to see on a Tuesday afternoon?' she gloated.

The village green was coming into sight, against a backdrop of blue sky and bright sunshine, and the women's dramatic chase had piqued the interest of several locals who were already gathered outdoors, chatting and enjoying their front gardens in the sun. Something was about to kick off and no one wanted to miss it – it was perfect sporting weather after all. A small crowd gathered as Patsy strode onto the grass, grabbed one of the young men huddled by the swings and roundabout and hauled him around to face her.

'What the hell!' the young lad shouted in terror, feeling Patsy's vice-like grip on the back of his collar. His friends took a wary step backwards, their mouths dropping open.

'What the hell? What the HELL indeed!' Patsy exclaimed. 'What the hell have you been stealing from my shop, more like!' The other boys, none of whom looked older than eighteen, looked guiltily wide-eyed and poised to run. All pretence at bravado had disappeared as they stood looking terrified in their matching 'uniform' of Nike trainers, black Lonsdale jogging bottoms and knock-off designer logo sweatshirts.

'If you know what's good for you, you'll stay exactly where you are!' Patsy roared. The boys stood stock-still. Not least because several of the concerned (and nosy) crowd of neighbours who had noticed a 'situation' occurring on the green and had surreptitiously strolled over were now purposefully blocking their potential exit, but also because Patsy's deep, rasping voice was so authoritative. Even Daphne was in silent awe of her commanding power.

'Gerrroff me!' The boy was whimpering now, but Patsy refused to release her grip on his collar.

'Which one of you rats stole from my shop?' she demanded. She looked first at the boy caught in her grasp and then at the trembling lads on the other side of the circle that had formed. Daphne marvelled at the crowd that had gathered: everyone looking grim-faced and determined to get to the bottom of the thefts that had been pervading this quiet enclave of rural England since March. *I suppose this is what one would call community spirit*, Daphne thought. She noticed that even Augusta had joined the crowd, looking secretly gratified that Patsy had taken things into her own hands, and was that

Helena standing in the background with a shocked expression? Daphne was distracted by Patsy's balled first before she could be sure. She grabbed her arm, desperately trying to stop her from swinging a punch at the boy.

'Well!' Patsy thundered at the boys again, shaking her arm from Daphne's grip and staring each boy in the face while still holding on to her first terrified victim. 'Do I need to question you all individually?' She took another step towards them and they shrank back in unison.

'It was *him*!' At least five of them – including the boy in her grasp – pointed to a gangly, bespectacled boy standing in the middle of the group. The unlikely looking culprit turned and made a bid for freedom, but his escape was foiled by the adults standing shoulder to shoulder around the playground.

'Was it you?' Patsy called out towards the boy. 'And the burglaries? Were you part of those too?'

The boys all looked up in surprise. 'Burglaries – what? No! We ain't taken part in no burglaries. I just took sweets from the shop – they dared me to!' the main culprit wailed, tears forming in his eyes.

In the distance a blaring police-car siren could be heard approaching the centre of Pepperbridge. A concerned citizen had considered it wise to involve the police before Patsy took the matter into her own hands.

'What about my sister?' Patsy asked, her voice cracking with emotion.

'Who?'

'The other woman who used to be in the shop. Which one of you scallywags pushed her off the ladder?'

All the boys stared blankly at Patsy, then at each other.

They had no idea what the crazy woman holding on to their friend was talking about and they were far too terrified to lie.

'Did one of you come in to steal from my shop the night my sister fell?' Patsy repeated furiously, starting to shake the boy in her grasp. He was now crying inconsolably. 'Did you hurt my sister?'

'No, no! But I saw a man in there once arguing with her!' he said through his sobs.

Daphne's eyebrows raised in interest at this.

Patsy's hand slackened. 'What man?'

'I don't know. I hadn't seen him before. He was wearing combat trousers.'

At that moment, Inspector Hargreaves and PC Clarke strode purposefully onto the green and the villagers quickly disbanded.

Seeing the police officers approaching with stern expressions on their faces, Patsy finally released her grip on the boy.

'I'm going to tell my mum on you – you . . . you nutter!' the boy shouted over his shoulder having regained a modicum of feigned confidence as he now sprinted across the green towards the police who, for once, appeared to be the lesser of two evils.

'That may well be, Ms Warburton, but you really cannot start stalking around the village like a vigilante and taking the law into your own hands,' Inspector Hargreaves reprimanded Patsy after escorting her back to her shop. 'I'm telling you this for your own good, not for his! That lad could get you into an awful lot of hot water if you're not careful,' he warned her.

Daphne stayed quiet, conscious of Inspector Hargreaves's exasperation.

'If you have any future concerns, please just let me know and I'll deal with them. Understood?' The inspector could barely contain his frustration.

'But what about the man that the boy said he saw arguing with Nancy?' Patsy asked, apparently no less fixated on discovering more about Nancy's death after her telling off.

'Well, I'll have a word with him about that again, but to be honest it will probably amount to nothing. There's nothing to suggest that your sister's accidental fall was anything but an accident. So, we have no crime and therefore no motive to investigate.' Inspector Hargreaves noticed Patsy's dejected expression and softened his voice. 'Look, I understand how hard the past few months have been for you, Patsy. Loss is an awful thing and we all loved Nancy. She was such a character, and a real fixture in the village, but the truth is that any one of us could have had a mild disagreement with her; she was, after all, a very opinionated woman,' the inspector said before diplomatically adding, 'as well as being much-respected, of course'. He cleared his throat and adjusted his tie. 'I really wouldn't read too much into it if I were you.'

After the inspector had left, Patsy looked sorrowfully at Daphne. She seemed deflated, her shoulders hunched, the adrenaline of the past twenty minutes fizzing out, leaving regret and frustrated sadness in its wake.

'I know that you think I'm off my rocker, Daphne,' she said quietly, 'but honestly, Nancy would not have fallen off a ladder. She was only just joking with me about revealing some explosive gossip before I went upstairs. It was the last time I saw her alive. Her mind was sharp as a pin, I'm telling you.'

'I know Patsy, I know. It's hard to get my head around too.'

Feeling utterly helpless, Daphne wished there was more she could do to help her friend.

Back inside A Fine Vintage, with the hum of Radio 4 playing quietly in the background as she methodically and carefully waxed the top of a beautiful mid-century dressing table, Daphne thought about Patsy's refusal to accept that Nancy had accidentally fallen from the stepladder. She couldn't help wondering what the 'explosive bit of gossip' that Nancy had intended to share with Patsy had been. The sisters were known for their uncanny ability to extrapolate the deepest secrets of unwitting members of the community. Nancy had always been a keen observer. She would watch and hover quietly, noticing every hand gesture, hidden look or illicit smile. Warburtons' was an unlikely hotbed for scrutinising human behaviour. Her dismissive manner would lull shoppers into a false sense of security, unaware that she was watching their body language like a hawk. Whether she was perched on a ladder, unpacking boxes or scanning groceries, she had constant oversight of her domain.

One evening shortly after Nancy's funeral, Patsy had told Daphne that her sister had prided herself on being an excellent self-taught lip reader. Nancy had often joked that she had specifically learned the skill for the purpose of catching people out and discovering their hard-earned secrets but in reality she had learned it when their father had been diagnosed with dysarthria after a stroke. Nancy had been the only one able to understand what he was saying as she studied the movement of his lips towards the end of his life due to his inability to communicate by writing. What had started out as a necessity had quickly turned into a useful tool as she continued to practise on unsuspecting strangers long after her father had passed away. It was an unusual pastime, perhaps, but you had to make your own entertainment when you rarely left Pepperbridge – and someone had to keep everyone on their toes.

Daphne preferred to think of Nancy gathering these nuggets of gossip in a little notebook for her own private entertainment rather than using the information gathered and noted down for more sinister purposes of control. She imagined that's exactly what the Augustas and Mariannes of this world would do if they had access to such insider knowledge of other people's private affairs.

Daphne thought back to the day that Nancy had died. *What had their last conversation been?* Helena had come into Warburtons', she remembered that, and Nancy had reacted to her with typical disdain. A classic case of village snobbery towards a woman who had fallen in love with a suitor beyond her perceived station. But that wasn't the only cause of Nancy's disapproval. Daphne recalled that there had been something else too.

Hadn't Nancy mumbled something about Helena not being the one she was worried about? Patsy hadn't heard it, but Daphne had. She'd dismissed it at the time as part and parcel of Nancy's general disapproval of Helena, but when she came to think about it, it wasn't directed at Helena at all. *What had that all been about?* Daphne wondered. *And who* was *she more worried about?*

'What do you think of Hugh Darlington, Patsy?' Daphne asked a few hours later when Patsy had had time to cool off. With half an hour to spare before school pick-up, Daphne had just popped into Warburtons' for a quick chat and a cup of tea, hoping to reassure herself of her friend's return to a less agitated state of mind.

'What do I think of him? What do you mean?' Patsy replied, glancing up from the horse-racing pages in the sports section of the *Norfolk Post*. Horse racing always calmed her down in times of stress. She turned the radio down slightly so she could hear Daphne more clearly.

'You must have known him as a boy, when he first lived here. What do you think of him now?'

'I hardly see him. In fact, if I'm honest, I don't think that we've spoken two words to each other since he's been back from Australia. We didn't mix with people like that back in the day. He may have popped in when he was very young, but I can't remember him much. Nancy was the one who knew them all up there at Darlington Hall. She helped with the silver service on a couple of fancy occasions when they needed extra staff. She said they were just a bunch of typical toffs really. Oh – and he was good at the piano or something. The mother used to force him to play it for everyone at the end of the evening. Nancy said he was amazing. Concert-level, if I recall correctly. That was his thing – music. He could play every instrument going apparently. I think his father may have had wandering hands though – now *he* was meant to be a nasty piece of work. That's about all I know. Hugh Darlington certainly hasn't been in here since he's been back. No need I suppose – especially when he can send Helena for anything important.'

'Oh, right,' Daphne replied, thinking of the grand piano in the entrance hall at Darlington Hall and intrigued to hear of Hugh's evident history with it. 'One last thing,' she said, standing up and preparing to head to the school, 'why did Hugh end up going to Australia in the first place? No one has explained why he left, and I don't really want to be intrusive and ask Helena.'

'Well, according to Nancy he was sent away to boarding school at eight and hated it so much that he kept running away. He was always failing stuff – exams and tests – and doing badly in general, poor thing. Apparently, he and the father used to have some real humdinger fights about him hating school. Nancy said he wanted to be a musician. Anyway, when he finally left school, he wanted to join a band but his dad said 'over his dead body'. His mother tried to get them to compromise; she wanted Hugh to go to music school, but that was a no-no for Lord Darlington as well. Then the father found him using drugs and literally threw him out,' Patsy said, eyebrows raised. 'Called him a waste of space and a disgrace to the family; said that if he didn't get his act together, they'd disown him entirely. I think they ended up sending him to some sort of rehab camp in Australia as a punishment, but he ended up leaving it and working at various sheep farms or something like that and just stayed there. Not knowing where he'd gone caused his mother so much distress that his father had refused to let anyone try to locate him when she died. Said that they had washed their hands of him years ago and that he didn't deserve to see his mother again – even in death – so I guess the brother took the same stance when the father popped his clogs too.' Patsy shrugged. 'Why did you want to know, anyway?'

'Oh no reason. Just nosiness,' Daphne admitted. But she was starting to feel uneasy. Things didn't add up, but before she shared her suspicions, she needed to check one more thing.

Chapter 13

Daphne had spent the evening hosting Minerva and Silvanus for supper at Cranberry Farmhouse. The children loved it when Minerva and her son came over for Thursday night post-swimming-practice 'play dates'. James tended to be designated taxi driver, since these 'play dates' often ended up with a glass of wine or two for the mothers while they all tucked into a homemade shepherd's pie accompanied by home-grown vegetables.

Daphne and Minerva had had a few too many glasses of red wine, discussing the village drama and coming up with theories. With a slightly sore head, she was back at Darlington Hall the following morning. It was a Friday and they had almost finished preparing the final room for the decorators. The wallpaper stripping and sanding down of the architraves and skirting boards had proved to be a back-breakingly dirty and lengthy job. The scale of what they had undertaken was not for the faint-hearted. The large rooms were as high as they were wide, but at last the end was in sight, and although happy with the results, Daphne vowed silently to herself that she would probably never again offer to take on such an ambitious job – furnishings and design were definitely more her forte. However, despite their aching arms, the painting was scheduled to start on Monday morning and everything was on track for a soft launch of the B & B in time for the summer season.

'Did I see you in the crowd yesterday afternoon – when Patsy tried to perform her citizen's arrest?' Daphne asked Helena, casually injecting a note of humour in an attempt to lighten the mood. In reality, the situation had been no laughing matter. Patsy had been out of order to grab the boy, but Daphne knew that she had been acting in the throes of grief.

Helena looked cautiously at Daphne. 'Yes, I was. We'd run out of sugar soap so I'd driven to the shop. I didn't want to say anything because I know that Patsy's your friend, but oh my goodness, that was insane!' She was wide-eyed, as though still in shock at what she had witnessed. 'I told Hugh and he couldn't believe it either. Why on earth does she think that someone pushed her sister?'

Daphne shook her head gently. 'I don't know but it's likely to be down to overwhelming grief. She can't get over the fact that her sister has really gone.'

'Heartbreaking what grief can do to you,' Helena replied.

'Indeed,' Daphne said, feeling suddenly protective of Patsy and trying to think of a way to segue into another conversation. She taped the glass panes of the window with decorator's tape.

'How's Hugh today? Has he left the snug yet?'

'Well, he's still not doing great, but he has left the snug at least and moved to his office, so that's something I suppose. He's still not back to his old self though. I think that it might take a while. I'm hoping that he hasn't got PTSD or something else.'

'Is he showing signs of PTSD?' Daphne asked with concern.

'Well, he's taken to locking the door of the room that he's in and listening to loud music. He keeps telling me that he's fine and that he just wants to be left alone, but it's incredibly worrying. I think that he is showing signs of depression, if I'm honest.'

'Perhaps he should see a doctor,' Daphne suggested.

'Oh no. He's refusing to see any doctors, and he gets in a temper if I try to insist on anything. Even if it's for his own good. It's ... it's been really difficult.' Helena's green eyes were glimmering with tears. Her hair, usually held back neatly with an Alice band, hung limply to her shoulders. Now that Daphne was really looking at her, she noticed that Helena was thin and drawn, her skin almost translucent, with dark circles under her eyes. She suddenly looked far younger than her thirty years. Almost like a teenager. 'I'm sorry,' she apologised, embarrassed. 'I'm always complaining about something or other at the moment.'

'Not at all,' Daphne reassured her, reaching out to pat her shoulder. 'You have every right to be upset. And so does Hugh. You've both been through a very traumatic situation – and very recently too. It's hardly surprising that you're both affected by it.'

Helena looked at Daphne gratefully.

'What did Hugh say about the newspapers? Did his christening photos cheer him up at all?' Daphne asked, watching Helena out of the corner of her eye and feigning nonchalance as she continued taping.

'He hardly looked at them to be honest, Daphne. He said that that period of his life was completely over and that he had no interest in stirring up old memories.' Helena slumped back on her heels and looked at Daphne again. 'I'm so sorry, I know that you were just trying to do a nice thing, but Hugh seems to have no interest in the past. He said he just wants to move forward and make the best of what he has now.'

'I can understand that,' Daphne said kindly. 'It sounds as though he didn't have an easy relationship with his family. Perhaps the memories are far too painful, and he'd rather not revisit them.'

'Yes, I think that they are. That's exactly it.'

'It must be hard living in this house though, if that's the way he feels,' Daphne said quietly.

'Yes, there's definitely a contradiction in his decision to live here. Why doesn't he just walk away from it? After all, it's a huge financial burden. But it's his legacy and he's the last remaining Darlington, so he really wants to give it a try – and, of course, I'll be right by his side to help him,' Helena said with as much determination as she could muster.

Hugh was lucky to have patient, long-suffering Helena, Daphne thought.

'I suppose it wasn't necessarily the house that he stayed away from – but the people in it,' Daphne said contemplatively.

'Exactly. Perhaps this is a way to rewrite history and make

it a happy home again? Doesn't everyone deserve that chance? The chance to create the memories they deserve. Doesn't a house like this deserve that chance too?'

'Yes, you're right. Of course you're right, and I sincerely hope that it all works out for you in the end.' Feeling guilty of her suspicious thoughts of the previous day, Daphne was silent for a moment while they continued taping the edges of the window frames and along the tops of the skirting boards. Yet that same niggling sense of doubt kept popping towards the forefront of her mind. Despite her best intentions to stop interfering, she felt compelled to keep digging.

'Has he played the piano for you yet?' she asked Helena casually.

'The piano in the entrance hall? No – he can't play. Neither can I, which is a shame, but I'd love to learn. I've always wanted to, but we could never afford the lessons when I was growing up.'

Daphne digested Helena's answer silently, thinking about what Patsy had revealed. Then she remembered the grainy photo of a young Hugh sitting at the same piano with his mother standing by his side. What had the caption said? Hadn't it mentioned a Grade 8 piano exam? Incredibly impressive, especially for a young teenager. He'd obviously had a gift for music, as Patsy had mentioned yesterday. Yet now he refused to play – or couldn't play. *Which was it?*

The evidence pointed to something so macabre that Daphne almost felt ridiculous contemplating it. She watched Helena innocently and methodically cutting pieces of tape to run along the edges where the paintwork would soon go. If Daphne's hunch was correct, then Helena's world was about to shatter around her. The poor girl didn't deserve that, but nor did she deserve to exist in a lie that Daphne feared was the dark reality.

'Do you think Patsy will get over it?' Helena asked suddenly. 'Her theory that Nancy's death wasn't an accident, I mean?'

Daphne hesitated for a second, wondering how to answer, but perhaps it was time to start planting a seed in Helena's mind too. 'In all honesty, I don't think so. She's like a dog with a bone – especially now that one of the boys has claimed they saw Nancy arguing with someone.'

'The night she died?' Helena's jaw dropped.

'Well, that's the thing. He didn't say when it was, so the two things might not have anything to do with each other.'

'Does she think it was the tramp – the man they found in the garden?' Helena asked, wide-eyed.

'Possibly, but apparently he hadn't arrived in the village back then – when Nancy was still alive.'

'Oh gosh – she thinks it was someone else then?'

'Honestly Helena, please don't worry. I'm sure that Patsy will get to the bottom of it. You know the Warburton sisters. They've been here as long as anyone. Apparently, Nancy even used to document everyone's misdemeanours in a notebook. So if there was a significant quarrel with anyone, Patsy would have found out all about it already and that's the end of it,' Daphne said, keen to reassure Helena. She didn't want her friend to feel any more unsettled than she already seemed. 'Anyway, the boy may have just seen Nancy arguing with a tourist that she got snippy with. You know how she was. I'm sure it's nothing.' Daphne wasn't entirely sure about this theory but thought it best not to reveal her true thoughts to Helena. Hadn't the stranger been wearing camouflage trousers according to the young lad that Patsy had apprehended? The tourists who came to the village tended to be smartly dressed pensioners searching for tea rooms and historically interesting architecture. Camouflage trousers made her think of bird watchers and local farmers.

'Let's hope so,' Helena agreed. In the distance, the sudden thud of a door slamming made both women jump.

'Hugh – is that you?' Helena asked, getting up and calling out as she hurried to the open door. 'Hugh?'

A creeping sense of unease made Daphne shiver. *Had Hugh been listening to their conversation at the door? Wasn't he supposed to be asleep downstairs?*

'Just the wind, it seems,' Helena said with relief when she returned a few seconds later. 'I'd forgotten I'd opened a window at the end of the landing.'

'Oh right. That's good then,' Daphne smiled weakly and continued taping the skirting boards, trying to dismiss her rising anxiety. 'There's another emergency council meeting this evening,' she said. 'I think that Inspector Hargreaves is going to lecture us all about not taking the law into our own hands. He'll probably give Patsy a slapped wrist for grabbing the young chap. I'm intrigued to see how Patsy handles a public telling-off.' She laughed at the thought of her feisty friend standing up to the inspector. There would probably be a lot of tie-fidgeting on the inspector's part.

'What time does it start?' Helena asked. Her interest surprised Daphne. Hugh and Helena had not once turned up to a council meeting in Daphne's recollection.

'Oh, it's usually a five-thirty start officially, but it won't get going until just before six. If it goes smoothly then we're usually done by about six forty-five or seven at the very latest. These emergency meetings have been coming thick and fast so it shouldn't be a long one tonight. Do you fancy coming?'

At approximately 6 p.m. that evening, Daphne was sitting on an uncomfortable plastic chair wedged in between James and Marianne, listening to Augusta introduce a weary-sounding Inspector Hargreaves. The children were at home with Silvanus and Minerva. Minerva had unsurprisingly declined her invitation to attend the meeting with a wry smile and a roll of her eyes, stating: 'I'd much rather spend the evening with ten-year-olds than listen to adults spouting hot air . . .'

It was still light outside, and although the early evening air felt mild and even balmy, the inside of the hall felt like a sauna due to a faulty heat pump that remained constantly on, causing everyone to shuffle around uncomfortably in their seats. She had checked in on Patsy on her way over, but Patsy, anticipating the inevitable telling-off from Inspector Hargreaves, had decided to sit this particular meeting out. She was planning to close the shop early – since most potential customers would be at the meeting – and watch her *Poldark* boxset instead. Patsy had no desire to be made an example of and she was still fuming at not being able to grill the boy further on the argument he'd seen Nancy having in the shop.

Helena had also sent a text apologising for her no-show. Hugh had locked himself away in his study again claiming that he was too far behind on work to be disturbed by anyone – even Helena – so she was doing her best to try and get him to eat a proper meal.

At any rate the meeting was over by 6.45 p.m., as predicted by Daphne. The sweaty and relieved parishioners of Pepperbridge returned home suitably chastised, having been reminded that all suspected criminals must be dealt with by the police and never the general public. Inspector Hargreaves threw Daphne a pertinent look when he told the villagers in no uncertain terms to stop meddling, and emphasised that braying mobs surrounding the village green were not an acceptable part of civilised society. To which Mr Tomlinson had shouted out that the village stocks had been an acceptable method of punishment in the old days and Mrs Bertrand replied by asking whether Mr Tomlinson was, in fact, one-hundred and fifty years old considering that was the last official time that the village stocks were used. During the subsequent presentation on the Neighbourhood Watch scheme, Mr Tomlinson and Mrs Bertrand continued their spat across the room with increasingly personal retorts, while Julia Sugden wanted to know whether anyone had smelled the high-quality weed on the green.

Perhaps Pepperbridge had returned to its unremarkable and petty ways after all the recent drama, Daphne thought, finding unusual comfort in that thought as they stepped out into the much-needed fresh air.

Chapter 14

Saturday mornings were Daphne's favourite time of the week. James would usually get up first and head downstairs to make two mugs of steaming tea before bringing Byron upstairs for his weekend privileges of snuggling under the duvet between them for an extra-comfortable hour of snooze. It was the only time he was allowed to languish on the bed while James and Daphne read the weekend papers and drank their tea, putting the world to rights.

If luck was on their side, the children would wake up later than usual, until one or other of the twins decided that it was time for the chaos to begin and thus would do something suitably mischievous to make his brother squawk. The entire rabble would eventually gather downstairs in the yolk-yellow kitchen at the large farmhouse kitchen table in front of the Aga to breakfast on special weekend treats such as pancakes with bacon and scrambled eggs, all topped with maple syrup. It was a tradition that had started when Daphne was pregnant with Imani, long before they had moved to Norfolk.

At relaxed moments like these, with Byron curled up at her feet and the morning light streaming through the drawn curtains, Daphne felt able to ignore her compulsion to investigate the latest local mystery. She could simply enjoy the life that they had worked so hard to carve out for themselves. Only birdsong and the occasional sounds of distant cars and tractors interrupted the blissful peace and quiet.

Daphne looked at James who was squinting at the Saturday newspaper. He steadfastly refused to believe that he needed reading glasses, blaming his obvious issues with reading on their bedroom being dark due to its beamed ceiling. She smiled, thinking, *This is the life. Any other issues can wait until Mond—*

BEEP. BEEP. BEEP. She was shocked out of her relaxed state by the sound of her phone beeping and vibrating on the bedside table.

'Who on earth is calling at this time on a Saturday morning?' James asked disapprovingly but without moving the papers an inch further away from his nose. 'I'm sure that they're making this print smaller and smaller,' he complained as he narrowed his eyes even further at the sports pages.

Daphne picked up her phone. 'It's Patsy! Why would she be calling now?' she said before sitting up in bed and answering the call. 'Hello Patsy, is everything OK?'

'No, Daphne, it's really not,' replied Patsy, sounding uncharacteristically frightened. 'Someone broke in last night, and they hit me over the head.'

'Oh my God!' Daphne cried out and jumped out of the bed, prompting James to finally put down his paper.

He looked at her in confusion, mouthing, 'What's happened?'

Byron hopped up and started to bark; the bubble of lazy weekend relaxation had definitely been burst.

'Someone broke into Patsy's shop!' Daphne explained to James.

'No, Daphne – not the shop,' Patsy clarified. 'They broke into the flat. They were upstairs and going into the bedrooms. I came out of the sitting room when I heard rustling and banging and they walloped me on the head.' She sounded tearful as well as frustrated.

Daphne was almost speechless with shock. *Poor Patsy.* 'Are you all right? I hope you haven't been badly hurt ... Where are you now – at home?'

'No, I'm still at the hospital, but they want to discharge me soon and I was wondering whether you could come and pick me up?'

'Of course, I'll be there in under an hour!'

'What on earth is going on?' she said to James when she'd hung up. She was facing him but not really looking at him as her mind galloped, trying to work out the sequence of events. 'Why would they want to break into the flat and not the shop? Who could it have been?'

'You have no idea who it was? You didn't see their face, their clothing? Anything?' Daphne asked again.

'No, Daphne. Just as I told Inspector Hargreaves, I didn't see a thing. I heard someone rummaging around in the hallway and then – whoomph – the next thing I knew I was on the floor, and they were running down the stairs. I managed to call 999 and then I must have blacked out because the next thing I knew an officer in uniform was holding my hand and an ambulance crew were loading me on to a stretcher.' Patsy was sitting in the passenger seat of Daphne's Morris Traveller as the vintage motor trundled along winding B roads bordered by open fields filled with bright yellow rapeseed flowers. Saturday morning traffic this far from a major town or city was almost non-existent; the only other vehicle they passed was a livestock truck packed with sheep.

'I'm so sorry, Patsy, that's awful,' Daphne replied, genuinely shocked.

'The inspector thinks it may have been the boys from the village green coming for revenge, but why would they have come upstairs when they could have raided the shop? There was money in the till, and nothing has been taken from the shelves, apparently. The inspector says that whoever broke in had made a start on the bedrooms before I disturbed them.'

'The bedrooms?' Daphne repeated. 'But why on earth would they be going through your bedrooms?' Neither Patsy nor Nancy had been known for wearing jewellery, let alone for owning anything precious or valuable. Everything of value would have been down in the shop – the contents of the till and the products stacked on the shelves and behind the counter. Even their bulky old television looked like a relic in Daphne's opinion. The truth was there were no fancy gadgets or expensive items to be found in the Warburtons' fifties-throwback flat and she couldn't imagine anybody thinking otherwise. Had they been there to specifically attack Patsy?

'I can't believe how much they searched the flat,' Patsy said, visibly exhausted and unsettled. 'They'd been through the drawers in both rooms and had even dragged the mattress off a bed.'

'What on earth can they have been looking for?' Daphne asked, glancing quickly over at poor Patsy sitting looking bewildered in the passenger seat before indicating right to take the next turning into Pepperbridge. Patsy's worry was palpable, and Daphne's own heart was beginning to beat a little faster.

'I've no idea, but it seems as though it was "something specific" rather than a random search.'

'What do you mean by that?'

'It felt as though whoever broke in was looking for some-thing. Something significant. That's why I don't think it was that boy or any of his friends. Not only that but look – there they are – still on the playing field.' Patsy nodded towards the village green as they drove past. 'Surely if they'd just robbed my flat and hit me over the head, they wouldn't be standing there so nonchalantly as if butter wouldn't melt,' she said, rubbing her bandaged head and then wincing in pain at the touch. 'They may look daft, but I doubt they're that bold.'

Moments later, Daphne pulled over and parked Aggie in front of Patsy's shop.

'Any idea how they got in?' she asked as she jumped out and walked around to open the door for Patsy and help her out.

'I suspect that they used my spare keys. There was no sign of a break-in, and I usually leave them behind the counter.

Inspector Hargreaves says that they're no longer there. I feel so stupid but in all the years we've had the shop that's where the spare keys have always lived – even my parents left them there.'

'Wait – Patsy – what time did this all happen?' A sudden thought crossed Daphne's mind as they walked the few steps from the car towards the shopfront.

'Some time between six and six-thirty, I think. I'd locked the shop up early and I was already upstairs having a TV dinner in the sitting room.'

'That's when we were all at the community meeting,' Daphne confirmed. 'I wonder whether the person thought that you would be there,' she said carefully.

'Well, if they did then at least that's a start. And it couldn't have been anyone who was at the meeting.' Patsy handed her keys to Daphne to unlock the door.

'No, that's exactly what I was thinking,' Daphne said, coming to a horrible conclusion. 'Patsy, Nancy's notebook. Do you know where it is?'

'Nancy's notebook? You mean the one she used to jot her bits of gossip in?'

Daphne nodded eagerly.

'Well, yes – it's in the McVities biscuit tin behind the breadbin in the pantry. Why? Do you think that has something to do with it? It's completely useless, you know. She wrote everything in some sort of code. It all looks like gobbledegook to me but I can't bring myself to get rid of any of her things, so I left it there,' she finished sadly.

'Is it still in the pantry? Was it taken yesterday?' Daphne's stomach plummeted.

'Funnily enough, the pantry was the one place the filthy beggar didn't go into – mind you, it's only a cupboard really. You wouldn't know it was there unless you *knew* it was there.'

'Oh Patsy, I'm sorry, I think I know who it was. The worst thing is that I think it's my fault that they came looking!' Daphne felt completely distraught as Patsy looked at her incredulously.

'Who Daphne? Who do you think it was? Ouch!' Patsy leaned back against the shop counter to steady herself for a moment as she clutched her head. It had begun to throb again. 'I think I may need to lie down … Will you call Inspector Hargreaves?'

After carefully guiding Patsy through the shop and up the back stairs, Daphne nodded and asked, 'Do you think you'll be OK on your own for a while?'

Patsy looked shocked. 'Of course, Daphne, but first tell me – who do you think it was and what has the notebook got to do with it?'

'I may be wrong – I just need to make a few calls first. I promise I'll tell you the minute I can. Are you sure that you'll be OK on your own?' Daphne looked at her friend with concern, but time was of the essence.

'You really can't tell me now?'

'I can't wait another second, Patsy! You'll understand later.'

'OK, OK. You go and do your thing. My head is spinning and I can hardly think straight right now, but promise me that you'll let me know as soon as you're sure of anything. Here, take the spare keys and lock up on your way out. Inspector Hargreaves had the locks changed last night and he delivered me new sets of keys this morning, so I feel safe. But Daphne,'

Patsy said in a concerned voice, her eyes narrowing with worry, 'whatever your hunch is – please be careful.'

Daphne had locked the shop door behind her and ran the few doors towards A Fine Vintage. Opening the door quickly she hurried inside, grabbed her phone from her handbag and began to ring Helena, her heart pounding in her chest. 'Pick up, pick up, pick up,' she pleaded.

On her third attempt, Daphne's call was finally answered.

Daphne spoke frantically into the silence on the other line. 'Helena, listen to me, please,' she begged. 'You don't have to say anything, but I think that you might be in danger – it's Hugh – at least, I don't think that he *is* Hugh. Not Hugh Darlington anyway. Look, I'm probably not making any sense, but please just get out of there and meet me at the police station immediately. Don't say anything to Hugh and I'll explain more later, I promise ...' she babbled, realising that she was sounding panicked but fearing that they might be running out of time. If her hunch was right, then an interloper pretending to be Lord Hugh Darlington had just tried to claim victim number three in an attempt to conceal his real identity.

The long, tortured sigh on the other end of the phone may have sounded familiar, but it certainly didn't sound like Helena.

'H-Hugh?' Daphne asked tentatively.

'Daphne,' he confirmed and proceeded to hang up.

But just before the line went dead, Daphne heard Helena's tearful and distressed voice in the background calling out: 'Hugh ... please, you don't have to!'

'Damn,' Daphne cursed under her breath and called

Helena again. It rang and rang but this time no one picked up. *What have I done?* Daphne thought, terrified of the events that her phone call may have just triggered.

Departing from A Fine Vintage as speedily as she had arrived, Daphne ran back to Aggie, retrying Helena's number to no avail and ruing her decision to drive an ancient, slow and unreliable car. 'The one time I'd like to have a battery-operated key,' she muttered to herself as she tried to call James to raise the alarm of what she feared was going on. It went through to his voicemail. *Where is he?* she thought with rising panic. She left him a flustered and – she hoped – vaguely intelligible message instructing him to get hold of Inspector Hargreaves as soon as possible. 'Ask him to meet me at Darlington Hall without further delay and I'll explain things when he arrives,' she said. She wondered whether she ought to have called 999 immediately, but what if she was wrong? What if she was about to make a huge fuss over nothing? Helena's voice though ... there was no mistaking the panic in her tone before the line went dead.

Gripping the steering wheel with shaking hands, Daphne careered out of Pepperbridge, taking the most direct route to Darlington Hall. Pulling away, she narrowly missed Augusta, who was stepping off the kerb.

'Sorry, Augusta!' Daphne yelled.

'I was just coming to see you!' Augusta shouted angrily, waving her arms and indicating for Daphne to stop, but Daphne had no time to waste. Helena was in trouble and Daphne refused to leave her alone and vulnerable.

Her suspicions about 'Hugh' – if that was even his name – had been coming thick and fast over the past week. She had sensed that there was something a bit off with regards to how he carried himself from the start. A strange lack of confidence in his surroundings and an underlying sense of being overwhelmed.

At first, Daphne put this down to his twenty-year absence from Darlington Hall. Surely anyone would feel unsettled returning to their childhood home, steeped in difficult memories, after two decades living on a different continent. With no family, struggling finances and a crumbling estate to sort, anyone would be stressed. But as she spent more time in his presence, she realised there was more to his unease than a struggle to adapt to returning to England and his family home. She had caught Hugh hesitating when she had asked him simple questions about the house or where things were located, like whether a door connected to another room or opened a cupboard. She hadn't been trying to catch him out, just asking practical questions that you'd imagine someone familiar with Darlington Hall could answer. Surely, someone who had grown up in a house – even of this scale and size – would instantly know the layout of the rooms.

He had never given her an incorrect answer, but Daphne had been struck by the strange delays in his answers. A fleeting look of incomprehension had often been followed by a textbook-like explanation that sounded rehearsed rather than intuitive.

And what about the well-known passion of young Hugh Darlington for the piano? *Why had that disappeared?* By the time someone reached Grade 8 level, they didn't just lose that skill. There might be mistakes and forgotten notes after a twenty-year hiatus, but surely the basics would come back.

But no, 'Hugh' had said that he couldn't play at all. And then there was his unusual accent; Hugh's upper-class English enunciation, among the Australian twang, sounded passable enough, but at moments Daphne had noticed it seeming contrived – as though he was intensely concentrating on the way he spoke as well as what he was saying. Hugh was like the lead in a play that he had rehearsed over and over again: a Jay Gatsby-esque character locked in a nightmare pretence where he was performing the role of someone else.

These signs had been subtle and, as Daphne steered her Morris Traveller into the sharp bends of the single-track lane to Darlington Hall, she realised that she probably wouldn't have noticed them if she hadn't been spending so much time there.

However, she suspected that Nancy – with her unmatched eagle eye – had noticed. As one of the few remaining residents who had worked at Darlington Hall during Hugh's childhood, Nancy was one of the only people in Pepperbridge who might actually remember Hugh from the old days. She had obviously noticed something.

'It's not her I'm bothered about,' she had said on the day she had died. *Was that a clue?* Had Nancy also suspected that the man calling himself Lord Darlington was not in fact the real Hugh at all, but a convincing imposter? Was that the gossip Nancy was planning to impart to Patsy? Daphne's mind whirled, piecing it all together.

The accidents and the burglaries had all taken place since Hugh's return. First Nancy's 'fall' and then the 'accidental' death of the man in the kitchen garden. Regretting her earlier dismissal of Patsy's doubts about her sister's death, Daphne now agreed wholeheartedly that these terrible events were not a grisly coincidence. It all added up, and it all went back to Hugh – or whoever he was.

How had she been stupid enough to dangle the carrot of Nancy's little black book of secrets in front of unsuspecting Helena? Daphne was furious with her naivety. Poor Helena must have gone straight back to 'Hugh' and unwittingly informed him that his secret was still not safe.

Hence the break-in into Patsy's flat last night, when he would have assumed that she would be at the emergency council meeting with the rest of the village – except that she wasn't. Daphne shivered at how close Patsy had come to being another victim of Hugh Darlington's impersonator, and now it had come to this.

Daphne's foolishness had endangered Patsy, after everything she had been through, and it had probably done the same to Helena after the phone call. Sweat running down her back, she cursed under her breath.

Less than two years since Daphne had last found herself at the heart of a local murder case, she was hurtling along a country road en route to the scene of what had almost certainly been yet another murder in the parish. This time, a man who had already potentially killed twice to keep his secret hidden was at home with an innocent woman who may have only just learned that he wasn't who he claimed to be – that her entire life was a lie.

Daphne had to get to Helena as quickly as possible.

Chapter 15

Thankfully the door to Darlington Hall was unlocked. Daphne pushed it open as quickly as she could, relieved as she hadn't wanted to alert them to her arrival and ring the bell in a bizarre pretence of normality. She entered the main hall as she had done so many times previously; it felt different this time. Larger, darker somehow, more cavernous and eerily quiet.

'Helena!' she called out, breaking through the unsettling silence. Her voice seemed to echo. 'It's Daphne – is everything OK?' Her eyes darted around cautiously. For a moment, she felt like an idiot. *What if Hugh had nothing to do with the crimes after all? Have I been making something out of nothing?* Daphne's stomach dropped. If she was wrong about this, then she was about to make the biggest fool out of herself – and she would probably lose a lucrative job to boot. But if she was right . . . well, that was an even more horrifying prospect.

Tiptoeing further into the hall, her footsteps sounding unbearably loud despite how gently she was going, Daphne tentatively glanced at the drawing room door. It was open and it was as good a place as any to start looking.

'Hugh' was standing with his back to Daphne. Seeing him, her heart rate sped up even more. He was staring silently out of the window towards an ancient yew hedge that bordered the pathway to the kitchen garden. The view through the window looked calm and idyllic, with yet another clear cobalt blue sky that belied the lack of calm she was feeling standing on the inside. He seemed to be lost in thought; his stance was strangely wide, as though he needed stability to stop himself from falling – or running. Daphne could see the faint glimmer of a humourless smile flicker across his mouth from his side profile; his expression was at odds with the grave situation. The closer Daphne stepped towards him, the more she could see that Hugh wasn't looking through the window at all. Now she could see that his eyes were focused on the reflection visible in the glass panes of the large Gothic windows. He was glaring straight at Daphne's reflection, and, close-up, his smile was more of a grimace. A chill ran down her spine.

'Hugh,' Daphne said hesitantly, 'where's Helena?' She scanned the drawing room for exit routes, acutely conscious that her amateur sleuthing had taken her way out of her depth.

'Let's cut the crap, Daphne. You know that's not my real name.' With little need to continue the subterfuge, his voice had settled deeply – and perhaps with relief, Daphne suspected – into its naturally melodic Australian twang.

'Hmm, yes, I had realised that ... Hugh – or whatever your name is. But that's not important right now. I just want to know where Helena is. Please can you tell me?' she asked firmly, trying to conceal her desperation. She hoped he couldn't hear the frantic thumping of her heart.

'It wasn't supposed to end this way, you know,' he said, ignoring Daphne's question.

'End? What wasn't supposed to end this way? Hugh – I'm sorry, I don't know what to call you ... Where is Helena?' The urgency in her voice was obvious now. If Helena wasn't here then she sure as hell didn't want to be either.

Daphne began to back slowly out of the drawing room. She glanced to her left, looking towards the dark wooden staircase in the main hall as she shouted up to the landing, 'Helena? Are you OK? Where are you?'

'Hugh' remained still but his mood was inscrutable, and Daphne had seen enough to be terrified of what he was capable of. She continued edging backwards, anxious to not be alone with him. At Daphne's estimation he had been responsible for at least two deaths in the village: Nancy Warburton; and the man in the glasshouse. The situation in the glasshouse had never quite made sense – no thief would sit around building a fire and waiting to be caught after committing a burglary two minutes away and attacking the owner of the house. The unfortunate man had obviously been sitting there oblivious to the supposed thefts up at Old Hall when he was killed. She prayed silently that there were no further murders still to be discovered.

It had come to her with complete clarity the moment she had realised what the intruder had been looking for at Patsy's flat: Nancy's tell-all notebook. Although in truth she'd had her suspicions and had started to piece things together long before that. From the moment she had looked at the photographs of Hugh Darlington at the library she had sensed that the man she knew as Hugh and the younger version were not the same person. Then she had suddenly recalled the way the homeless stranger had shielded his eyes from the sun as he thanked her and everything had clicked into place. The boy in the Darlington family photos at the library had been standing and shielding his eyes in exactly the same way, with the same expression and the same stare.

'Don't you want to know why?' he asked, stopping Daphne in her tracks.

'Why?' Daphne responded, startled by his unexpected question. 'Why what? What have you done to Helena?' The imposter's strangely relaxed manner was deeply unsettling. *Please arrive soon, Inspector Hargreaves*, she thought. *Hurry up.*

'He wanted me to do it. It was part of the deal ...' he continued. His eyes seemed to focus on something behind Daphne's shoulder before refocusing on her. Spooked, she turned around but there was nothing there. Hearing his footsteps, she turned back towards him, almost giving herself whiplash with the speed of her turn. With only a few more steps he would be within lunging distance. He was a tall and muscular man and she understood without question that with his speed and frame, she probably wouldn't be able to outrun him – let alone overpower him if the need occurred. He was no elderly Doctor Oates. Thankfully he still seemed subdued, and his tone was strangely calm.

'What deal?' Daphne asked, playing for time while she

tried to work out how to find Helena before hopefully escaping together from Darlington Hall and its dark secrets.

He was looking straight into Daphne's eyes, although his own appeared glassy and occasionally unfocused. He'd taken another step forward and Daphne was now in fight or flight mode, poised to either throw a punch or flee within a millisecond if he edged any closer.

Suddenly his mood changed, like a switch had been flicked. 'It's the bitch's fault,' he spat, shaking his head as if to clear it. 'The old hag. I was never good enough. She said I'd be a nobody – well she was WRONG,' he shouted furiously. 'I was a somebody. I am somebody. I am LORD BLOODY DARLINGTON!' He laughed bitterly at the absurdity of his statement and then sighed. His head hung sorrowfully, his gaze lowering to the polished wooden floors.

Who is he talking about? Nancy? Helena? Who? Daphne began to wonder whether he might be drunk or intoxicated with something else. 'Who do you mean? Helena? You know that she loves you, Hugh . . .' Daphne's attempt at reassurance faltered and her voice trailed off uncertainly.

'No!' he exclaimed so angrily that Daphne nearly jumped out of her skin in shock. 'Not Helena . . . Not my sweet, beautiful, loyal Helena . . .' His voice softened and he paused long enough to give Daphne the opportunity to take stock of the situation.

What is that peculiar smell? Is that smoke?

'No . . . not Hels. She has nothing to do with this particular story. I'm talking about Nanna Prince. Nanna bloody Prince . . .' he said finally.

'Nanna Prince?' she asked. *Who on earth is that and how*

does she fit into all this? She desperately hoped that their conversation might buy her some time to work out how she could escape to find Helena.

'She was a plucky old bird ...' he said, almost as if to himself, obviously reminiscing about this mysterious relative. He had a distant look in his eyes.

'She brought me up – at least that's what she told people. Dragged me up kicking and screaming more like. Like a fox playing with a chicken before killing it,' he said wryly.

'So you weren't close ... with your grandmother?' Daphne knew that she was just repeating the man's revelations back to him, but he seemed to want to talk about this woman and if it distracted him for long enough, she could figure out her next move. She desperately hoped it worked because the smell of smoke was getting stronger and there wasn't a fire lit in the entrance hall or the drawing rooms as far as she could tell. 'Tell me about her, Hugh. Tell me about Nanna Prince.'

'You know my name isn't Hugh. It's Henry. Henry Johnson.'

Henry's recollection of his childhood was a game of two halves. Before and after. Happy and miserable. There were no grey areas, no mediocre moments, no middle-of-the-road memories. It had been heaven for the first eight years followed by pure hell thereafter. He knew that his early memories were most likely recalled through rose-tinted glasses, but regardless, anything would have seemed magical compared to the torture of being brought up alone with his grandmother. He couldn't even say that she had 'meant well', the term so often used to excuse the unpleasant behaviour of mean-spirited people who really ought to know better. She was bitter and angry for reasons that he could never fathom, and her bilious spite seeped into her treatment of her young grandson at the very time he had needed her the most.

Growing up, his grandmother had 'helpfully' and frequently reminded Henry that he had taken the worst characteristics of both his errant parents. The bedtime 'stories' she told him frequently underlined the gormless stupidity of his father, who had failed to provide a roof to go over his burgeoning family's heads once he and Henry's mother had found out that they had accidentally fallen pregnant with Henry. This had resulted in them all being forced to go and live with Nanna Prince in Tasmania, south of the Australian mainland. Another favourite tale of Nanna's was the fecklessness of his mother – her daughter – who, despite a solid grammar-school education and an unblemished academic record, had dropped out of university in the second year, chosen a 'useless excuse of a man' to have a child with, and carelessly expired in her early thirties from cancer. As far as Nanna Prince was concerned, her daughter's death was further evidence of her failure to properly bring up her now-motherless son.

Eileen Johnson had left behind a devasted young husband who without his soulmate had suddenly seemed to lose all purpose in life; Henry's grandmother recounted her interpretation of events without a shred of empathy.

'What about me?' he had asked with wide, tear-filled eyes.

Nanna Prince mercilessly threw the question thrown back at him, 'What about you? You obviously weren't their priority.'

His father, Liam, had apparently been left so devastated

and bereft that, in Nanna Prince's words, he had become 'even more stupid and incapable of finding work than before Eileen's death'. It hadn't helped that Nanna Prince had criticised and hounded him daily and stripped any final shred of dignity from the man who had once turned up on her doorstep with her pregnant daughter, looking so hopeful. Henry had been told that his dad had ensured his own demise by drinking himself into a youthful grave not far behind Henry's mother.

Liam's only win in life it seemed had been to prove his mother-in-law right out of spite and live up to the self-fulfilling prophecy of her cutting words. He had been good for nothing beyond loving his wife, and not even having a son could save him. The mutual satisfaction in his bitter (and in her words 'inevitable') demise was the only emotional connection that they ever shared. She had watched him implode though drink and he had watched her watching him.

She had then turned her disappointment on what was left behind. His son. Her grandson.

The years that followed had been hard. The only relative that Henry was aware of, Nanna Prince had taken it upon herself to remind him daily of how unwanted and how burdensome his presence was, while at the same time becoming increasingly dependent on him as a companion, handyman and general dogsbody.

At the age of seventeen, once he had finished school and received his high-school diploma, a worn-down Henry did the thing that he had been dreaming of for the past decade. He left his grandmother sleeping in her bedroom, crept silently out of the house, and caught a night bus destined for a sheep farm on the outskirts of Albany on the south coast of Western Australia.

His decision had been inspired by an old issue of *National Geographic* where he had once read an article on the oldest towns in the west. Stuck in a cramped, soulless city bungalow and exposed to Nanna Prince's relentless cruelty, Henry had fallen in love with the images of the region's beautiful coastlines, breathtaking white-sand beaches and karri forests. They had looked like a vision of paradise and signified a type of freedom that he had never known. He longed to escape.

Months later, while waiting for his grandmother in the doctor's surgery, he had read another article where a particular farm had stood out to him. He took the magazine home and it lay dog-eared and worn under his bed for more than a year. Advertised as a family-run sheep farm that welcomed people wanting to explore rural life, it described its focus on sustainable farming ecosystems and using biodiverse methods instead of the usual chemical farming practices. As the child of a parent who had died due to addiction, drugs and even alcohol now repelled him as an adult. He blamed them both for his unhappiness throughout his childhood and felt drawn to the idea of moving to an intentionally non-toxic environment and learning how to become self-sufficient. Self-sufficiency and farming meant that he could exist on his own one day. Far away from people. Nanna Prince had proved to be more than enough 'people' for him to handle in one lifetime. He had no desire for anyone else in his life who could desert him or abuse him.

He'd saved up money from his many Saturday jobs, and from working after school at a local garage. The one saving grace of his grandmother's general lack of interest in him was that she didn't want to know what he did with his spare time, which meant she couldn't leech his wages from him. She was so convinced of his lack of ambition, so sure that he was up to no good and wasting his time taking drugs (a myth that he was more than happy to allow her to assume during their rare monosyllabic conversations), that he managed to work and save money right under her nose. In fact, by the time Henry was eighteen, he'd saved enough for a one-way ticket from Tasmania to Western Australia, heading straight for the paradisial south coast that he'd seen pictured *in National Geographic*. The utopia he had spent years escaping to in his imagination.

The next time he saw Nanna Prince, she was dead. Two years after his departure he had received a telegram to say that that she had had a heart attack and died in her garden. Despite hating himself for feeling the need to do so, he had allowed her to know where he had travelled to by sending cards on her birthday and at Christmas – not that she had ever bothered to reply via the return address. If only she had tried to love him, she would have realised that all he had craved was a close and supportive relationship.

She had paid for all of her funeral costs in advance and left her house and all of her worldly goods to the local cat shelter. The final slap in the face for her only grandson.

Henry stood in silent isolation at her funeral – no one attended except him and the chaplain – and vowed from then on that he would make something of himself. He remembered how she had belittled his father, and how that belittlement had triggered his father's self-loathing. He would not allow Nanna Prince's judgement of him to shape his life.

It had been aways in his nature to keep himself to himself. When you are told from a young age that you are worthless and that no one loves you, it's hard to believe yourself worthy of even friendship, and so Henry remained a loner for the most part. Meeting Hugh Darlington was the first time in his life that he had come close to making a genuine friend.

Their unlikely alliance had started after Henry kept on being called 'Hugh' while working on a new sheep ranch in Western Australia. He had been living a rather nomadic life, working at various ranches covering everywhere from the Wheatbelt to the Outback and was now closer to the southern coastal region dominated by endless rolling plains and low-lying hills. It had been seven years since Nanna Prince had died, and although Henry was now in his mid-twenties, he was yet to fulfil his goal of proving his worth. It infuriated him that he was still affected by Nanna Prince's abuse. With the added indignity of now being mistaken for somebody else, he felt as though he were disappearing. Being mistaken for 'Hugh' wasn't a rare occurrence; since joining the new ranch it had happened with such frequency that Henry had sought out his apparent doppelganger to see how similar they really were.

Henry and Hugh's first meeting had been when seven farmhands were sent to fix a break in a large section of fencing on the western perimeter. On the overnight drive out, in the back of a cramped Land Rover, Henry finally came face to face with the real Hugh.

He had realised who Hugh was the minute he poked his

head through the door. The two men had stared at each other in surprise, eventually both unable to stop grinning and laughing as they realised that they did indeed share an uncanny resemblance – not only in looks but in height and stature too. They even wore the same style clothing: white T-shirts under tatty denim shirts with faded combat trousers that had seen better days.

This moment had marked the beginning of an unlikely friendship so strong that they were soon referred to as 'the twins' or 'the brothers from other mothers' on the ranch. For two lonely men who had experienced cruelty, rejection and loneliness during their childhoods, this bond was a gift that grew to feel genuinely fraternal.

Their friendship had deepened over drunken stories of unpleasant childhoods, and equally unpleasant family members – Nanna Prince for Henry and an unloving rogue of a father for Hugh. Henry had always noticed that Hugh's accent had more than just a subtle English undertone to it, concealed by a light Aussie topping, but his friend was vague about his background, and understanding what it was like to harbour family secrets that one didn't always feel like addressing, he chose not to pry. Hugh would open up if he chose to, and that was good enough for Henry. When he was drunk, Hugh's accent was reminiscent of the way that Hollywood actors like David Niven and Laurence Olivier spoke in the films that Nanna Prince had watched during his childhood. It was properly posh and there was no denying it. He couldn't help but be intrigued by Hugh's upbringing.

Hugh may have been in the bad-childhood club, but Henry suspected that Hugh's version had featured a fair bit of privilege. Not that he minded – after all, Hugh was hardly an aloof aristocrat in his regular uniform of ripped jeans and filthy T-shirts and hard work on the ranch. He was warm and friendly, constantly entertaining everyone with his ever-present guitar and stupid self-effacing jokes. He was one of the lads, regardless of what his background had been. Their favourite double act was impersonating each other's accents. Hugh did a seamless Aussie and Henry managed to capture Hugh's strangely posh, Australian-tinged English accent perfectly.

The biggest problem their friendship had encountered was Hugh's growing dependency on alcohol and drugs. The soft kind at first. Just the odd smoke that would help him laugh uncontrollably and forget about his worries. At first, Henry had sometimes joined in, when it was still casual. For a brief moment, Henry had also wondered if drugs could offer him the same sense of escape from his insecurities, but memories of his father slumped over the front doorstep with his grandmother firing expletives at him chastened him quickly. Steering clear of even casual drug use, Henry watched helplessly as his friend fell further into a spiral of addiction.

He had tried his best to help Hugh over the years, even taking him to a rehab centre to try and dry him out once and for all, but Hugh would always fall back into his old habits. Henry was forced to acknowledge that Hugh's addictions were long-established and would likely lead to his early death – a thought that he couldn't bear. Every once in a while, Hugh would disappear entirely, only to return to the ranch with promises that he had cleaned up and that this time would be different, but it never was. Eventually, the ranch refused to have him back and he ended up bunking with Henry, sleeping on his floor while Henry tried to work out what to do with him – the only real friend he'd had in his life.

It hadn't escaped Henry's attention that years had gone by and yet neither of them had made much of their lives. Hugh's potential had been stifled by his struggle with addiction, but what was Henry's excuse? He had risen up the ranks to become assistant farm manager – which was a big deal on a sheep ranch of this size where thousands of sheep were at stake, and he was responsible for livestock management as well as the challenge of handling dozens of farm hands – but it was still someone else's farm. This certainly wouldn't have been sufficient to impress Nanna Prince. Despite Hugh's problems, he was Charming, with a capital C, at least when he was sober, and Henry imagined that his grandmother would have been won over by Hugh's aristocratically accented charm. Completely unearned traits like that had impressed the old woman more than hard graft and supposed family bonds. He couldn't believe that she still consumed so much of his thoughts. Would this have impressed Nanna Prince? Would she have approved of that? Would she have thrown a crumb of love for anything that he had achieved? All he had ever wanted was her approval. To know that he had been loved by her. Or anyone at all, really. He just wanted to be loved enough for someone to stick around, and now it seemed that even his best friend was hellbent on abandoning this life too. His biggest fear was that he would end up as bitter, twisted and alone as his old Nanna.

Hugh had told Henry that he'd found out about his mother's death by accident – no one in his family had tried to tell him. Almost seven years later, he had learned about his father's passing in the obituaries section of an English newspaper in town. This had prompted a huge bender for Hugh. He disappeared for three months, retuning stinking to high heaven in clothes that had barely been changed, having slept rough and – by the look of it – been beaten up more than a few times. Henry was just thankful that his dear friend was alive.

The day that Hugh had received the crisp, monogramed letter that changed everything was imprinted in Henry's mind.

On this occasion, in a state of increasingly rare sobriety, Hugh had solemnly opened the letter at the rickety little kitchen table while Henry made them coffee, steak and eggs with fried potatoes, a breakfast speciality that had become a ritual when Henry was going through a sober period.

'What is it, mate?' he asked, watching Hugh read the letter and place it back down on the table silently. 'A parking ticket?' he joked, knowing full well that his friend didn't own a car.

'No.' Hugh's accent was distinctly English, with no hint of its usual hybrid Australian tinge.

Henry looked at him with concern. 'What's up?'

'My brother is dead,' he said without emotion. 'I'm the new Lord Darlington.'

Several hours passed and Hugh had still shown little to no emotion about the passing of the final member of his immediate family. Henry couldn't quite tell whether his friend was numb with shock or genuinely didn't feel anything. He chose to believe the former.

'I knew it!' Henry practically shouted later that evening as they sat on the floor of his rented digs drinking shots of whisky. For once, Henry had found it hard to refuse a drink, owing to the awful news that his friend had so recently received. 'I just *knew* you were a lord or something stupid like that. It's that bloody accent. None of the other Poms ever speak like that! Lord bloody Darlington if you don't mind. Well look at *you*!' he laughed, trying to lighten the mood as his friend sat po-faced and humourless with his back against the foot of Henry's bed.

'So, when do you go back and what do you have waiting for you? Pots of cash?' Henry asked, intrigued as to what being a fully-fledged 'lord of the manor' really meant.

'No idea, and I'm not going back. I haven't been back for years and I'm not going back now.'

Henry was taken aback for a few moments and a shocked silence hung heavily in the air between them.

'But . . . Jeez, Hugh,' Henry offered eventually. 'You've got the world waiting on a plate for you back there. Everything a man could want. A big house, a title – land! Your own bloody land – imagine! Not somebody else's. You won't need to answer to anybody else for the rest of yer bloomin' life! Of course you're going back. Who in their right mind wouldn't take that opportunity?'

'No, Henry. I'm not going back,' Hugh replied quietly. 'I don't want it. Nothing could drag me back there. They can burn the whole bloody lot in a bonfire for all I care,' he said with conviction.

Henry raised himself up from the floor. He suddenly felt incredibly angry. Hugh had the world at his feet. Everything that anyone could possibly want, and here he was talking about discarding it as if it were an unwanted overcoat. *Was he mad?*

'You selfish brat. You arrogant idiot.' Henry criticised Hugh with such emotion and anger that he was almost on the brink of tears. 'Do you know what I'd give to get a chance like that? To be offered a new life? To get out of this hamster wheel and try something different? Do you know how hard it is for *real* people like me to get on and amount to something? And there you are turning your nose up at something that others would kill for. If you won't do it for yourself, think of other people. Think of me! Your old mate Henry, remember? Your brother from another mother, remember? Just go over and sell it and come back with the money and let's live a life of Riley here!' Henry was half laughing, half crying now and feeling unsteady from all the whisky he'd so uncharacteristically consumed.

Hugh was staring silently at Henry. He had listened intently to his emotional outburst and he didn't seem to be angry at his friend's hard-hitting words. 'You do it,' he said suddenly.

'What?' Henry replied, his head beginning to spin slightly.

'I said you go. They haven't seen me for twenty years. No one has. You could easily be me twenty years on. People can hardly tell the difference between us.'

Henry had stopped swaying and was now looking at Hugh with incredulity. 'Don't be daft,' he replied after a moment of shocked silence, unsure whether Hugh had been joking or not.

'I'm serious. All we need to do is apply for a passport with your photograph in instead of mine. It'll be easy. I can teach you everything you need to know. It's not hard. No one knows me any more and they won't expect much from me except to sign a few papers, take the cash and come back to Australia. Do it for me, Henry. I can't go back. I can't face it. Please. You do it. Pretend to be me.'

Chapter 16

Despite the increasingly acrid smell, Daphne barely moved an inch as Henry Johnson – as she now knew him to be – recounted his story from start to finish with barely a pause, his voice occasionally breaking with emotion. Despite the earnest delivery of his words, she wasn't entirely sure whether she believed that he was the unwilling accomplice in such an elaborate ruse, but regardless of what she believed, here he was, in place of his apparent 'friend' and partner in deception, the real Lord Darlington.

Torn between making a run for it to search for Helena, and simultaneously wanting more answers, she remained at the entrance of the drawing room and continued to quiz Henry. 'So, was that Hugh then? In the kitchen garden?'

'Yes,' Henry nodded sadly, his head hanging low and his body almost imperceptibly swaying with – *genuine emotion?*

But Daphne was having none of it. Despite having the potential to stray into dangerous and possibly life-threatening territory, despite the thudding of her heart, she had to persevere. The man in the kitchen garden and Nancy Warburton were both dead, and she had a strong suspicion that the man standing in front of her was responsible for both of their deaths.

'If he didn't want to come back to England to claim his inheritance himself then why was he here? How did he end up back in Pepperbridge and why was he sleeping rough?' she asked.

Henry paused, visibly ashamed, before answering the question in a dejected tone, filled with hopelessness and regret. 'Because I stopped answering his messages . . .' he said dully.

'His messages?'

'Yes, we were in constant contact from the beginning. He remained in Australia, but he was my guide to Pepperbridge throughout. Hugh was advising me on what to say and what to do and who was who . . .' Henry looked up momentarily to gauge Daphne's expression, but she was giving nothing away.

'He told me who to contact, what to sign and who to avoid. We knew it might take a while, but the plan was for me to get the ball rolling to sell off the estate bit by bit and then return the cash to Hugh in Australia. He had no intention – at the time – of ever setting foot in England again. We had access to his family account, which was transferred into his name, so it should all have been pretty straightforward.'

'So, what changed his mind?'

Henry hesitated for just a second, then shrugged his shoulders, evidently figuring that as he was already in for a penny he might as well stay in for a pound. He had obviously reached the end of the road. 'I started to enjoy it,' he said.

'Enjoy it?' Daphne repeated, eyebrows raised.

'Yes. I started to enjoy being Lord Darlington. Started to enjoy trying to sort out the finances and looking after the estate. I realised I was good at it. I began to feel that it was something worth saving and that it would be such a waste to split up this centuries-old family legacy and sell it to some developer as though it didn't mean anything.'

Daphne realised that Henry was swaying heavily now. *Was he slurring his words?* She jumped slightly as he checked himself abruptly and walked over to lean against a red-leather Chesterfield armchair, steadying himself.

'I mean, who wouldn't give their eye teeth to be born into this? Why would you walk away from it? I was given nothing. Not even the one-way fare for a bus ride. Hugh was given *this*!' He gestured towards the interior of the drawing room with its grand proportions, fine art and beautiful furniture.

Daphne found it hard to disagree, but that wasn't the point. 'But Henry, this wasn't yours to take,' she replied tentatively, fearful of pushing him too far, but unwilling to stand there and allow him to justify what he had done.

'No. It wasn't mine to take, but I guess I lost myself for a while . . .' he said sadly, his tone lowering. 'It had all seemed so easy. She made it seem so easy—'

Daphne's ears pricked up. 'She made it seem so easy? What do you mean? Who made it so easy?'

Henry looked up from where he was now slumped against the worn old armchair.

Daphne could smell it again. Something definitely appeared to be burning.

'My loyal, sweet Helena,' he said finally, before collapsing onto the floor.

'HUGH! I mean – Henry!' Daphne shouted as she ran over to him, putting her hands on his shoulders and shaking them. 'What have you taken? Where is Helena? What have you done with her – is she all right? Henry, you need to tell me!'

Henry's eyes flickered opened again, and he tried to focus on Daphne's face. 'It wasn't meant to turn out this way . . .' he repeated over and over again as his eyes rolled back.

Daphne was desperate for a response to the one question that needed answering. Her mind had been working quickly, trying to decode what Henry was talking about. 'Henry – did you kill Nancy because she found out who you were? Did you kill Hugh because you wanted to keep his identity a secret? Please, Henry – I need to know!' she gabbled, sweat beading her forehead, trying to engage his attention before he slumped back into unconsciousness.

'I didn't kill anyone, I would never have hurt Hugh,' Henry murmured, looking hazily at Daphne. 'I loved Hugh. He was like family. He was the best friend I ever had. The only friend I had – until Helena.' His eyes flickered suddenly and he began to mumble an increasingly indistinguishable sentence. 'But it's not her fault . . . the baby . . . she just wanted to protect me. Us . . .' And with that he drifted into unconsciousness, once again leaving Daphne trying to work out what on earth was going on and who the real villain in this story was.

'Who wanted to protect him? Nancy? Helena?' She had an awful feeling that all was not as straightforward as she had originally thought.

Chapter 17

Helen Carter had grown up the youngest of five boisterous and confidently opinionated sisters, in a household filled with gregarious, loud and wonderfully strong women. It ought to have been the perfect hothouse for her to become the type of confident young woman who laughed in the face of patriarchal stereotypes. But being the youngest by eight years she had fallen through the cracks and lacked the robust independence of her sisters. As a baby, her crying had been drowned out by the louder and more articulate cries of her four much older and far more demanding sisters. Eventually she had learned that she could never compete with the four other girls. She had learned early on that if her voice could not be heard among the din then assuming a façade of compromise, compliance and self-sacrifice was the only weapon at her disposal to keep her life on an even keel. Her choices had rarely been her own. Her clothes and toys had been a relent-less chain of hand-me-downs, leftovers and afterthoughts. Always known as 'the baby' rather than by her given name, Helen's identity had been so squashed by her assertive sisters, Hannah, Harriet, Honor and Hazel that after a while she had simply given up, retreating into herself and her books, and creating a fantasy world where she was the main protagonist. A fantasy world that revolved around a dream that one day she would be rescued by a handsome prince who worshipped her for her individuality and intelligence. He would take her back to his castle where she would be able to choose her own clothes and sleep in her own room, high in a turret, filled with books that she had chosen. Helen and her prince would, of course, live happily and quietly ever after without a sister to share her things in sight.

It hadn't taken Helen long, however, to realise that there would be no fantasy rescue party coming for her. Her mother and grandmother had told all the Carter girls as much. 'Men are a waste of space and only needed for one thing', they had often said, cackling with a mixture of mirth and stoicism.

'When you have a strong mother, you respect your-self – you don't let anyone talk down to you or walk over you – certainly not a man,' her grandmother would remind them all periodically.

Why was it then, Helen had wondered, *that when I speak up no one listens?*

Because you're the baby, silly, she had rationalised to herself. *The baby has to find other ways to get what they want!*

Thus, Helen had realised that she would have to be her own knight in shining armour.

School and academia had been the one area of her life where she had hoped to achieve a semblance of independence, or at least escapism, but even at school she had been compared to her sisters and penalised for their sins far in advance of committing any of her own.

The Carter girls – or the 'H-Bombs' as they were often jokingly referred to – had been notorious for their fearlessly rowdy nature, their love of collecting and discarding boyfriends – as well as detentions – and their ability to tie their teachers up in knots with sassy responses and wilful backchat. When a young and timid Helen had started high school, it was widely assumed that she would be just another difficult chip off the old block. Without much faculty support, and too blinded by their own preconceived assumptions to see the sparkling intelligence behind her quiet demeanour, she had single-handedly pushed and excelled her way through her studies to escape the shackles of a village where being a 'Carter girl' raised eyebrows or prompted jokey signs of the cross. Helen's teachers' surprise at her achievement of three excellent A levels in no way hindered their ability to take full responsibility for her success. She had nonetheless left for university filled with relief and optimism, hoping that her life was about to change for the better.

But university hadn't changed anything. She had found no sense of empowerment in escaping from village life. If anything, her privileged Russell Group university with its collection of historic buildings standing within a thousand years' worth of world heritage architecture simply underlined the petty restrictions and social injustices that that were part and parcel of life everywhere. If she had found people from a similar background it may have been fine, but due to an error with the accommodation office she had accidentally found herself living in a hall of residence that seemingly judged students based on what class and you were born into and how much financial freedom you had. Intimidated, her quiet nature caused everyone to talk down to her or around her – just as her sisters had. In her first year, potential friends would approach her, their eyes drifting away when they realised that not only did she not have much to say for herself but she was also 'one of those' who had to work to pay her way and couldn't go clubbing on a whim. Her resentment began to grow.

Far from university paving her way for independence, it had simply made her feel even more of a spectator destined to remain a cog in the wheel of other people's far more extravagant lives.

She had been born into a household where she had started at the bottom of a pile and remained there, suffocating under the effort of trying to make her own way. All that university had taught Helen was that power and freedom were an accident of birth, and her own 'accidental birth' – as her mother had often jokingly (and unintentionally hurtfully) referred to it – had given her no momentum to attain anything beyond returning home for more of the same.

In spite of the naysayers in Pepperbridge, her sisters hadn't done badly at all, just as the family matriarchs had predicted. As her mother had proudly stated, 'Strong women beget strong women – always remember that.' Hazel was now a veterinary assistant. Honor was assistant manager at the same stables as her mother had been, Harriet was a mother of twins and helping out part time at a local nursery, and Hannah, the eldest, had moved away to join the armed forces – apparently never quite ready to detach from the joys of communal living. Not bad at all for a quartet of apparently 'unruly hooligans', as Augusta Papplewick had once described them. But Helen had wanted so much more for herself. She had hoped that she would be different, that she would be the one to escape Pepperbridge properly and make something bigger and better of herself.

Returning to the village from university with nothing to show for it besides a few letters after her name and a hefty student loan, she had been close to admitting defeat. Big things didn't seem happen to quiet girls from small villages. After a few years spent dreaming about travelling or moving to London, she accepted the truth that she was destined to remain the silent understudy forever waiting in the wings, watching other people's dramatic and interesting lives evolve on stage. While she, even by remaining silent, would be forever mistaken for one of the prejudged rabble of 'Carter girls'.

A series of unfulfilling jobs that could accommodate her responsibilities at home came and went while she nursed first her grandmother and then her mother in their final years – both heartbreakingly dying within years of each other due to the same horrific disease. It seemed that being strong when it came to external threats had not extended to watching out for signs of insidious threats from within. Despite being told on numerous occasions to do so, her mother had refused to be screened for the breast cancer that took her own mother. Her sisters had helped out occasionally, but the responsibility had been overwhelmingly hers. No one had imagined that she might want her own life – she was the baby after all.

Finding the handwritten card on the post office notice-board advertising for a 'household manager and assistant' at Darlington Hall had seemed to be just another in the long list of directionless jobs that Helen had taken over the last few years. The upshot was that she would at least get up close and personal to see how the other half lived for the first time in her life. Her dreams of being rescued had long since been abandoned, but Darlington Hall had been a permanent fantasy fixture in the lives of most of Pepperbridge's long-standing families. Most people had someone in the family who had worked up at Old Hall at some point in their lives. At one time it had been a thriving household hosting plenty of social events and employing permanent staff, but as with many houses of its size, the need to cater parties and tend house guests had long since dwindled.

Like most in the village, Helen had heard the news that the new Lord Darlington had returned home after twenty years abroad. She knew that he was proving to be a bit of a mystery, just shy of forty years of age, at least a decade older than she was, and that he had been loath to show himself much in and around the village. 'A bit of a snob and definitely right up his own backside, he'll need to muck in with the rest of us if he wants to get on in this day and age,' one of her sisters had surmised.

Helen had walked up to Darlington Hall one early autumn morning to attend an interview. With her old banger of a car in the garage for the third time that year, she had walked using the back route through the fields that bordered the road to Cringlewic and up the hill that eventually led past what looked to be the most beautiful walled garden. She had stopped by a large, lone chestnut tree with branches adorned by a riot of orange and brown leaves, and she had soaked the whole gorgeous scene up. From the back, Darlington Hall looked like a fairy-tale castle with a single turreted window catching the golden light of the morning sun. It was absolutely spectacular: just like the fantasy home Helen had imagined as a lonely young girl. Who would have thought that people could live like this?

Arriving nervously at the front door, Helen had spent a few minutes searching for the doorbell before realising that she actually had to pull down a long cast-iron pole that she had at first assumed was a piece of broken doorway hanging down. She laughed self-deprecatingly, feeling more than a little out of her depth, and angry at herself for being thrown by some-thing so basic before even walking over the threshold. She was nervously smoothing down the front of her skirt when the door had swung open and an equally flustered-looking man stood in front of her. He had been wearing old jeans with a moth-eaten old jumper – not what she had expected from a lord who had just inherited a Norfolk estate. Neither had she expected him to have such rugged and appealing good looks, sandy hair that caught the autumn sun, and a tanned and youthful face that belied his forty years. Where was the weak-chinned and arrogant fop that her sister had described? They had stood there silently for a moment, both acknowl-edging the meeting of a kindred spirit.

Helen had fallen in love instantly – with Hugh, with Darlington Hall, and with the life that she could envisage herself having there – although in which order she could never be sure. She sat opposite him in the study for twenty minutes, and while he asked her a series of basic questions to determine her suitability for the role she realised that this was her destiny. She had never wanted anything so badly.

Hugh had felt a strong connection to Helen too, and she had sensed this straight away. He had seemed lonely, and it was obvious from the turn the conversation had taken that he had already decided to hire her on the spot. The moment he had noticed her flustered embarrassment on the doorstep, he had let his guard down.

While Hugh had been making his decision, Helen had been thinking that living in Darlington Hall would not constitute a mediocre life. This would be beyond her sisters' wildest dreams, but more importantly, it would be beyond her own wildest dreams. It would mean that every sacrifice, every compromise and every disappointment to date had been leading to this. This was the life that she had dreamed of escaping to during her childhood when she had prayed so hard to be rescued and to feel seen. She could tell from the way that Hugh was interacting with her that he wanted to hear her opinions. To have someone listen to her meant so much. This man, a man with titles and money and power – he wanted to hear her viewpoint. She hadn't felt this heard since, well – ever. She felt so grateful, grateful for his lack of judgement about her voice and background, the lack of preconceived ideas about who she was or where she came from. She certainly hadn't expected this sort of reception from someone who had so obviously been born with a silver spoon in his mouth. The two decades Hugh had spent in Australia had clearly enabled him to transcend the judgemental English class system.

Helen had stayed with Hugh for the entire day, walking around the multitude of rooms, the endless corridors, as they discussed their thoughts with interest and compassion. They had both felt instantly comfortable in the other's company, despite the obvious age gap. The ten-year difference hadn't bothered Helen in the slightest. Hugh looked a bit weathered and worn perhaps, but it only added to his charm.

During their first walk around Old Hall together, she had been shocked to hear that he was intending on breaking up the estate and selling it off section by section. She was aghast. *Who would willingly desert a place like this?* she had thought, pretending to understand while internally feeling devasted at the prospect. She was too close now to allow this opportunity to slip away.

A few months into her employment, she had come up with the idea of renting out rooms on Airbnb to help with stabilising the estate finances. Rather than sell Darlington Hall to a hotel group, why not see if they could build it up room by room and create something of his own? Hugh, she said, had the potential to be the saviour of the estate. Turning things around could be his legacy, Helen explained. After planting the seed in his mind, she nurtured it and watched it grow, carefully massaging his ego and bolstering his confidence along the way. It had taken a while, but eventually he admitted that he was warming to the idea. First though, he needed help in simply sorting out the estate as it was, including organising and controlling the tenant farmers and the tenanted cottages that bordered the larger estate. These should have been providing an income, but with no member of the family having been in charge for the best part of a decade and a management company who seemed to have been gladly taking advantage of his absence by siphoning off funds, his hands were full trying to keep the estate afloat. She could see that these things consumed Hugh's every waking hour, but through his anxiety, she could sense that he too was slowly beginning to fall in love with the idea of saving his childhood home.

Every evening before she returned home, they would sit and eat supper together. She had made a point of finding out his favourite foods and she always prepared something that would make him smile. She mothered him and cared for him gently and sweetly. Showed concern for his worries and reassured him that all would be fine. It wasn't going be easy to turn the estate around, she agreed, but she urged him to try. Every day on their walks through the grounds, she helped him to see the beauty of the historic building and the abundant garden, reminding him what he would be giving up if he sold it off. Helen had pushed him to appreciate what he had at his fingertips. As the weeks went by and autumn morphed into a hard winter, her reassurance and nurturing care began to embolden Hugh. The burden of carrying the Darlington Estate didn't feel so bad when there was someone constantly by your side cheering you on. He had never had someone care for him and encourage him in this way before. Helena's belief in him was intoxicating.

Helena had never been afraid of hard work, and from what Hugh was explaining about the sorry state of affairs he had inherited, there was destined to be a lot of it. This magical place, Darlington Hall, was worth it and slowly, ever so slowly, as if hypnotised by her unwaveringly positivity, Hugh began to agree.

It had not taken long for him to come to depend on her in more ways than he could ever have imagined. Within a few months she was no longer leaving the Hall at the end of the day, and soon their future plans became a collective endeavour. She could see that her presence calmed him, soothing his anxiety like a soft balm. His gentle and caring Helena, who constantly supported and made him believe that anything was possible. She made him believe that he was important, worthy of this unexpected legacy – that he could take on the world. She had sensed that having someone believe in him was not something that Hugh was used to and so she nurtured that feeling in him with a carefully concealed ferocity that hid the obsession growing within her.

This was no altruistic endeavour. She was in love with Lord Darlington, true, but she had also never felt such belonging, such freedom and such a passion as she did for Darlington Hall. Within these rooms she was able to take up space. When Hugh was busy elsewhere on the sprawling estate, she would enter each room and sing and shout and dance and be herself for the first time in her life. Best of all though was the fact that to the outside world she could be anyone she wanted within the walls of Darlington Hall. She had been given a second chance at reinvention and this time she would not waste it. No one who came knocking could judge her without also having to respect the fact that she was now the chatelaine of such an important house. One day she intended to become Lady Helen – no, Helena – that sounded much grander. Lady

Helena Darlington of Darlington Hall. There would be some who would oppose it; she wasn't naive enough not to realise that. She was one of the 'H-Bombs' after all. However, they could try, but they would eventually leave – yet she would remain at Hugh's side, and ultimately win.

Her skills of seduction were not the most sophisticated, but her well-practised skills of feigning compliance, willingness and submission were second to none. Years of having to compromise through gritted teeth had taught her how to softly manipulate a situation to get her own way – and these skills came in useful with Hugh. Within the first few months of moving in to live with Hugh as his girlfriend, she realised that she was willing to do anything to ensure that he kept a hold of Darlington Hall and that she would remain by his side to see it. Anything at all.

The cracks in Hugh's demeanour had been there from the beginning. He had often seemed slightly nervy and anxious and at first she had put this down to financial stress. However, it was when he had started to jump at the beep of a text message, scurrying away soon afterwards to respond or speak in private and returning looking even more stressed than before, that she began to suspect that something was seriously wrong.

At first, she'd had a sick feeling in the pit of her stomach that maybe the seemingly innocent Lord Darlington had left a secret girlfriend back in Australia. A girlfriend who was getting fed up with his absence, putting pressure on him to return. She had guessed this after staying awake one night to sneak Hugh's phone into the bathroom. She was determined to work out who was calling him and what she was dealing with. Losing Hugh was not an option she was prepared to consider. With a locked phone and not knowing his password, she had nearly jumped out of her skin when a number with an Australian code had flashed up on the screen. *Australia then . . .* At least this persistent caller wasn't close by.

She had started to watch Hugh like a hawk, assessing his mood changes and figuring out what the main triggers were. The messages would throw him into a spin that would result in a bad mood that lasted hours and sometimes even days. This would often be the time that he talked about selling up and liquidating his assets. *Did he owe money in Australia? Was someone dangerous chasing him?* she had wondered, perplexed. *Why did this caller have such a hold over Hugh?*

It was during this time that Helena had ramped up the pep talks, the confidence-bolstering and the love. She had even hinted at the idea of a family of their own rewriting history for the better – noticing how his eyes lit up at the thought of a family. The biggest thing that had been lost to him over the past twenty years.

She had finally felt that she was making headway the day she saw him put his phone in a drawer in his study and start to use a new one. The texts disappeared, his mood improved, and life seemed to move forward once more. But still she felt uneasy. She could sense that Hugh was still hiding something. The jumpiness he exhibited whenever there was a ring at the doorbell. His reluctance to talk about his family. His occasional confusion about details surrounding the house. He rarely wanted to venture into the village.

It was when the letters started arriving that it started to go downhill again. *Who was writing these letters? What were they saying?* His temper would flare, and she had to do her best not to bite back. She couldn't do anything to upset her chances of making Darlington Hall her permanent home.

The worst moment had been after what had started off as a lovely evening. She had cooked what she hoped would be a romantic meal, setting the scene with candlelight and music. Everything had been going so well until she had asked him to play the piano. She knew from the music books that sat untouched in the piano stool that he had been the one to use it many years ago. Every book had his name on it. There were even certificates to prove his skills and at the very bottom, a selection of photographs showed young Hugh at the piano. The photos covered a period of years, up until he was about fourteen, Helena guessed. She had momentarily thought it was strange how different he had looked back then, but she supposed that everyone changed over time.

His response to her innocent request had come out of nowhere. A fury like nothing she had seen him display before. She'd reeled in shock as he had stalked out, leaving her standing at the piano wondering what had just happened.

It was then that it had struck her: Hugh was most aggrieved when he was forced to confront anything from his life before Australia. Anything that intimately tied him to his past living in Darlington Hall. Present and future were safe spaces, but the past was a minefield. It wasn't simply to do with his difficult upbringing, she was quite sure of that. It was more specific, as though speaking about his past took an effort of thought and memory. He often looked like a man who was about to take a test exam – the biggest test of his life, or a test *about* his own life.

Helena's suspicions had been confirmed on a biting cold

day in early February when they had visited Pepperbridge together. She had needed to visit the post office and Hugh had needed to get his head out of mounds of paperwork. He had been unusually upbeat when she had asked him if he would be able to pick up some tea bags from the convenience store while she ran quickly to catch the last post of the day. He had reluctantly agreed. Curious, she had run back to the shop as fast as she could, eager to see how he interacted with the Warburton sisters. An ideal experiment, she had thought, to see whether Hugh's reluctance to speak about the past was specific to her.

She had walked quietly towards the shop, pulling her coat firmly around her and being careful not to slip on the frosty pavement. She had stopped a short distance from the door but close enough to peer through the glass front, noticing a young lad who was also hovering just outside, staring through the doorway. He appeared to be watching some sort of minor altercation occurring inside, and when the voices became slightly more raised, had obviously decided against going in and jumped back on his bicycle, cycling away. She inched closer towards the boys' recently vacated vantage point.

Hugh's back was to her, obscuring her view of whoever he was speaking with at the counter, tea bags in hand and a disembodied voice speaking calmly but tersely at him. She had recognised Nancy Warburton's gruff-sounding voice.

'Well, let me tell you, I'd know him anywhere – and he ain't you!' she had rasped loudly and triumphantly, not caring who heard her accusations.

'You're being completely ridiculous!' Hugh had retorted quietly but angrily back – far less eager for his dirty washing to be aired for all and sundry to hear. 'You haven't seen me for twenty years, of course I seem different. Besides, I hardly think we moved in the same circles!'

'Say what you like, but you're not pulling the wool over my eyes,' Nancy had snarled at Hugh's speedily retreating back as he had stormed out.

Helena had already run a few yards back in the direction that she had come from. She stopped and pretended to look at a sign in the window of shop further up the road, her heart beating furiously.

'All done?' she'd asked brightly, pretending to just catch sight of him, hoping that he was unaware that she had just witnessed the tense exchange.

'Yep, all done,' he'd said through gritted teeth, striding angrily towards the car.

' . . . and you'll need to pay for that!' Nancy had called out through the door, pointing at the tea bags in Hugh's hand.

He had turned around, walked back to the shop entrance and flung a twenty-pound note through the shop door. It landed on the floor.

'Is everything all right?' Helena had asked nervously in the car on the way home.

'Why wouldn't it be?' he'd snapped back.

'Well, you seem a bit tense, and you just threw money through a shop doorway,' Helena said cautiously, trying to keep her tone as light as possible. There had been no point in pretending that she hadn't just witnessed that bit.

Hugh had been silent until they had reached Darlington Hall. As they approached the front door, he abruptly turned to her and said, 'Helena. All of this,' he had gesticulated towards Darlington Hall, 'it's not real. It's just a dream. It's not viable. It's . . . it's all too complicated. I'm going to sell up.' All traces of his earlier anger were gone, and a heavy sense of disappointment and dejection lingered in its place.

That was the moment that it had all become clear to her. She now understood his reasons for hiding, for trying his best to escape questions about the past. This man was not Lord Hugh Darlington at all, but someone posing as the real heir. She could sense it with all of her heart and soul, but rather than disappointment came a feeling of renewed determination. A call to battle. She had to protect this man and therefore her own situation at all costs. However he had found himself here, whatever game he had been playing up until now . . . she was going to help him play it better.

Helena hadn't questioned him any further that evening. She had just pretended to accept his decision without going into to depth as to why. She had bigger things to worry about. Like what to do about that old trout Nancy Warburton before she let the cat out of the bag.

Chapter 18

By now the burning smell had become impossible to ignore. Daphne didn't know whether to locate Helena or attempt to revive Henry, who was now limp and doubled over. She quickly checked his pulse and monitored his breathing, trying to fathom a reason for his abrupt collapse. It didn't appear to be entirely alcohol-induced; he'd been slurring his words slightly, but he hadn't been staggering or inarticulate, and surely he'd have had to drink a huge amount to be incapacitated enough to fall unconscious? There were no half-empty bottles in sight, and she couldn't smell alcohol on his clothes or breath. His breathing wasn't laboured, which ruled out choking or pain, and his forehead was cool – showing no indication of a fever. His body hadn't gone into spasm, and he hadn't been struggling or clutching at his chest before he fell, so it didn't appear to have been the onset of a sudden heart attack or other such illness. However, from the dead weight of Henry's head as she attempted to check his breathing, he was definitely unconscious, and he didn't appear close to waking up any time soon. The last time she had seen someone in that state was that fateful day with Doctor Oates, but at least then she had been witness to the cause – truth be told, she had *administered* the cause! Right now, she was overwhelmed with confusion and uncertain where danger lay.

What on earth is going on? Daphne wondered, taking a deep breath to steel herself. She looked down at Henry and then over in the direction of the increasingly intense burning smell, which seemed to be circulating downwards from the wooden gallery in the upper part of the Great Hall. Time was running out. Burning smells and centuries-old houses built with an abundance of flammable materials weren't exactly a match made in heaven. She would need to somehow get him out before delving further inside the house to find Helena.

Decision made, Daphne held Henry underneath his armpits and tried to drag him towards the front door. At least if she wedged the front door open he would be close to fresh air – if she could get him there. He was incredibly heavy in this unconscious state and over a year of lifting antique furniture had certainly not prepared her for this situation.

She was struggling under the effort of dragging Henry. It didn't help that his feet kept getting caught up in the beautiful faded Aubusson rugs that hampered their progress across the Great Hall. In the past, she'd admired their stunning woven tapestry designs, but now she cursed the rugs' presence as sweat dripped down the back of her neck.

'HELENA!' she tried calling out while simultaneously

dragging Henry a few more inches towards the front entrance. 'Helena! Where are you?' *And where the hell are James and Inspector Hargreaves?* Had James not picked up her message yet? Why weren't they here already?

Chest heaving and with much difficulty, she had finally managed to drag Henry as close to the front door as she felt would be safe to leave him. She yanked open the heavy oak door so that air and light suddenly flooded through into the hall, breaking through the gloom. The atmosphere didn't seem quite as oppressive and menacing as it had only a few minutes ago when she had stood listening to Henry's confession.

Now Daphne steeled herself to confront the woman who she now suspected was not the passive victim she had imagined. Regardless, she could smell smoke and that meant that Helena may be in danger. Daphne could not ignore that possibility. She leaned momentarily against the mahogany dresser that backed onto the entrance vestibule and caught her breath, frantically searching her pockets for her phone to call the fire brigade and looking down once more at the limp Henry. He was now in the recovery position on the cold hallway tiles with his head in full view of the front door should anyone arrive in the next few moments.

She yanked herself away from the dresser and stood upright again, jabbing 999 on her mobile with a shaking finger and raising the phone to her ear only for it to cut off after a few moments. 'This bloody connection!' she muttered angrily. She still didn't know where Helena was and her lack of response when Daphne had repeatedly called out was unnerving. There was nothing for it but to follow the smell and see whether it had anything to do with Helena's absence. If not, then at least she could help put out whatever was happening before it spread further.

She began approaching the longer far corridor that led into the East Wing. A lingering trail of smoke was coming from there, and from high up in the gallery. She felt safer starting with the ground floor and the rooms she knew, rather than immediately trying the main staircase. The smell of smoke may have been milder coming from behind the connecting door that led to the study, the back staircase and the soon-to-be-refurbished guest rooms, but she had to see if Helena was through there before she ventured upstairs.

She hauled open the door that mirrored the front door in shape and weight if not quite height. Panicking now at how quickly the smoke rolled towards her as it opened, Daphne confirmed that the smoke was billowing down from upstairs. 'Helena – are you up there?' she called desperately towards the back stairs, praying that she would at least hear a small sound that would give away the younger woman's location.

The study was empty, as were the rooms she had passed before reaching it. Should she try the kitchen before trying the stairs? But that would mean doubling back, and there were more rooms up ahead. *What if Helena isn't up there, and you're putting yourself in danger for no reason at all?* Daphne thought briefly about her children and James and then thought of a happy-looking Helena somewhere elsewhere, oblivious to the chaos ensuing back at her home. Should she risk her own safety for a shot in the dark when she had a family depending on her back at home? However, Helena had definitely been at the house when Daphne had called earlier.

What had happened to her in between that call and Daphne arriving at the house to find Hugh – or as she now remembered, Henry – standing all alone in the drawing room? She took her phone out and tried to call 999 again. If James or Inspector Hargreaves weren't on their way, then at least she could try to get an ambulance and the fire brigade over here as soon as possible. *Where the hell were they?*

'Damn – no signal again!' Daphne cursed, registering the lack of bars on her phone with despair and knowing that it would get worse the further into the house she went. Could she risk running back to the front door to try to reconnect her phone, or should she keep going?

She was quite far into the house now, way beyond the entrance hall, down the back corridor and into the left wing that led towards the back stairs. She thought better of returning to the main hall – it would waste precious time and who knew if she would even get a connection. If Helena was in any danger – even if she was somehow guilty in this big mess – then time was of the essence.

Rushing past every room and pushing each door open was taking too much time. Decorating just the three bedroom suites meant Daphne had almost forgotten how many unused rooms there were at Darlington Hall, and now she realised what a ridiculous task this might be. None of the rooms were small. Helena could be anywhere in this house.

'Help ... please, someone help me ...' A voice – almost a whisper, croaked from somewhere in the distance. It was weak, but she had definitely heard it. A female voice coming from upstairs, followed by coughing and spluttering.

Her heart skipping a beat, Daphne changed direction and

returned to the foot of the back stairs – one of three more modest sets of staircases that the servants would have used to access the upper floors. They were less ornate and far narrower than the grand front entrance stairs and, worse, they were engulfed by dark black swirls of heavy smoke. *This doesn't smell like burning wood smoke,* she thought quickly to herself. This smelled like fabric was burning or like something was melting.

'Helena – keep speaking please! Which direction are you in?' Daphne called out as she reached the first-floor landing, her arm covering her face as she attempted to breathe through the smoke. She couldn't see or hear fire; it was all just the thick and potent stench of smoke at this stage – for which she was hugely relieved.

'Here ... I'm here!' croaked Helena from a room several yards down the landing, it seemed. Daphne had never been this way before. Daphne guessed that the gallery would be somewhere on her right.

Surrounded by smoke, Daphne felt her way along the wall. The smoke, although dense, wasn't yet too thick to see through, but it was beginning to sting her eyes and make them water from the effort of trying to see through it. Daphne could hear that Helena was calling out from behind a door located to the left-hand side of the hallway – her voice seemed fainter now somehow, despite the fact that she could tell she was getting closer. She pushed open the door – relieved to find the handle turned easily – and was immediately pushed back by thick black smoke and the heat of flames. Straining her eyes to see, she shielded her face from the heat with an elbow. There, in the middle of the room, tied to a chair and rocking back and forth, was Helena. Behind her was a four-poster bed with its heavy brocade drapes ablaze with flames. A scarf that had been tied around her mouth had slipped down and was hanging around her neck. Her eyes were bulging and stream-ing in the smoke as she coughed and spluttered, rocking her body in the chair to try to edge towards the door.

'My God – Helena!' Daphne screamed, her eyes sud-denly wide despite the fire. Had Daphne got it wrong? It was the turreted room; she could just about see through the smoke beyond Helena that the window looked out towards the fields that she had walked across so frequently in recent weeks

Daphne tugged and pulled at the ropes binding Helena's legs and torso to the chair, trying not to breathe in the smoke.

'Can you stand up?' she asked the terrified-looking woman. 'I can't untie this left one, we're going to have to get you out still attached.' She choked. A tearful Helena looked back, her eyes streaming; her face sweaty, red and covered in black sooty streaks; her hair in disarray. Helena nodded. She leaned towards Daphne, attempting to stand with the chair still tied to her left ankle.

The two women dragged and pulled their way out of the room, the chair still attached but the knot visibly loosening with each laboured movement and Helena coughing and choking through the thick air.

They were in the hallway when the rope on Helena's leg was finally loose enough for her ankle to be painfully pulled through, leaving the chair toppled over to one side and the younger woman bruised but at least untethered … but it wasn't over yet. They needed to get downstairs. Helena looked over at Daphne, still coughing and choking on the acrid smoke, and taking huge gulping mouthfuls of air.

'Come on,' Daphne ordered, once she had managed to catch her breath. 'We need to get out of here and I need to try the fire brigade again as soon as possible.'

Helena, propped up by Daphne's arm, her legs barely holding her upright, could only muster a small nod. Her large eyes stared: terrified, red-rimmed, raw and watering.

Daphne nodded back and continued to half carry, half lead the other woman down the servants' stairs. It was slow progress and the smoke was descending thicker and faster around them, but at least she now knew the source – and the further they got the safer they would be.

She looked over at Helena hesitantly. She had so many questions, but now really wasn't the time. What she had just witnessed had been too horrifying to try and make sense out of it right now – a woman bound to a chair in a burning room? What had Henry been thinking? Was it even Henry? She'd just began to deduce that Helena was behind it all – it didn't make sense . . .

Daphne's head was beginning to spin with theories – or was the spinning caused by smoke inhalation? She had just found Helena bound and half gagged, tied to a chair in the middle of a burning room, so why did she still not trust her? Of course, on the face of it, she had every reason to feel uneasy – only moments ago, she'd heard the confession of stolen identity from a man she had until recently known as Hugh Darlington, and now she was fleeing a burning house with his fiancée, who he had tied up and left to burn ... but why? Because she had found out his true identity and had threatened to reveal his secret? He hadn't seemed too unwilling to reveal the truth to Daphne fifteen minutes ago. Why would he have felt compelled to leave Helena to burn to death over it? And if he had confessed everything to Daphne after somehow starting to regret his actions, why on earth had he not gone upstairs to rescue Helena himself, or at least alerted Daphne to her peril and allowed her to try earlier?

No. Something didn't sit right, especially after Henry's impassioned declaration of brotherly love for the real Hugh Darlington, a declaration that despite defying all sense of logic, she sensed rang true. A pit sat in Daphne's stomach, her doubts mounting.

They had managed to negotiate their way through the back hall and were about to come upon the large dividing door between the back quarters and the main hall. Hugh's office was to their right. Daphne, her breath ragged and labouring under the effort of holding up Helena as well as herself as they manoeuvred towards the exit, could wait no longer. She had to ask Helena what had happened.

'Helena – what's going on?'

Daphne could feel Helena's heavy breathing pause for a millisecond before she continued panting, visibly shocked by the question.

'But he, it's obvious ...' she stuttered, 'he, he, Henry – he tried to kill me! He tied me up and left me in that room.'

'But why? When? After I called?' Daphne went on, aware that Helena's body had become stiff and rigid, in direct contrast to its heavy reliance just a few seconds ago. Her voice too had seemed less croaky, stronger and – had she imagined it? – slightly irritated by Daphne's questioning.

'Yes, that's right, *you* called and said something about knowing who he was, and that's when he turned on me.' Helena's tone almost seemed accusatory. But sensing Daphne's eyes watching her carefully as they progressed slowly down the hall, her voice suddenly softened. Her eyes widened, and her face took on a helpless, Bambi-like expression. Her body crumpled towards Daphne. They had reached the connecting door. Daphne needed to pull it open with more force than she could muster with Helena leaning on her, and turned her body to allow Helena to prop up against the wall, while she reached for the handle. Knowing that Henry was collapsed a few yards away from them on the other side of the door, she had to ask just one more question: 'Why would he need to tie you up, Helena? Why would he need to go to such lengths to get rid of you when he would only be charged with murder when you were found? What would he have to gain?'

'Because he's a murderer, Daphne! He killed the real Hugh Darlington!' Helena could barely contain her exasperation.

Daphne hesitated and turned. The smoke once again began to filter its thin tendrils out towards them, causing her throat to restrict. She spluttered a cough.

'Henry said he would never have hurt Hugh, Helena ... and I believe him. He said he was willing to give it all up. That he didn't want all of this.' *There.* She'd said it. She didn't believe that the broken man who had confessed before her was the man who had hurt the real Hugh Darlington. That man had looked pained and tortured. He hadn't looked like a heartless killer.

Helena suddenly heaved her body away from its feeble recline against the wall and stood tall and bolt upright. Daphne's words had prompted her usually doe-eyed and sweet-natured face to harden. Her green eyes glinted with annoyance through the smoke.

'Don't you *ever* get tired of interfering?' Helena blurted out viciously, causing Daphne to jump at her forcefulness. 'Poor Henry "didn't want all of this"? Who in their right mind wouldn't want all of this? Only an idiot would willingly walk away from this!' she said furiously, gesturing towards the smoke-filled hall. Her face was contorted with incredulous anger.

Helena's vitriol had shocked Daphne, but only for a second. The questions were forming rapidly in her mind.

'How did I hear you calling out from behind the bedroom door, Helena?' Daphne asked slowly. It had been troubling her from the moment she had arrived upstairs. She had heard Helena's voice calling out for help – but it had seemed to have been leading her rather than coming from one spot. The first time she had heard the weak words as she passed the stairs on the ground floor – surely it must have come from the landing directly above and not from behind a room several metres away that was becoming engulfed with fire? *Had Helena really been incapable of escaping that chair?*

'Did you murder Hugh Darlington, Helen?' Daphne asked staring directly into Helena's eyes and hoping to catch her off guard. She had purposefully called her Helen rather than Helena, and noticed her slight wince in reply.

Helena, indeed surprised by the question, was standing stock-still, with an increasingly fearsome defiance to her stance and expression. Daphne hadn't been able to hold herself back from asking, but she hoped beyond hope that Helena would prove that her hunch was incorrect. She wanted Helena to instantly deny any involvement and declare how preposterous it was to even consider such a wild theory. She truly wanted to believe that there was a more logical, less terrifying explanation. A different version of events than the one that was currently living rent free in Daphne's imagination. All Helena had to do was deny it. *Please Helena*, Daphne thought, *please say that's not true.*

Instead of speaking or denying anything, Helena began to expel a low and animalistic guttural growl, a growl that turned from a moan into roar of rage and that ended in a piercing scream. The stinging pain of a slap came first, before Daphne knew what was happening. Helena's fists were flying towards Daphne's face, her hands pummelling into the side of her head and cheek in a crazed attack that ricocheted over and over again towards Daphne's face.

Helena – small, sweet Helena – had turned into a raging harpy.

Daphne held out her hands in front of her face to defend herself. *What was happening?* Her last question had triggered Helena in a way that was like flicking of a switch. Gone was the gentle and loyal fiancée – a role that she had played to perfection over the past few months – and in her place was a furious harridan, wild-eyed, wild-haired and hell-bent on stopping Daphne's questions.

'Pry, pry, pry!' Helena screamed. 'Bloody Miss Marple! Why the hell couldn't you leave well alone? It was none of your damn business.' Her sharp nails clawed at Daphne's face as Daphne backed away, defending herself with one hand and scrabbling around behind her with the other as she blindly attempted to turn the door handle to escape. It had proven hard enough to open doors with one hand when Helena was walking limp-legged and leaning against her, but now it was near impossible with Helena flying at her with thrashing fists and clawing nails. Daphne defended herself with one hand, using the other to frantically feel backwards, trying to find the door handle again.

'Stop it, Helena, stop it! You're acting like an insane person!' Daphne cried out futilely, in between coughs, her jaw throbbing, bruised and swollen with pain as she finally managed to heave the door open. But Helena launched herself at Daphne with enough force to slam it shut again, only barely missing Daphne's hand getting trapped.

Her snarling face was only inches from Daphne's. 'Henry killed Hugh. It was nothing to do with me. I knew nothing. Henry tied me up and then tried to kill me to cover up *his* crime, then he tried to kill himself. That's what happened. *That* is the truth, you meddling bitch!' she screamed at Daphne, her hands flailing towards Daphne's face again as if trying to erase her accusatory words.

Tired of fighting and getting nowhere with attempting to exit the corridor with Helena so close behind her, Daphne ducked down, allowing Helena's fist to hit the door. Using the full force of her body, she pushed herself against Helena's legs, causing the younger woman to lose her balance and topple backwards onto the hallway runner. Daphne grabbed Helena's feet before she could kick out, securing them with her own knees, and managed to pin her arms to her sides. Helena may have been angry, but thankfully she was still smaller than Daphne. The women stared and panted furiously at each other while choking in the smoke-filled atmosphere. *What next?* Daphne thought in panic. *I can't keep her pinned down for much longer . . .*

Helena managed to thrust herself forward, headbutting the edge of Daphne's jaw as she continued to rage and thrash out. Growing weaker and struggling with the smoke, and with her bottom lip badly bleeding, Daphne realised that she didn't have the strength to stop Helena for much longer before she collapsed into a coughing fit that was threatening to wrack her chest and take over her entire body.

Would Helena try to kill her if she released her? Is that what was happening here? Had Daphne yet again been caught out by attempting to explore a situation that was best left to the police? She thought of her family back home and bit back her tears.

Suddenly Helena went limp. Exhausted, finally, she allowed her hands to fall on either side of her body, Daphne's hands still attached to her wrist. The women were silently watching each other through the smoke.

'I'm pregnant,' Helena announced flatly, without emotion.

Chapter 19

Both women lay exhausted on the floor next to the inner hall door. Looking up towards the back staircase and watching the smoke spiral down, Daphne was aware that they should try to leave but at this moment she didn't have the strength to lift even a limb and she could see that Helena was the same. The two women stared at each other, panting and trying to regain their strength.

'Why, Helena? Why?' was all that Daphne could muster.

Helena paused for just a moment and then proceeded to tell Daphne the whole story as the smoke continued to creep slowly down the stairs behind them.

She had tried to reason with Henry on more than one occasion. She had already made sure that there was no one left standing in his way to finally claim the Darlington seat.

She had faced the task with pragmatism that belied her seemingly soft and helpless exterior. Nancy Warburton had been the first to go and was easy enough to silence. The stupid old woman had tried to take the moral high ground from the vantage point of the top of a ladder. *How ridiculous.*

It hadn't been Helena's intention to hurt her initially. She had simply wanted to know what Nancy had intended to do with the tricky nugget of truth that Henry was not in fact the real Lord Darlington. Was she hoping to blackmail him? Or worse still, to immediately inform the police that there was a fraud being committed and have him – and even Helena herself – prosecuted? What would have happened then? Would she have simply proven to those who suspected nothing otherwise that she was just a typical Carter girl – always willing to cause trouble and bend the rules? No, she was different. At least she was at first. She had been hoping to reason with Nancy – nothing more, nothing less ... but something in the way that the older woman had sneered at her, calling her a 'thieving little gold-digger who didn't even know when she'd been conned herself' had incensed Helena beyond control.

Nancy had assumed that she had one up on Helena, but Nancy had underestimated the younger woman, and how wrong she was. Helena was far cleverer than anyone gave her credit for. Hadn't she already proven that by being the first of her family to attend university? Evidently, academic prowess wasn't enough to satisfy the likes of Nancy Warburton. What she didn't know was that Helena had worked out that the real Hugh Darlington had remained behind in Australia long before Henry had realised that she was aware, and she'd certainly had a hunch that something was up a while before Nancy had threatened to reveal Henry's identity.

Nancy's little conversation in Warburtons' that fateful afternoon with Henry had been the catalyst to Nancy's demise. In Helena's opinion, meddlesome Nancy Warburton had manifested her own fate by being such a spiteful and supercilious bitch.

The night of Nancy's death, when Helena had only intended to barter for Nancy's silence, had been a minor inconvenience. She had suffered at the hands of judgemental gossips like Nancy Warburton all her life in Pepperbridge, so the old lady's patronising stares and snippy little asides were nothing new. People like Nancy Warburton and Augusta Papplewick were the worst of the lot: always grasping on to nasty, damning stereotypes like dogs with a bone. The stereotypes they relied on refused to allow people to change; they stopped people growing. It was the worst kind of village snobbery. Snobbery that locked people in boxes and never let them escape.

Nancy had sneered at Helena as she teetered confidently on a high rung of the ladder, her tights loose by her ankles, criticising Helena's mother and grandmother, both unable to defend themselves from the grave. Helena had seen red for the first time in her entire life. Oh, she had had plenty of dark thoughts before, but she had never acted on them. She'd done a few minor things that she wasn't proud of but had made her feel good at the time – like pouring a little bleach into her roommate's face cream in the first year of university – oh how her face had flared in a deep rash! And double-charging wealthier students buying unnecessary products when she worked at the checkout in the university town supermarket – *who needed truffle oil in student digs?* These acts had always given Helena a little thrill.

Now here was Nancy Warburton, alone in her shop with no one else around, giving Helena that familiar superior sneer. It had only taken a moment to edge closer and give the ladder a tiny shove. Well, perhaps not such a tiny shove, judging by the force at which Nancy had fallen sideways and cracked her head on the edge of the counter. The sound had shocked Helena before she had scuttled out quickly. She hadn't checked to see whether Nancy was still breathing but the force of the impact and the way her head had twisted at an unnatural angle had suggested not, and the potential impact of her actions had stunned her into retreating quickly and quietly into the night. She had waited fretful and terrified for days, but no one had come for her. No one had seen her enter the shop or leave it. As far as everyone was concerned, Nancy's fall had been an unfortunate accident. For something so unpremeditated she could not have planned it better if she had tried.

A sense of calm power had fallen over her the moment she had realised that she had got away with it. At least Henry would be out of danger for now. Perhaps she was worthy of being called a H-Bomb after all.

But then along came Hugh. The *real* Hugh Darlington, back on English soil. It had just been phone calls at first. Specifically calls that Hugh appeared to answer from a separate handset when he assumed no one was looking. The relentless calls had alerted Helena to the fact that something was seriously wrong. Searching through Henry's locked drawers, she had tried to find his secret phone to investigate what was increasing his angst – such palpable distress. Was it another woman or was it bailiffs, perhaps? Was Darlington Hall in financial trouble? Searching discreetly through Hugh's files when he was away from the Hall had put that theory to rest. The financial affairs of Darlington Hall may have been a complicated mess but as a business it was still more than financially viable.

What she had found out hadn't surprised her hugely – she had already guessed most of it. The Australian dialling code. The overheard masculine voice that sounded English. The disappearance of all physical evidence of Hugh's past – no photographs, removed paintings and the fleeting blank looks when a question arose about his family that he ought to know before he came up with a suitable answer. An absence of old friends and certainly no desire for family to be in contact. The complete severance of life before the last two years. No, it hadn't surprised her. She knew a reinvention when she saw one.

After all, she had spent her entire life pretending to be one person – quiet, docile, innocent, malleable Helen, while concealing the embittered, vengeful Helen that lived just below the surface and logged every single misdeed and slur aimed at her. One day she would show them. She would show everyone that she was better than this. Better than the reputation that she had unjustly accrued by virtue of being a 'Carter girl'.

Discovering while searching through his old texts that her Hugh, her Lord Darlington, was plain old Henry Johnson, who had also been pretending to be someone else, made her feel almost normal. She had found a kindred spirit. A knight in shining armour. Someone else who wanted to escape their past, to reinvent himself.

Henry's deception had never troubled Helena. It was his willingness to give up the spoils of his deception that had shocked her to the core. He'd been handed the opportunity for a new life and a new beginning on a plate. He had a title, an estate and the potential to generate a steady income. Why would he hand it all back? The real Lord Darlington had surely forfeited his right to claim the Darlington title and fortune the minute he had refused to return to England to claim it for himself. How did the childhood rhyme go – 'finders keepers . . .'? This opportunity had been handed to Henry fair and square, and it had become Helena's mission to convince him that he had every right to it.

She had watched as the calls had been followed by letters, and then the letters had been followed by something that seemed to suck the blood from Henry's body and turn his face as white as a sheet. Helena had instantly realised what had happened. She had heard the dogs barking furiously from the kitchen garden before Henry had returned with them looking as though he had seen a ghost. It could only mean one thing. The real Lord Darlington had finally returned home. But for some reason, he had decided not to waltz in and claim his house or his title. He really did despise his family and the estate was tarred by association; he simply wanted to sell Darlington Hall and release the money so that he could return to Australia free of his depressing past.

Henry had seemed to be backing down and crumbling. Lord Darlington had returned and put him in his place, and Henry was jumping to attention like the lacky he really was.

How could he give up on everything they had fought so hard to restore?

That was when Helena had finally decided to confront Henry, but seeing that his resolve to retain his new identity was swiftly vanishing, she had swiftly changed her mind and felt compelled to take matters into her own hands. She hadn't yet revealed that she knew his real identity, hoping to capitalise on his desire not to let her down. She had hoped that doing it for both of them would be what it took for him to refuse to step down and hand everything back over to Hugh Darlington, but she had soon realised that it would take more than just resolve. The real Hugh Darlington was still walking around, and while he was doing so, whatever hopes she had of remaining at Darlington Hall were in danger.

Helena had formulated the plan after hearing about the random break-in in the village. It had been a one-off, but Helena had carefully kept the petty thefts going once she realised they could be used to her advantage. It had been easy enough – especially in a village where people rarely locked their back doors and everyone was obsessed with attending the same boring Parish council meetings on a regular basis. The threat of malicious danger lurking around the quaint enclaves of Pepperbridge and Pudding Corner had been an absolute gift and had set her imagination running rampant. Lord Darlington didn't appear to be in a hurry to reveal his real identity, and so Helena had decided that she would give him a new one. That of thief, vagabond and violent criminal. It played directly into the busybody hands of the residents of Pepperbridge, who were only too happy and willing to blame a stranger to the area. But what if he was reprimanded, and his identity was revealed? She would have to ensure that there wasn't a shadow of a doubt that he was the culprit, without giving him the chance to deny it or confirm otherwise.

Spiking Henry's drink had been simple enough. She'd already done the same thing to him the evening she confronted Nancy in order to secure her alibi. Henry wasn't a heavy drinker – in fact, he said that he had sworn off it for years – but he did drink when he was morose or anxious. He would stay in the study, fretting and working his way through paperwork, and occasionally working his way through a decanter of brandy. She had managed to acquire a vial of gamma-hydroxybutyrate from the older brother of one of the boys on the green who lived near Cambridge. The boys themselves may have been relatively harmless, but everyone knew someone and you just needed to know who – and how – to ask. More commonly referred to as GHB, it was known for its sedative and anaesthetic effects, and she had received frequent warnings about it as a student. Adding a few drops to Henry's glass, she had bid him good night and it had taken less than an hour for the effects to start working. She had peered through a crack in the doorway to see him swaying at the desk and eventually he collapsed face down on it.

Hitting him on the back of his head with the bronze had been a harder task. She hadn't wanted to hurt him badly, but it had to be hard enough to knock him out and had even drawn blood. Then she had hauled him out of the chair and allowed him to collapse onto the floor, arranging him as though he had been whacked around the head from behind. She'd gone through his papers and got herself up to speed with what was happening on the estate before trashing the room. She took Henry's wallet, and anything else that looked like it might be worth taking in the eyes of a burglar.

Wearing Henry's wellington boots, Daphne had made her way by torchlight down to the kitchen garden. She had walked quietly to the last glasshouse where she knew Hugh Darlington would be waiting after she had left a note in his belongings asking him to meet Henry to 'talk things over' the day before.

Unsurprisingly, Hugh Darlington had seemed shocked to see her. He had been cooking something over a fire and he had looked at her apologetically. His manner was gentle if a little confused at her appearance, although he clearly knew who she was. 'Hello ... I was expecting Henr— err – Hugh ...' he had corrected himself quickly, unsure of what anyone knew – if anything.

'Oh, he'll be here shortly,' she had reassured him.

'Are you sure, he hasn't seemed that keen to see me so far!' He smiled wryly with more than a hint of sadness laced into his tone.

If he had thought it was strange to see a small woman standing in the semi-darkness of the glasshouse wearing an old rain mac over a nightdress and a pair of men's wellies then he had been too polite to mention it. Henry had told him about Helena, although he obviously hadn't enlightened him on the extent of her ambitions for Darlington Hall.

'Don't mind me – please go ahead.' Helena had motioned for him to continue cooking his meal – it had looked like tinned beans with mini sausages, and she'd almost gagged in disgust. Looking bemused but seemingly not feeling threatened, he turned his back on her and continued stirring the little saucepan. She had already spotted the shards of glass when she had been rooting around the day before. She had taken her hands out of her pockets; she was wearing heavy-duty gardening gloves.

'Do you mind if I come and sit beside you?' she had asked innocently.

He had turned around to look over her shoulder and smiled. 'I'm not here to cause any trouble you know,' he had replied with a sad smile. 'Of course, I don't mind if you sit here – it's warmer by the fire.' He continued to stir the food in the saucepan. He seemed at ease with himself, which made sense. This was his childhood home after all.

Helena had given him no cause to question her slow walk up behind him. He hadn't even flinched when she had stopped at his back; it was only after she had thrust the large shard of glass down through his back with all her might that he had made a sound. It hadn't been a scream or a shout or even a cry out in pain. It had simply been like a deep exhalation. As though she had just released the air from a large balloon. It had all been strangely quiet and quick. His hands had shot out in front of him and into the fire, giving her the idea of trying to distort his fingerprints like she had seen in films. He'd still been breathing – just – when she had shoved his face and hands into the fire, trying to angle his body as though it had been propelled in shock and fallen forward after being pierced by the falling glass.

She had then left the wallet and other items taken from the study in a bag next to him.

The only dangerous bit was throwing something up to the ceiling to try to induce a shower of glass to fall around his body. She ran the risk of being hit by the shards herself, but in the end, after throwing up several stones, she'd managed to hit a spot directly above Hugh Darlington's slowly expiring body, causing several shards of varying sizes to come crashing down on and around him.

Dragging a branch with leaves behind her to cover her tracks, she had exited silently and retraced her steps back up to Darlington Hall. There she had made one last check on Henry's unconscious body and returned upstairs to bed and to wait, the words *The baby has to find other ways to get what they want!* ringing in in her mind.

She had purposefully arranged an early meeting with Daphne for the following morning. It would be far more realistic if someone else discovered the fruits of one or other of her evening's labours, leaving her to play the damsel in distress.

The ruse had played out as planned. After weeks of frantic, increasingly anxious speculation, there was no reason suspect anyone else for the burglary when the spoils had been found right by the suspect's side.

She had noticed a few strange looks from Henry after he had been questioned by the police, as he simultaneously mourned the loss of his friend and tried to work out what had happened the evening before, but she had been able to feign innocence for much longer than she'd expected.

Things had come to a head the night of Patsy Warburton's break-in. Helena had hoped that Hugh Darlington's 'death by misadventure' would be the last bit of blood left on her hands, but then she heard via Daphne that Nancy had kept diaries and may have written down the juiciest nuggets of her many interactions. With the possibility of Nancy post-humously scuppering Helena's plans from beyond the grave, she realised that she would have to do something to stop the truth from leaking.

She had assumed that Patsy would be at the meeting with everyone else, just as Daphne had predicted, but alas, it was not to be, and Patsy's presence upstairs at the shop proved to be yet another inconvenience for Helena to manage.

The beauty of living in a village where bad things rarely happened was that no one was ever on the lookout for them. Dark corners were rarely avoided and noises in the night were ignored and put down to the most innocent of reasons. Patsy had been like a sitting duck. She practically walked into Helena's waiting path where she managed to knock her out with one swift blow to the head. By then she had felt rather practised in the art of knowing where to strike. YouTube had provided a wealth of information when Helena had researched where and how hard to inflict a blow to the skull for maximum impact. Alongside the cooking tutorials, day-in-a-life vlogs and DIY videos, Helena had wondered whether anyone else thought it was interesting how popular the 'how to attack your attacker' tutorials were.

Henry had been slumped upright on a sofa in the drawing room when she had arrived home. He was in exactly the same place and in exactly the same position as she had left him, the trusty gamma-hydroxybutyrate having worked its soporific magic once again. She had changed into her night-dress and curled up alongside him, snuggling close into the nook of his arm. At first she had pretended to sleep, but it was only after she had awoken and felt Henry shifting in the seat next to her that she had realised that she had nodded off too.

Henry had awoken confused and had complained of a crashing headache as Helena had alluded to the fact that they had been on the sofa all evening, even adding a few dramatic tears as she hinted how worried she was by his evident drinking problem. He had stared at her strangely that evening, looking from the empty whisky glass and back to Helena, trying to work out why he couldn't remember anything. It wasn't the first time that this sort of temporary blackout had occurred, and he was clearly unnerved. She had sensed him trying to work things out in his head as he sat there. She had even been able to tell the moment when he had begun to distrust her. She had asked him whether he wanted a hot drink and some headache pills as she stood in the doorway to the drawing room. He had suddenly paused and she had felt her own breathing pause at the same time when his eyes came to rest on her and stayed there: looking at her as if he were seeing her properly for the first time. It had sent a mild shiver down her spine, and she had been forced to make her excuses, feigning a headache of her own in order to head off to bed rather than stay under the relentless nature of his questioning gaze.

The next morning Henry had been in his office when he received the call from Inspector Hargreaves warning him to be extra vigilant. Someone had assaulted Patsy Warburton in her own home the previous night and there were fears that the original burglar hadn't been working alone after all. Helena had been standing at the door with a cup of Henry's favourite coffee when he had turned to look at her after setting the receiver down.

Helena had seen immediately that he knew; she could tell from the anxious, almost disappointed look in his eyes.

'Helena . . . what did you do?' he had asked sadly. He hadn't even expected her to deny anything, and so she didn't.

'I did it for you . . . Henry,' Helena had replied. 'For us.' She had corrected herself quickly, clutching her abdomen with her free hand. She had noticed a flicker of surprise cross his expression at the use of his real name, but it seemed that nothing could surprise him any more.

'How long have you known?' he asked quietly.

'For a while,' she responded, guessing correctly that he was querying her knowledge of Hugh. 'I worked it out when the real Hugh wouldn't stop calling your phone. I saw the messages between you . . .' she trailed off guiltily.

'Helena,' he paused, struggling for words. 'Did you . . . did you hurt Hugh?' He had looked devastated at the prospect of hearing what he now knew would be her inevitable response.

'I did it for us, Henry. For you, me and the baby!' More impassioned now, Helena walked over to him, setting the coffee cup down as she attempted to embrace his stiff figure. 'He didn't want this life! He didn't even want to come near the house – his own family home – what does that tell you! It was meant for us!'

'No, Helena – this wasn't for us – this was for you!' Henry had said, anguished. 'Hugh didn't deserve to die – not for me, not for you or anyone.'

'But he didn't want it! He didn't want any of this!' she had repeated frustratedly. Tears had streamed down her face as anger bubbled up in her stomach. 'I did him a favour. I did YOU a favour. Now there's nothing standing in the way of us making this work. Don't you see? It's easy now. You ARE Lord Darlington of Darlington Hall. Nothing can stop us from being the Darlington family!'

Henry had looked at Helena in appalled disbelief.

Was she losing him? Had she come this far only for him to reject her now – even with the baby?

He had walked into the hallway, heading towards the front door.

'Where are you going, Henry?' Helena's throat had constricted; she was filled with fear.

'I'm going to hand myself over to the police, Helena. What's happened here is wrong, and if you are pregnant, then God help us.'

'But I'm pregnant! Why would you throw all of this away when we could be a proper family? Isn't that what you've always wanted? To have a proper, loving family? We're here, Henry. Standing right in front of you. Hugh was an accident – I promise. I tried to convince him to go and he – he – tried to attack me!'

Henry had looked at Helena doubtfully. He had known Hugh Darlington well enough to know that it was unlikely that this version of events had occurred. Helena on the other hand, he realised, he hardly knew at all. Apart from her relentlessly sweet habit of pushing him towards keeping the Darlington family seat intact.

Helena's mobile phone had started to ring. It was on the table in the centre of the hall. They had both rushed to pick it up but Henry had narrowly pipped Helena to the post. He had heard Daphne's voice issuing an urgent warning to Helena.

'Helena, listen to me, please. You don't have to say any-thing, but I think that you might be in danger – it's Hugh – at least, I don't think that he *is* Hugh. Not Hugh Darlington anyway. Look, I'm probably not making any sense, but please just get out of there and meet me at the police station imme-diately. Don't say anything to Hugh, and I'll explain more later I promise ...'

Helena had heard Henry let out a long, tortured sigh, fol-lowed by the singular word: 'Daphne'.

Panicked and fearing what Henry was about to reveal, a now tearful and distressed Helena pleaded with him, 'Hugh ... please, you don't have to!' while simultaneously grabbing the phone and ending the call before he could say another word. 'You don't have to tell her – or anyone. Please let's just sit down and talk sensibly about this.'

But it was no good. She could tell that Henry was com-mitted to revealing the whole truth: about himself, Hugh's murder, everything.

He had looked at her and simply asked, 'Nancy too?' Helena hadn't been able to deny it. Henry had looked away.

He walked into the drawing room, and Helena followed him, promising that she would confess everything to him.

He had stood by the window, his back partially obscur-ing the magnificent view across the gardens and the bright sunshine surrounding him through the glass like a halo. She pleaded for him to reconsider revealing the truth, but he had only shaken his head, looking sadly at her as though she were a stranger.

'Don't worry, Helena. I won't tell them your part in any of this. You will remain innocent. I'll tell them that I did it.

That I was behind it all.' Despite everything, he still loved her. Although now he seemed to hate her in equal measure too. He told her that he realised that he had felt like this once before. That strange mixture of love and hate. He had loved his Nana Prince too.

Helena had screamed at Henry, slapping and kicking him, but he had remained standing impassively at the window, numb to her physical and verbal assault, knowing that this dream that they had fleetingly shared had come to an end. Eventually she had realised that her wild outburst was futile. Henry was not willing to take the lie any further. Deep down he was an honest man with no real stomach for deception, let alone violence.

She had stormed out of the drawing room. She had to think quickly. Would he really confess to the things she had done and take responsibility for her crimes? She'd come so far and sacrificed so much and now everything was falling apart around her. How could she be sure that he wouldn't drag her down with him?

Helena had realised that she needed to look like a victim too. She had to ensure that she was perceived as a helpless victim rather than a willing accomplice if the police came. Running to the kitchen, she had found a box of matches and the bottle of GHB that she had concealed in the cupboard. Returning to the study, she had grabbed a whisky glass, filled it almost to the brim with the malty, amber liquor and then poured a large dose of GHB into it. *What was the dose that was mentioned in the video? 3.5ml would be enough to kill him – wasn't that what they said?* Feigning calm, she had taken both the spiked glass and a second untampered glass back to the drawing room. Meeting Henry's bereft eyes, she suggested they have a final drink, for old time's sake, before handing themselves in together.

Henry had met her gaze as he had drunk the GHB-laced whisky. She had sensed that he had known she was lying. When had he come to recognise the way she would become coy and childlike when she wanted someone to believe in her innocence? She had done too much to give up so easily – could he sense her desperation? What was he thinking? Was he wondering what sort of person was willing to kill innocent people – for a house and a life that wasn't meant for them? Did he realise that that was the whole point – all of this *was* meant for her? He had looked down at his glass before finishing its contents. In that moment, Helena wondered whether he even suspected that she put something in it, but didn't care – his world had imploded and perhaps nothing mattered any more. He had lost Hugh, he had lost Helena and it seemed that he didn't want this tainted dream any more. What was left?

Helena had watched him down the whisky, kissed him on the cheek, taken the glass and walked slowly towards the door. She could hear the engine of an old car wheezing up the long gravel drive. *Daphne. Why did that snooping woman think it was her job to solve every mystery in the parish?* She would be at the door within a couple of minutes.

'I love you,' Helena had mouthed to Henry while he remained frozen beside the drawing room window, staring expressionlessly back at her. At that precise moment she had really meant it, but she was too strong to give everything up now, especially not – as her mother had warned her – for a man.

As she had rushed upstairs in a desperate bid to secure her future, Helena realised that he hadn't mouthed anything back.

Upstairs, she had run to the turreted bedroom. She knew that the four-poster bed in there was filled with heavy fabrics and had a ridiculous amount of paperwork piled to the side, covered with dust. She'd lit a match and thrown it on the bed, then managed to tie one arm and one ankle to the rungs of a ladderback chair while listening to what was going on downstairs. Of course it had been Daphne Brewster coming to rescue poor, defenceless Helena. Helena had almost laughed out loud at the irony. Almost, but not quite. She was worried that Daphne had arrived too quickly for the drugs in Henry's whisky to have taken effect. There had been enough GHB in that glass to take down an elephant. *Would Henry change his mind about confessing?* Helena panicked. *What if he pins the blame on me after all?*

Helena needed to get Daphne away from Henry before he revealed anything that would implicate her. She dragged the chair across the room. The fire had taken hold and smoke was beginning to billow out from the heavy velvet bed curtains. *Time is of the essence*, she had thought anxiously, realising that she was precariously close to becoming one of her own victims. It was all about to go up in flames – literally.

'Help!' she had called from the door. Feebly at first and then, realising that Daphne couldn't possibly hear her from downstairs, with rising volume. Next she would have to leave the room to yell down. 'Help, please, someone help me – I'm up here!'

Chapter 20

If it hadn't been for their heavy breathing and increasingly frequent coughing fits, then the silence that had fallen between the women would have been deafening.

Overwhelmed by shock and delirious from smoke inhalation, Daphne could hardly begin to process Helena's full and unadulterated version of the past few month's events.

Her hands, which until moments ago had been pinning Helena down, had gone as limp as her would-be assailant's. Helena's shocking confession had rendered them both temporarily speechless, and Daphne's prior attempts to defend herself and restrain Helena had subsided when Helena had seemed to surrender and back down.

'Are you really pregnant?' Daphne eventually asked her, breathing laboured yet still managing to ruminate on the revelatory statement that had preceded the purge of shocking disclosures.

There was a slight pause as Helena started to cough and then stopped, wiped her streaming eyes and stared wearily into the distance. Her heavy breathing slowed to a normal pace as though she had suddenly taken control of herself, and she let out a long, sad sigh as she stared directly into Daphne's eyes. Despite the smoke, Daphne could almost physically see the fight draining away from the younger woman's body. She looked at once calm but defeated. The game was up. The lying, it seemed, stopped here. 'I was ... for a fleeting moment. I wanted to be so badly and I was so happy. It was a reason for all this – do you understand? I wanted things to be so very different for "her" ... at least, I hoped it would be a girl.'

The restrained simplicity of Helena's answer spoke volumes. There was genuine longing in her voice. It made sense of why Helena had given up fighting so abruptly and had become – albeit resignedly – so willing to reveal her guilt to Daphne. *Had she finally had enough of lying? Enough of killing to get her own way now that there was no longer a potential family to fight for?*

'Why have you told me all of this, Helena?' panted Daphne, as she began to slowly pull herself up onto her knees. 'You were obviously trying to pin the blame on Henry. Why confess to me now?' she continued, her throat aching.

'You knew. I could see it,' Helena replied stoically through a spluttering of coughs. 'What's the point of continuing to deny it? I'm so tired, Daphne. I'm so tired of fighting to prove why we ...' Daphne corrected herself quickly, ' ... I mean, why I deserve all of this. The funny thing is that I wasn't like my sisters at all. Not really. I wasn't the disruptive one. I wasn't the argumentative one. I wasn't a rebel or even naughty ... and yet ...' She smiled ruefully at Daphne. ' ... here I am. The worst of the lot.'

Daphne stood up, her body momentarily wracked by a coughing fit that threatened to topple her over and straight back down to the floor, before reaching down and offering her hand to Helena. The smoke was almost unbearable and her eyes and throat stung. She could barely breathe. 'Come on. We need to get out of here. For both our sakes ...'

Through the acrid shroud of smoke that swirled thickly around them, Daphne saw that Helena's expression had changed once again. Although her eyes were streaming she looked determined. Her head had now turned away from Daphne and was looking back towards the stairs. Daphne could sense from her suddenly weak grip that she was poised to run and flee back towards the source of the smoke.

'No!' commanded Daphne fiercely. She stared directly into Helena's eyes and gripped her reluctant hand. 'No more lives.' She softened her voice in response to Helena's startled look of silent despair. 'Please. No more lives for this silly old house.'

Helena's shoulders dropped in acknowledgement, all fight in her gone. Resigned and weary, she reciprocated Daphne's grip and hoisted herself up. The sound of sirens grew louder as police cars and fire engines blared in the driveway. Daphne finally yanked open the door that divided the entrance hall from the left wing, the glare of flashing blue lights lighting up the back hall through the smoke. The two women stumbled out, coughing and spluttering through the heavy hallway door to see a harried Inspector Hargreaves and an extremely anxious-looking James running towards them. For the second time, the man still widely believed to be Lord Hugh Darlington was being carried on a stretcher to a waiting ambulance.

'What on earth has happened here?' Inspector Hargreaves

barked in surprise when he saw the two dishevelled and soot-stained women staggering hand in hand into the great hall. A halo of giant smoke plumes surrounded them.

'It's a long story, Inspector ... but I think that Helena can fill you in,' Daphne explained as she fell gratefully into James's arms.

Chapter 21

July

Good friendships are an incredibly rare and special thing, Daphne mused as she waited for her children in the Pepperbridge Primary School playground at the end of the school day. *There are friends that we cherish through thick and thin,* she thought as she gave Minerva a quick wave of acknowledgement. Her friend was scuttling quickly into the school office to sign up for an increasingly sociable Silvanus's unlikely debut in the Year Five football team.

'Fancy coming back to mine for tea and cake?' Daphne shouted out just before Minerva disappeared inside.

'Definitely – we'll see you there!' Minerva called out eagerly.

There were friends that could prove to be challenging but

were solid in the long run – once you understood them of course. She thought of her late friend Nancy's gruff exterior, which belied her reliable nature, although even Nancy had got it wrong at times. Would she have acted differently if she had realised the impact her judgement would have on others?

Then there were the friends who appeared strong and dependable on the outside, always solidly waiting to lend an ear or make you laugh, but who were as in need of the occasional reassuring hug and sympathetic ear themselves. Just like Patsy, who Daphne had enjoyed a lovely long chat with only that morning over a shared slice of homemade Victoria sponge cake and two mugs of builder's tea.

There were the ones who liked to believe themselves to be friends, but who were in fact far too caught up in their own interests and bitter rivalries to be truly concerned with anyone other than themselves ... Her eyes rested fleetingly on a sparring Marianne and her arch-nemesis Augusta as they stood together in the centre of the playground, the older woman loudly reprimanding the younger with heavily laced sarcasm as she reminded her yet again that the yellow zig zags outside of the school gates didn't in fact mean 'Reserved exclusively for Mrs Marianne Forbes'.

Then there were the 'friends' who used you to mask their true character and intentions. The ones who initially seemed genuine, but who instinctively knew how to manipulate you to get their own way. Her mind strayed, as it did frequently, to poor, desperate Helena Carter, who was currently awaiting trial for two counts of murder, two counts of assault and one count of attempting to pervert the cause of justice. Daphne had visited her once at HM Prison Bronzefield in Surrey, a surprisingly modern building surrounded by parkland, but Helena had been withdrawn and quiet, only saying, 'I'll be fine. I'm one of those "Carter girls" after all.'

Lastly, there were the friends who not only stuck with you through thick and thin but who also forgave you for every misdemeanour, every slight and every betrayal. The ones who believed in you and wanted only the best for you, even when they knew you were flawed. The real Hugh Darlington had been one of those friends to Henry Johnson. Hugh Darlington had reluctantly returned to England to remind Henry of their original agreement for Henry to settle the estate and release enough funds for him to return to Australia to live a modest but comfortable life. However, he had also returned to leave a will that had been secretly drawn up prior to Henry's departure, long before his friend had assumed his new identity in England. He had also written a letter stating that should the two friends' deception ever become common knowledge, he wanted to legally acknowledge that he had been a willing party to it and that he wished the contents of the will to be upheld and his entire estate to remain in the hands of Henry Johnson. Thus ensuring that in the event of his own untimely death, and without issue, that all his worldly goods, including title, estate, income and holdings be legally transferred into the hands of his good friend.

He had travelled to Bury St Edmunds, signing and dating the letter in front of two witnesses in a coffee shop on the morning before his death at the hands of Helena, and had been intending to return to Australia a few days later. He had known from the increasing lack of response that Henry had wrestled with the idea of staying in England and intentionally stealing his identity as well as his inheritance permanently, but he had also known that the Henry Johnson he had known and loved as a friend would not have had the heart to go through with it, so he had decided to give it all to him anyway. During the weeks that he had spent rediscovering the country where he was born, he had made his peace with it. Occasionally sleeping rough or renting the odd hostel room here and there, it had been a similar experience to much of his time in Australia. He always had the glasshouses to return to – just like he had escaped to them as a child and hidden for days on end when he had run away from boarding school, too fearful to enter the Old Hall and confront the wrath of his father. He had even visited the gravesides of his parents and brother, laying flowers at his mother's headstone and pouring a toast of a bottle top of scotch on both his father's and brother's graves. He may not have liked either of them, but they deserved one last toast before he made his final farewell. Growing tired of England and missing the rugged freedom of Australia, he had been happy to walk away from it all, with genuinely no desire to keep the title or the estate for himself. Ironically, and despite the last year's events, Henry had ended up being Hugh's closest friend, and the only person he had ever been able to rely on. Henry had become his family and, as such, he had been happy to pass his legacy on to someone whom he felt had not had the same supposedly 'fortunate' accident of birth that he had been given – despite his acknowledgment that the consequences of that unearned birthright had not led to a happy or settled mind.

The law had found a now fully recovered Henry not guilty of any charges pertaining to the deaths of either Hugh Darlington or Nancy Warburton. There had been no conspiracy on his part beyond the mutual agreement between himself and Hugh to tie up loose ends with the estate and there was clear evidence that Hugh Darlington had been a more than willing participant in that particular ruse. He would be facing the less serious offence of tampering with a passport and entering the United Kingdom without a visa. Helen Carter had admitted that she had acted alone and without the knowledge of Henry – perhaps a sign that her affection for the erstwhile imposter had been genuine and true – at least for a while.

Henry was therefore partially free in body if not in mind and spirit and was now clear to legally receive the surprise inheritance so generously and selflessly left to him by his old friend. Despite everything. It would take months if not years of untangling red tape to complete the probate for a full handover, and that was assuming that Henry could get past his feelings of guilt and that there would not be a long-lost relative entering the picture to contest Hugh Darlington's wishes. Who knew what would happen in the future, but for now, Henry Johnson – formerly the fake Lord Hugh Darlington – was a single man in accidental possession of a good fortune – a large house that had suffered only partial fire damage and an incredibly picturesque walled kitchen garden. Not bad for a small boy who – according to his grandmother – was destined for nowhere and nothing and who had never been anybody's priority.

Daphne's children, Imani, Archie and Fynn, ran joyfully into the playground as the final school bell rang. They clamoured and squawked around Daphne's legs, chatting to their friends and begging parents for play dates.

'Yes, yes, Imani, Silvanus is already invited to come back for tea!' Daphne responded to her daughter's enthusiastic questioning with a laugh.

'Yesssss!' Imani punched her fist into the air with happiness. ' ... and by the way, Mummy, please can you call me Immy again?'

All was normal once more for the residents of Pepperbridge. Even the youths had moved on from the village green as the new cricket season had commenced after a temporary lapse. The 'youth problem' had been easily solved by scones, jam and cricket.

Daphne smiled wryly to herself as she pulled out of School Lane in Aggie, the children safely belted up in the back and Byron strapped into his car basket on the passenger seat. She thought about the conversation she'd had with James that morning.

'Daphne ...' he'd said slyly as she'd stretched her arms in bed, listening out to see if she could hear either the dog or the children and wondering whether she could squeeze in five more minutes under the duvet.

'Yes, darling? she'd replied, yawning.

'Do you think that you could possibly avoid befriending or hunting down any supervillains for a few years?' James had continued, only half-joking.

'Oh, I think I could manage a year or so ...' she had replied, contemplating the question with faux seriousness. ' ... But of course that means you'll have to provide some excitement to distract me!' she'd chuckled as he'd rolled over to kiss her just as Byron barked loudly to be let out.

When all was said and done, she was still very happy living

in Pudding Corner in the quaint parish of Pepperbridge. It felt like home. True, Inspector Hargreaves had told her to stop her sleuthing – despite having helped him solve two murder cases in as many years – and they were missing a few old and friendly faces in the village, but life still went on in these quaint lanes. Villages like Pudding Corner and Pepperbridge had seen people come and go for lifetimes. Some stayed for a season, some came for a reason, but many stayed for a lifetime – if they were lucky . . . Those that left prematurely became part of the folklore of the area – the subject of myths, historical gossip and mystery, and those that managed to stay a lifetime seemed to fall back sleepily into the open arms of the fields and villages that had harboured them so carefully during their lifetime. These villages had been the silent witnesses to secrets both harmless and grim, they had been the backdrop of love trysts and betrayals, of an abundance of happiness and the stage set for a deluge of tears and hidden misery. Above all, they had always been and still were, a peaceful home to many, and despite the rather-too-frequent discoveries of bodies in potting sheds and kitchen gardens, Daphne loved it.

Acknowledgements

Behind every creative endeavour lies an incredible team encouraging, supporting and making things happen. Without them the world of Pudding Corner could not have been released from the confines of my whimsical mind to the book you see here today. I'd like to thank the following people from the bottom of my heart.

Christina Demosthenous – for your unwavering belief in and love for this imaginary world.
Oscar Janson-Smith – for your calming and level headed presence.
Eleanor Gaffney – for your uplifting organisational skills.
Emily Moran – for your unrivalled and joyful enthusiasm.
Corinna Zifko – for your tireless efforts to get me seated at the table.

Jamie Brenner – for expertly managing my time and sanity.
Christopher Charnley – for always having my back.

With special mentions to the Design and Sales teams at Dialogue Publishing, my management team at Dopamine Studios and Ellen Rockell for her incredible cover illustrations.

Bringing a book from manuscript to what you are reading is a team effort.

Renegade Books would like to thank everyone who helped to publish *The Body in the Kitchen Garden* in the UK.

Editorial
Christina Demosthenous
Eleanor Gaffney

Contracts
Stephanie Evans
Sasha Duszynska Lewis
Isabel Camara

Sales
Megan Schaffer
Kyla Dean
Dominic Smith
Sinead White
Georgina Cutler-Ross
Kerri Hood
Jess Harvey
Natasha Weninger-Kong

Design
Ellen Rockell
Charlotte Stroomer
Sara Mahon
Sasha Egonu
Luke Applin

Production
Amanda Jones

Publicity
Corinna Zifko

Marketing
Emily Moran

Operations
Rosie Stevens

Finance
Chris Vale
Jonathan Gant

Audio
Ellie Wheeldon

Copy-Editor
David Bamford

Proofreader
Saxon Bullock